BRIDES OF THE WEST

Ruth

LORI COPELAND

Tyndale House Publishers
Carol Stream, Illinois

Visit Tyndale online at tyndale.com.

TYNDALE and Tyndale's quill logo are registered trademarks of Tyndale House Ministries.

Ruth

Designed by Libby Dykstra and Jacqueline L. Nuñez

Edited by Diane Eble

Scripture quotations are taken from the *Holy Bible*, King James Version.

Ruth is a work of fiction. Where real people, events, establishments, organizations, or locales appear, they are used fictitiously. All other elements of the novel are drawn from the author's imagination.

For information about special discounts for bulk purchases, please contact Tyndale House Publishers at csresponse@tyndale.com, or call 1-800-323-9400.

Previously published in 2002 under ISBN 0-8423-1937-9.

First repackage first published in 2007 under ISBN 978-1-4143-1538-6.

Second repackage published in 2021 under ISBN 978-1-4964-4197-3.

Printed in the United States of America

27   26   25   24   23   22   21

7   6   5   4   3   2   1

To three very special Christian young women
who will someday be brides:
Brittany King, Kelsey King,
and Bethany Chambers

Prologue

I've survived a lot of things, I'm right proud to say, for someone who grew up in the back-woods of Missouri and all her life thought the whole world consisted of Poppy's front yard and a one-room shack.

Glory sat back on the Siddonses' settee and tapped the tip of the pencil against her teeth. The parsonage hummed as women scurried about preparing for the afternoon celebration. Ruth said that it was important to record special days. Ruth was smart about such things—smart and sassy when the mood hit her. And today couldn't be more special: Glory was marrying Jackson Lincoln Montgomery.

She bent and hurriedly scratched out her story. . . .

When Poppy died, my life changed overnight. God's timing, Ruth says. Guess God thought it was about time for me to grow up, but to be honest I'd been real happy where he'd put me. I loved Poppy and the old cow and the few setting hens we had. Our mule, Molasses, died shortly after Poppy went to be with the Lord. The animal just laid down in the middle of the road and went wherever old mules go when they die. I felt empty then. The animals had kept me company after Poppy died.

My favorite memories are of those winter nights after the chores were done, the animals fed and bedded down. I loved those cold evenings by the fire when Poppy would spin yarns and play the old violin. Those were good times. No matter what you might believe, I know God had seen farther down the road than me, which was right good of him, since before I joined up with the wagon train and Jackson Montgomery, I couldn't see beyond today and didn't know enough to come in out of the rain.

I learned many a new thing on the trail to Denver City. Some folks lie, like my uncle Amos, who tried to say the gold Poppy gave me was rightfully his. That was a big windy. The kind of lie you go to the burning place for telling.

Uncle Amos was mean and wouldn't know the truth if it spat on him. But some men are just plain despicable. Tom Wyatt is such a man. He tricked Jackson Montgomery into

*bringing a wagonload of mail-order brides
clear from Westport, Missouri, to Denver City,
Colorado. We were young orphaned women
between the ages of fourteen and sixteen, who
were expecting to have fine, strong, God-fearing
husbands waiting for us. Instead, Patience,
Harper, Ruth, Lily, Mary, and I found an
evil, greedy disgrace of a man who wanted
girls with strong backs and ample resilience to
work the gold mines of Colorado. There were
no matrimony-minded men awaiting us—only
a gold mine and years of hard work. When
wagon master Jackson Montgomery discovered
the swindle, he helped us get away, with the aid
of his friend Marshal McCall.*

*Anyways, everything turned out fine for
me. Jackson Montgomery asked me to be his
bride. If you'd hit me with a two-by-four and
called me stupid, I couldn't have been more
surprised, what with me not knowing how to
cook or sew or do any of those things Jackson
deserves in a wife. 'Course, when he whispered
in my ear that sewing and cooking was all
right, but a man could live a lot longer on
true love, well, I wasn't about to argue.*

*My only concern now is what will happen
to Ruth, Patience, Harper, Lily, and Mary.
The girls are like sisters to me; we're all one big
family now. Winter's coming on and before
the snow sets in, Jackson and I will leave for
California, where we'll make our new home.*

*The other girls can't leave because they have
nowhere to go. They are approaching the age
when the orphanage where they lived most of
their lives will insist they find jobs and support
themselves. Not a girl wants to go back to
Westport. The kind pastor in Denver City,
Arthur Siddons, and his wife have given them
a home until spring, so they will be all right
for a while.*

*I'm marrying Jackson today. This seventh
day of November, eighteen hundred and
seventy-three, is the happiest day of my life.
Mary and Harper made my gown out of
bleached muslin that the preacher's wife
supplied. Simple but pretty, though it wouldn't
matter to me if I wore duck feathers. I'll bet
when Jackson sees me, he won't be able to take
his eyes off me, nor will I take mine off him.
He'll be dressed in black pants and a shirt with
a string tie, and I bet he'll smell better than
sunshine on a spring day. These past days, I
have to say, I've never seen him looking more
handsome or seen love shining more clearly in
his eyes—and that's saying a whole bunch.*

*Everyone is here for the ceremony—the
girls and Marshal McCall, who joined up
with us for the last fifty miles on the trail.
Much to Ruth's dismay, the marshal is staying
around for the ceremony, but he has to leave
in the morning. He's been chasing an outlaw
for over a year, and the trail's getting hotter.*

*Now, mind you, Dylan McCall isn't hard
to look at either. He's almost as handsome
as Jackson, but he carries a bucketful of
stubbornness. Jackson can be ornery when
it suits him, but Dylan can be charming
and ornery at the same time—a dangerous
combination in a man, Ruth says. She has all
the learnin' in the bunch. Serious Ruth doesn't
care for the cocky marshal, though the other
girls titter, blush, and squeal at his harmless
bantering.*

*Ruth and Dylan mix like wheat and hail.
Ruth is serious, focused on the task. Unless
I miss my guess, Dylan rides life lassoed to a
cyclone. Those two can look at each other and
have eye battles that make you duck for cover.
Yet it seems to me they do look at each other
more often than they look at anyone else.*

*Ruth is every bit as ornery as Dylan, only
she doesn't recognize it. I said to Jackson just
yesterday, while snuggled in his powerful arms,
that it would be pretty funny if Ruth and
Dylan fell in love.*

*"Funny as stepping on a tack barefoot,"
Jackson murmured, and then he kissed me
long and thoroughly.*

*I wasn't so sure he was right, though by
then my thoughts weren't entirely focused on
Ruth and Dylan. Jackson and I started out
at odds with each other, too, and look where
we landed—we're so much in love, we can't*

talk without our tongues tying in a knot.
It wouldn't surprise me if Ruth and Dylan
discovered they have a lot more in common
than mulish pride, and they've each got a
wagonload of that. But as I wrapped my arms
around my honey's neck and closed my eyes,
happiness warmed me like a new Christmas
blanket. In this new, exciting world God's
allowed me, I believe most anything is possible.

1

On November 7, 1873, Denver City sat under a crystal blue dome. Ruth took a deep breath of crisp mountain air and fixed her gaze on the faultless sky. It was a truly remarkable day—beautiful in every way.

Sunshine warmed her shoulders as she listened to Glory and Jackson Montgomery repeat their marriage vows. Marrying outdoors was Jackson's idea. He was an outdoorsman; he wanted to be as close to God as he and Glory could get when they became man and wife. The audible tremor this afternoon in the wagon master's otherwise strong voice amused Ruth, but she supposed the quiver was natural for a man accustomed to being on his own and about to commit the rest of his life to one woman.

Ruth cast a sideways glance at the man standing next to her. Marshal Dylan McCall stood stiff as a poker, his face expressionless as he witnessed the ceremony. What could he be thinking? The egotistical man was surely commiserating with Jackson, thinking that he was glad it was the wagon master and not he about to be saddled for life.

Well, no matter. She was not like some women she'd noticed, inexplicably drawn to the marshal. Besides, it must be God's will that she never marry. True, her head still reeled and her heart ached from the unexpected news she received from the doctor yesterday—news that she would never be able to bear children. Perhaps it was just as well that the mail-order bride thing hadn't worked out for her. Wouldn't her new husband have been dismayed to learn that Ruth had no uterus? "A rare defect," the doctor had said, "but it does happen sometimes."

Ruth lifted her chin and glanced again at the handsome marshal with eyes as blue as the color of today's sky. If it was God's will that she never marry, then she would accept it as another one of life's injustices that God allowed for his own purposes. Getting married and having children wasn't the have-all-or-end-all of life. At least not for her. She'd make a good life for herself, especially now that Tom Wyatt's spiteful trick had been discovered.

Ruth understood why a man needed a wife who could give birth to children, someone to give him strapping heirs to help with the work. Knowing this didn't lessen her desire to be loved. But then most men were like Glory's uncle Amos. They made promises they never intended to keep and blamed other folks for their own shortcomings. The chances of her finding a man who would love her regardless of her barrenness were about as remote as her hitting the mother lode the local prospectors fantasized about. She had no such fantasies. Life was real, and sometimes hard, but it was the living of it in God's will that was important to Ruth, certainly not the finding of a husband.

With a mental sigh, Ruth shifted her gaze back to the happy couple. Glory was different. She loved Jackson and would give him a whole passel of kids. Ruth tried to imagine the feisty Glory as a mother. When the wagon train had first come across the homeless waif, they'd thought she was a boy—a young man *very* much in need of a good bath. It had taken several days for Glory to convince Lily, Patience, Harper, and Mary that Glory wasn't going to oblige. She was oblivious to her malodorous state, though how she missed them holding their noses Ruth would never know. The happy-go-lucky, will-o'-the-wisp Glory had no idea she wasn't socially fit. Finally the women took it upon themselves to throw her into the river, then determinedly waded in after her, wielding a bar of soap. Glory's squeals of outrage had not deterred them. When the boylike child had been scrubbed from head to toe, the transformation was amazing.

A smile hovered at the corners of Ruth's mouth. During those days on the trail, Glory had become like a sister, and Ruth wished her nothing but happiness. Still, it was hard to imagine Glory married, nursing a child—Ruth's thoughts cut off and she forced down a tinge of remorse. She could accept God's will for her life; she really could.

The preacher concluded the ceremony. As Jackson swept his bride into his arms and kissed her breathless, the small crowd clapped and whistled. There wasn't a doubt in Ruth's mind that the two were made for each other, although for a brief and unreasonable time Ruth herself had suffered her own attraction to the handsome wagon master. She enjoyed Jackson's friendship, but Glory truly had his love and that was only right. Ruth felt not a twinge of regret about the match.

Everyone had helped to prepare the after-wedding festivities. Tables covered in lace tablecloths and adorned with bouquets of dried fall flowers had been set up in front of the church. A large wedding cake festooned with a tiny bride and groom stood amidst the decorations. An air of festivity blanketed Denver City as fiddlers tuned up.

Well-wishers descended on the happy couple as Ruth drifted away from the confusion. She'd be back to extend her best to the new Mr. and Mrs. Montgomery when things settled down a bit.

Oscar Fleming caught her eye, and she smiled back distantly. For the last few days the crusty widower had been on her trail. There had to be fifty years' difference in their ages if there was a day, but that hadn't stopped Oscar. He smiled, winked, and showed a set of brown teeth worn to the gum every time he could catch her attention.

Ruth stiffened as the old codger sprinted in her direction.

"Afternoon, Ruthie!" he called.

Ruth mustered a polite smile, her eyes darting to the marshal, who was watching the exchange with a self-satisfied grin. "Good afternoon, Oscar. Lovely ceremony." She tried to sidestep the old coot.

"Hit was, hit was." Grinning, he blocked her path. "Thought maybe I'd have me th' first dance."

"Oh," she said, her gaze swinging toward Patience and Mary, but they were both helping a group of women set food on the tables. They were too busy to pay heed to her silent plea for help.

Oscar held out his scrawny arms. "How 'bout it, Ruthie? You and me cut a jig?"

Jig, indeed. Ruth swallowed, drawing her wrap tighter as she tried to manufacture a plausible excuse. She glanced up when a hand wrapped around her left arm and Dylan McCall politely interrupted. "Now, Ruthie, I believe you promised *me* the first dance."

Though weak with relief, Ruth seethed. *Ruthie.* How dare he call her that! Still, it was a chance to escape. She stiffly accepted his proffered arm and mustered a friendly smile. Anything was better than dancing with the old miner. "Why, I believe I did, Marshal." She smiled her regrets to Oscar. "Will you excuse us?"

Oscar's grin deflated, his chin sinking down to his chest. "Maybe later?"

"Of course," she conceded. *Much, much later.*

As the couple strolled off, Ruth pinched Dylan. Hard.

Though he winced, the marshal kept a pleasant smile on his lips . . . and pinched her back.

"Ouch!" She jerked free of his grasp and flounced

ahead, pretending to ignore him. The very *nerve* of Dylan McCall acting as her rescuer!

His masculine laugh only irritated her more. "Admit it, Ruthie," he called. "You welcomed the interruption!"

Ruth's face burned. "Not by the likes of you!"

He paused, chuckling as she marched to the punch bowl. She swooped up a cup, dunked it into the bowl, then quickly drank, dribbling red liquid down the front of her best dress in the process. She dropped the cup and swiped at her bodice, then felt punch oozing through her right slipper.

Her temper soared. It was Dylan's fault. He made her so mad she couldn't think straight. From the corner of her eye, she saw Dylan politely tip his hat and ease into the crowd.

"Oooooph!" Ruth sank into a nearby chair, steam virtually rolling from the top of her head. How that man infuriated her. If only he weren't so handsome and charming at times as well. . . .

•   •   •

Forever. Whew. The vows the newlyweds had exchanged lingered in Dylan's mind as he threaded his way through the guests. He paused to speak to the ladies. Lily and Harper bloomed under his attention, but his mind was on the ceremony.

Forever. The word made a man break out in a cold sweat—at least a man who liked women but didn't care to tie himself down to any particular one, only one, for the rest of his life. Not unless he was planning to die tomorrow.

He'd been accused of breaking women's hearts, and he supposed he had broken his fair share. They could be as pretty as ice on a winter pond or ugly as a mud wasp, and he'd allow them a second glance. Dylan didn't judge a woman by the way she looked on the outside. He'd learned long ago that the outside didn't mean much. He'd told someone once that when he met the right woman he'd marry her, but deep down he knew he'd never see the day. There wasn't a *right* woman. Not for him. There were just . . . women. All softness and pretty curves, but inside they weren't worth a plug nickel. Sara Dunnigan had taught him that. Women were out to use men, use them up for their own purposes. Well, he had *his* own purposes, and they weren't to share with any woman.

The married women turned to watch him walk away; Lily and Harper tittered. Dylan neither welcomed nor resented the attention. A woman's naive notice made him feel in control. He could always walk away, and he intended to always be able to do just that.

The receiving line had begun to thin as he approached the newlyweds. He shook hands with Jackson. "You're a lucky man."

The sincerity in his tone wasn't entirely contrived. Jackson *was* lucky. Glory was the one woman who could tame the wagon master, and Dylan wished them well. Jackson grinned down at his bride. If ever there was a happy man, Montgomery fit the bill today.

"It's your turn next, McCall!"

"Don't hold your breath, Montgomery."

Dylan leaned in and kissed the bride lightly on the cheek. Glory blushed, edging closer to Jackson. Beaming, Jackson drew her close.

"That's my girl. Beware of wolves in sheep's clothing."

Dylan lifted an eyebrow. "Me? A wolf?"

"The worst," Jackson confirmed with a sly wink. "Knew that about you right off."

The two men laughed.

The new Mrs. Montgomery frowned. "Jackson—"

Throwing the marshal a knowing wink, Jackson took his wife's arm and steered her toward another cluster of well-wishers.

Dylan milled about for a while, exchanging expected pleasantries and hoping he could leave soon. Events like this weren't his cup of tea. He spent the majority of his time alone, which he preferred. He was eager to get going to Utah. He would have left last week, but Jackson and Glory had talked him into attending the wedding. Jackson needed a best man, he said, and Dylan had reluctantly agreed, feeling torn between friendship and duty to his job.

Dylan spotted Ruth with Mayor Hopkins, her cheeks flushed, blue eyes aglow, thick, shiny, coal black hair hanging to her waist, laughing up at him. She'd never looked at Dylan that way . . . but then he supposed a woman like Ruth wouldn't. Men like him were loners. They had to be. Keeping the law was a dangerous business. Ruth, even with her independent streak a mile wide, would avoid a man like him, as well she should.

Dylan had stepped onto the sidewalk when Pastor Siddons threaded his way through the crowd toward him. "Marshal McCall! They'll be cutting the wedding cake soon. You won't want to miss that." The pastor beamed. "Etta Katsky makes the best pastries this side of paradise."

Smiling, the marshal acknowledged the invitation. The whole town was friendlier than a six-week-old pup. It was a good place for Ruth and the other girls to settle.

The two men stood side by side, watching the festivities. Arthur Siddons's pleasant face beamed. "Nothing like a wedding to make you feel like a young man again."

Dylan refused to comment. His gaze followed Ruth as she moved through the crowd. He'd never seen her smile like that, laugh like that, so happy and carefree.

Arthur looked up at him, a sly grin hovering at the corner of his mouth. "Right pretty sight, wouldn't you say?"

Dylan had to agree. "Ruth's a fine-looking woman. All the girls are."

The pastor nodded. "Mother was just saying how nice it is to have young blood in the town. Tom Wyatt and his boys are low-down polecats. The whole town's known that for years, but I have to say the devil was taken by surprise this time. Had it not been for you and Jackson, those six young women would be working the mines right now, without a hope for the future."

Dylan bristled at the thought. "The Wyatts ought to be strung up by their heels."

"Yes, many agree, but Wyatt's not done anything he can be legally prosecuted for. We know he promised the women husbands, but in a court of law he'd say the women, the orphanage, and Montgomery misunderstood. He would eventually set them free, once they worked off their debt to him. But considering the wages he'd pay, that would take a mighty long time. It isn't the first time he's used deceit to gain mine workers. Brought eight women out last year, and one by one they escaped. Found one this spring." The reverend shook his head. "Poor woman didn't make it."

A shadow crossed the marshal's features. "I thought once that Jackson and Glory had met the same fate."

"Yes, Jackson and Glory were fortunate to survive that blizzard." The pastor beamed. "Wouldn't have, without Glory's common sense."

"No." Dylan watched the laughing bride and groom. "She's quite a woman."

Arthur nodded. "Colorado's rough territory. A man can freeze to death in no time."

Sobering, the minister rested his gaze on Mary, who was smiling up at Mayor Hopkins. The couple seemed to be enjoying each other's company.

"Now, there's the one I worry about. The poor thing coughs until she chokes. Won't be many men who'd want to take on such a responsibility."

Dylan agreed. Mary's asthma would make it difficult for her to find a husband. He looked at Harper and Lily, who were busy setting out platters of golden brown fried chicken. Harper was so independent and quick-tongued it would take a strong man to handle her. Lily would do okay for herself, and Patience wouldn't have any trouble finding a husband. She was the looker of the bunch.

His gaze moved back to Ruth. She was now conversing with a tall, lanky man who looked to be somewhere in his late twenties. The couple made a striking pair. The young man's carrot-colored hair and mahogany eyes complemented Ruth's black tresses and wide blue eyes. But Ruth was going to be trouble for any man who took her on. She was as prickly as a porcupine—and as quick to raise her defenses. Made a man wonder what was inside her.

Not him, of course, but some man—some good man looking to settle down.

Patting his round belly, the pastor chuckled softly as he followed Dylan's gaze to the couple. "They make a fine-looking pair, don't they? Conner lost his wife a couple years back. Fine man, Conner Justice, so young to lose a mate. Lost Jenny in childbirth . . . baby was stillborn. His wife's death was mighty hard on him. Conner is only now coming back to community socials."

Dylan's gaze narrowed. It appeared to him that

Conner Justice was recovering quite nicely. He was standing a bit too close to Ruth for manners. The sound of Ruth's lilting laughter floated to him, a sound he hadn't heard often. She was enjoying herself for the first time since he'd met her.

Well, good for Ruthie. Maybe Conner Justice needed a new challenge, and the saucy brunette would certainly provide him one.

The pastor patted his belly again. "Well, the bride and groom will be cutting the cake soon." He stuck his hand out to Dylan. "Guess you'll be moving on?"

"I have to be in Utah by the end of the month."

"Worst time of the year to travel."

"I'm used to it."

Dylan preferred to travel in better weather. But when he'd decided to help Jackson deliver the brides to Denver City, he knew he'd be delaying his trip to Utah and would probably face bad weather. It wouldn't be the first time he'd been inconvenienced, nor would it be the last.

"Take care of yourself," Pastor Siddons said.

Dylan smiled. His eyes involuntarily returned to Ruth and Conner, while the pastor wandered toward the cake table. Ruth looked like she was having a fine time.

"Well, I am, too," he told himself, but right now he couldn't have proved it.

2

Shadows lengthened over the Rockies as the wedding guests danced and laughed the festive afternoon away. A grinning bride and groom, their faces flushed by wind and excitement, cut the wedding cake while the sun sank behind the mountaintops.

Crimson tinged Glory's cheeks as she smiled up at her husband and fed him the first bite. With good-natured humor, he fed her a piece; then one of the women invited the guests to step up and eat their fill.

Ruth felt herself being shuffled along with the crowd. Today's events had been magnificent—one of the best times she could remember. An aura of love surrounded the newlywed couple, and Ruth allowed the special feelings to seep through her pores. In her life, Ruth had known little love. When Edgar Norris, the only father she'd ever known, took her to the orphanage when his wife died, he'd left Ruth with a glowing promise that he would soon return. To a ten-year-old, *soon* meant "not very long." She remembered crying and holding on to his leg, begging him not to leave her. She didn't see how she could live without Paws—that's what she called Edgar—to greet her when she came home from school each day.

But Edgar Norris had lied to her.

He didn't come back; Ruth never saw the man again. Five years had gone by, and she didn't know if Edgar Norris was dead or alive. She made herself believe that she didn't care, but the Bible said she was to honor father and mother. Her real Mama and Papa died when she was four, and she had been adopted by the Norrises. But she had no idea how to honor a man who had deserted a child he'd promised to raise.

"What say, little missy? Is this our dance?"

Ruth froze when she recognized Oscar Fleming's feisty intonation. *Rats.* She'd been on the lookout for Oscar all afternoon, terrified he would seek her out. He'd tried to dance with every woman in attendance, including poor Mary, who had finally begged off and slumped down in the nearest chair to catch her ragged breath.

Summoning a pleasant smile, Ruth whirled, confronting the nuisance. "Why, Mr. Fleming—here you are again."

The old man's eyes twinkled. He opened both scrawny arms and extended them wide. "What say? Saved the best for last?"

"Oh, Mr. Fleming, I know you must be worn-out—"

"Oscar! Call me Oscar, my beauty." He moved in closer. "They're playing our song!"

Before Ruth could invent an excuse, Oscar swung her onto the platform and waltzed her around the wooden deck in a breakneck fashion. The old prospector certainly had oomph!

Ruth hung on to the squatty miner as pins flew out of her hair and landed beneath other dancers' feet. She flashed a smiling apology to couples who slipped and stumbled when their feet encountered the shiny hair fasteners. One man whirled to denounce her as he helped his partner up from the dance floor.

"Hee, hee, hee," Oscar hooted as he cut between two jigging couples, nearly tripping them with his wild maneuverings. "I knew I'd found me a ring-tailed molly!"

This ring-tailed molly was about to break her neck! Ruth, not accustomed to dancing, struggled to keep her slippers on her feet and her tangled hair out of her eyes. She caught a brief glimpse of Patience, Lily, Harper, and Mary on the sidelines, holding their hands over their mouths, amusement flashing in their eyes. She managed to get off a silent, beseeching look before Oscar gave her a couple of swift turns and then jumped in the air and clicked his heels.

"By gum, but you're a filly!"

Ruth lamely smiled, anxious for the dance to end. Instead, guitars and banjos shifted into a slow waltz. It took Oscar a couple of beats to make the physical adjustment. He jigged, then jagged, and then grasped her so tightly she couldn't breathe. His breath was stale and his clothes smelled of sweat. Ruth closed her eyes, praying for deliverance. She opened them again, instinctively searching for Dylan. She found him surrounded by a captive group of women as he leisurely ate a piece of wedding cake and exchanged friendly banter. Typical. Where was the courtly gentleman when she really needed him?

"You're one of them orphans Wyatt sent for, aren't you?"

Ruth's thoughts snapped back to Oscar, and her feet tried to keep time with his stomping boots. "Yes—I was on the Montgomery wagon train."

"Pity." The old fellow shook his head. "Wyatt's a known polecat around these parts. I could have told you him and his boys was up to no good." He swung her around, then propelled her roughly back into his arms—highly irregular for a waltz, as even Ruth knew.

"I like your name, Ruthie."

"Ruth," she corrected. "Nobody calls me Ruthie. My name is Ruth."

"Like in the Bible."

"Like in the Bible—only I'm not nearly as virtuous as that Ruth."

Oscar nodded as if that suited him. "You want to be a bride, do ya?"

Ruth felt heat shinny up the back of her neck. His foregone conclusion that she wanted to be married cheapened her forced decision. She hadn't *wanted* to be married; the orphanage had strongly advised her to agree to Wyatt's offer. She knew now that if a husband had awaited her in Denver City, the marriage would have been short-lived. Once the new groom learned that she was not able to conceive, he would have left for greener pastures. But she had no intention of confiding such personal information to Mr. Fleming. Now if only she could think of some way to abort this dance without hurting the old man's feelings.

"Do ya?"

"Do I what?" she asked sweetly, hoping to change the subject.

"Do you want to be a bride?"

"I suppose," she murmured, giving the expected response, though it wasn't entirely true.

"Well, hot diggity dog!"

Horrified, Ruth watched the prospector jump straight up in the air and click his heels again, then land on both knees in front of her on the wooden platform. He grasped her hand, his rheumy eyes peering intently into hers. The music started to fade and people stood rooted in place, all eyes focused on Oscar Fleming.

"Ruth . . ." Oscar paused and scratched his head. Then he brightened. ". . . whatever your last name is. Will you be my wife?" He grinned, flashing red gums.

A collective gasp came from the crowd. Ruth heard a drum beating in her ears and realized it was her heart. Harper's distinct giggle filtered through the beat.

Ruth's hand came up to her forehead as she tried to form a coherent sentence. Marry Oscar Fleming? A man old enough to be her grandfather! Her senses turned numb. No! She looked around, panic setting in. No!

But how could she tell Oscar no in front of all these people, people who were most likely his friends?

Her eyes darted for refuge, but there was none. Patience shook her head vehemently. Lily, Harper, and Mary all indicated the negative with their eyes.

Oscar peered up at Ruth hopefully.

"Oscar," she began, searching for strength and compassion. She didn't want to hurt the old prospector's feelings; he knew she had previously been receptive to marriage to a man she'd never met. What answer could she give that wouldn't wound the poor man's spirit yet leave no doubt of her refusal?

"I am very honored . . ."

"Hot doggedy!" Oscar bound to his feet and swept her up in his skinny arms, his face ecstatic. Ruth's eyes grew wide as he whirled her around and around. "I got me a *bride*!"

The crowd burst into a smattering of hesitant applause. With Oscar's declaration, Dylan McCall turned and set his cake plate on the table. A frown creased the corners of his blue eyes.

"No, Mr. Fleming!" Ruth protested when she realized the old miner had misunderstood. The band swung into an upbeat tune, and dancers flooded the platform to congratulate the newly betrothed couple.

"But I didn't . . ." Ruth protested with each congratulatory slap and sly wink Oscar received. Women stared in pity, and men grinned with an ill-concealed pride.

"Didn't think you had it in you, Oscar!"

"You old goat! Suppose we're going to be calling you 'Papa' before long!"

The crude remark brought a round of masculine guffaws that shook Ruth to her toes. She broke free of the crowd and ran toward the parsonage, holding a handkerchief to her mouth for fear she was going to be ill. Upon entering the Siddonses' foyer, she slammed the door behind her and took the stairs two at a time. Marry Oscar Fleming! She couldn't! She entered the upstairs bedroom and fell across the bed she shared with Patience and sobbed until exhaustion overcame her.

She dropped into a fitful sleep, her dreams filled with old prospectors spitting tobacco on clean kitchen floors. Oscar chasing her around the kitchen table, wearing a gummy grin, reaching for her . . . the stale smell of his breath . . .

Images floated in her dreams. Voices warned her: *Ruth, you can't marry that man, regardless of your desperate situation.*

"No," Ruth murmured, thrashing about on the bed. The thought of marrying a man nearly seventy years old was so dreadful that her head pounded and knots gripped her stomach. "I can't . . . please, God . . . I can't. . . ."

•   •   •

"Ruthie?"

Ruth stirred, opening her eyes. The room was

pitch-dark, and she took a minute to gather her thoughts. Her eyes felt sore and swollen. Then the afternoon's events came rushing back—Oscar, the proposal, the old man's misunderstanding.

"Ruth?" A match flickered, then caught a wick. Candlelight penetrated the darkness. Mary, Harper, Patience, and Lily gathered close around the bed, their eyes solemn with worry.

Burying her face in the pillow, Ruth began to cry. Patience sat down on the side of the bed and held her hand. "Oh, Ruth. What are you going to do? Everyone thinks you're going to marry that old man."

Ruth bawled harder. What *was* she going to do? Did Oscar's misinterpretation constitute a promise? It couldn't—yet everyone knew the girls were orphans and in dire need of husbands. How could Ruth refuse a legitimate marriage proposal and not appear to be self-centered and ungrateful? Oscar's age didn't matter. He was so old that he couldn't possibly consummate the vows. . . . The image of the old man jumping up and clicking his heels together—the way he threaded in and out of the dancers like a man half his age—oh, goodness! She sobbed even harder.

"Now, now," Mary soothed. She sat down opposite Patience. Each girl patted Ruth's back soothingly. "It isn't that bad. Why, Mr. Fleming seems to be kind . . . and lively. *Very* lively for a man his age."

Harper nodded her head, her dark eyes troubled. "A little too lively, if you ask me."

Lily shot her a censuring look. "No one did ask

you, Harper. And Mr. Fleming can most likely provide Ruth a very good home," she added.

Ruth flung the pillow aside. "Then *you* marry him."

Lily drew back as if bitten by a rattlesnake.

Bolting upright on the bed, Ruth wiped her eyes and blew her nose on the handkerchief Patience pressed into her hand. "I *won't* marry that old man. I won't. Even if it means I have to work my fingers to the bone and maybe even starve to death. I won't marry Oscar Fleming."

Patience's hand closed tightly around Ruth's. "Don't say that, Ruth. This might very well be an answer to prayer. At least you'll have someone to care for you. The rest of us face very uncertain futures."

All four of the women nodded.

"It could be a blessing, Ruth." Lily stood behind, smoothing Ruth's back.

Ruth shook her head mutely. God wouldn't be so cruel. He had revealed his will for her life when the doctor told her she was missing a uterus and could never bear children. No children. She was trying to accept the doctor's words, but the knowledge still stung. Now? Marrying Oscar would give her a temporary home, but it would never give her love and children, the things she'd once wanted most in life. It would take a miracle from God to give her those things now, and at this moment her faith couldn't stretch far enough to believe she'd merit such favor.

"Oh, it might be fun," Patience encouraged. "Oscar could be like—like a dear grandfather. You

could sew and cook and keep his house clean while
he sat in the rocking chair in front of the window,
drinking in the warm sunlight. . . ." Her words
trailed as Ruth turned withering eyes on her.

Patience smiled lamely. "Look on the bright
side—isn't that what Jackson told us?"

"There isn't a bright side, Patience." Ruth drew
her knees up to her chest and rested her head on
them. Lily gently tucked Ruth's skirts around her.

Harper humphed. "More like she'd get her exercise with the old coot chasing her round the house
twenty-four hours a day."

The eyes of all five girls turned as round as boiled
eggs. Silence shrouded the room.

Suddenly Ruth threw her petticoats aside and
straightened her hair.

"Where are you going?" Lily tried to restrain the
determined woman as she got off the bed.

Shrugging Lily's hand aside, Ruth marched to
the door. She hadn't wanted to resort to dire actions,
but if ever there was a time for urgency, it was now.
She couldn't let this ride another minute. She had
to see Oscar and apologize for the misunderstanding
and inform him she would not marry him. Then she
would face Pastor Siddons and his wife, Minnie, in
the morning and explain why she had turned down
a perfectly good marriage proposal, further impos-
ing upon them during the long winter, when the
Siddonses already had four additional mouths to feed.

"You're not going anywhere." Patience's eyes
firmed as Ruth's four friends formed a physical bar-

rier, blocking the bedroom door. "You have to at least promise to sleep on this and pray about it. In the light of morning you may discover that there could be a worse fate than marrying Oscar Fleming."

Ruth met the women's eyes stubbornly. She would rather have this out tonight and get it over with, but if they were going to be adamant about it, then so be it. Marching back to the bed, she dropped into it and yanked the covers over her head.

The candle went out. Silence fell over the crowded bedroom. Ruth felt the springs give as Mary crawled between the sheets on her side of the bed. Guilt gnawed at Ruth; she tossed and turned. The Siddonses had been kind enough to take all five women in until spring. By then other arrangements for Mary, Patience, Lily, Harper, and herself would have to be made. The good Lord knew the aging couple couldn't afford to feed five extra mouths. If Ruth wasn't so selfish, she'd marry Oscar. Maybe he would offer to look after Lily and Patience, or Mary and Harper. That would leave only two extra mouths for the Siddonses to feed during the long winter.

Patience had said to pray about it. Ruth tried . . . but images from her nightmares came back to her. Oscar chasing her around the house. . . . What if God wanted her to marry Oscar? She couldn't. She just *couldn't* marry that old prospector.

Cousin Milford. The name popped into Ruth's head. She hadn't thought of Milford in years. He was Edgar's youngest brother's son, and Edgar had always spoken highly of him. Milford lived in

Wyoming—somewhere. Pear Branch, Wyoming, if she remembered correctly. Milford would be in his late twenties by now, probably married with a wife and children. If she could get to Pear Branch, Milford would take her in for the winter. She didn't know why she hadn't thought of him before!

Now, how could she get to Pear Branch with winter coming on? She had to use logic. The weather would be formidable, but with the proper clothing and a good horse she might make it. She had to think of a plan. . . .

She heard the hall clock chime two. Easing from beneath the warm sheets, she covered Mary more securely, then tiptoed to the door. A minute later she crept down the stairway, wincing at the telltale creaks. Pastor and his wife slept in the downstairs back bedroom.

Ruth fumbled in the darkness to pull on Mary's boots and the coat she'd left in the hallway. She slipped out the front door, closing it softly behind her. Moonlight lit a path on the ground. The sleepy town was quiet at this hour. The hotel where Dylan and the newlyweds were staying was dark as pitch when she approached.

She couldn't believe what she was about to do. But desperate straits called for desperate measures. Hadn't her biblical namesake done something similar with Boaz?

Ruth eased the establishment's front door open and crept to the registration desk, where a candle burned low. The old clerk sat back in a chair sound asleep, his snores falling in even cadence. Even wide-awake, Mort Carol couldn't hear himself think, she'd been told. Turning the name register around, Ruth lifted the candle and located Dylan's name. Room 4. Glory and Jackson were in room 10.

The soles of Mary's thick boots clunked up the uncarpeted stairs. Holding the candle aloft, Ruth tiptoed down the hall and read door numbers. Two . . . three. Light snores resonated up and down the hallway. Mostly cattlemen stayed the night as they passed through on their way to deliver herds. This time of year the hotel was nearly empty.

Ruth paused at room 4 and knocked lightly. Holding her breath, she waited. Dylan McCall must sleep like a log. She'd have thought a marshal would sleep lighter, alert to unexpected trouble. So much for Mr. Know-It-All McCall's abilities—

She lifted her hand and knocked again. Suddenly the door flew open, and Ruth found herself staring down the steel barrel of a very unfriendly looking Colt. She dropped the candle as her hands flew up to shield her face. "Don't shoot!"

She heard a masculine rumble that sounded very unpleasant—like an old bear awakened from hibernation—before she was physically yanked inside. After kicking the door shut, Dylan reached for his shirt. "What are *you* doing creeping around here in the middle of the night!" He jerked the shirt on, then lit a candle. His features looked sinister in the shadowy light. "Fool woman."

"Fool!" she mocked. "I could have burst in here

and shot you dead if I'd wanted. You didn't hear my first knock."

"I heard it."

"You did not."

He glowered at her.

Ruth quickly decided she wasn't making any points with him, and that was her sole purpose for being here in the middle of the night. Pastor Siddons would faint if he knew she was visiting a man's hotel room at this hour. Brushing past the glowering marshal, she moved deeper into the room. "I have come to ask a favor."

"No."

"Just like that? No?"

Dylan calmly buttoned his shirt. "Maybe . . . if you come back in the morning."

She whirled to face him. "You're leaving in the morning, aren't you?"

He sat down on the side of the bed, running his hands through rings of tousled curls. The gesture reminded her of a young boy—a very good-looking, young, impatient lad.

"So?"

"I need your help."

He looked up. "My help." He laughed.

"Your help." Taking a deep breath, she clunked over to where he sat. "You have to take me with you in the morning."

For a moment he frowned; then the cad threw back his head and laughed harder. "In a pig's eye. I don't want to upset your fiancé."

Bravado crumbling, she knelt before him. "Please, Dylan. I *can't* marry Oscar Fleming—I can't. If I remain here in Denver City, I'll have no alternative."

His eyes hardened, and for a moment he reminded her of a spurned suitor. An illogical sense of elation filled Ruth, then dissipated just as quickly when she realized that the arrogant boar was only showing his usual insolence.

"Then why did you agree to marry the man?" His tone was flat and final.

"I *didn't* agree to marry him! Oscar misunderstood!"

"Misunderstood?" He *pffi*ed. "How does a man misunderstand yes from no?"

A hot blush crept up Ruth's neck. "I didn't exactly say no . . . I said, 'Oscar, I'm honored,' and he took it to mean yes."

Dylan stared at her. "'Oscar, I'm honored.' Hmm. Wonder how he mistook that for a yes."

"Honored *but*," she argued. "I was going to say *but I can't marry you*. No! I was going to say a firm no."

"Then why didn't you? How hard is it to stop and say, 'No, you misunderstood'?"

Ruth knew he had a valid point. She should have stopped Oscar, but she was dumbfounded by the proposal, and the crowd was pushing around her, and Oscar was jumping up and down crowing like a proud rooster. She had bolted like a coward, leaving Oscar with the impression, no doubt, that she was suffering from a hefty dose of shyness and premarital jitters.

Desperate now, she grabbed both of Dylan's hands. "Look, I'll work my way. If you'll take me as far as Wyoming, I'll cook, wash your clothes, be your servant." Ouch! It galled her to say that, but she was a woman in dire straits.

"Take you with me?" he scoffed. "With winter setting in—take you to Wyoming? You are out of your mind."

"I'm not out of my mind; I'm desperate. Can't you see that?" She sprang up, her temper flaring. "You insensitive jackal! I can't stay here and marry Oscar Fleming. You *have* to take me with you— it's—it's the only gentlemanly thing to do!"

Maybe if she appealed to his chivalrous side. She knew he had one because she'd seen him turn on the charm with more than one unsuspecting woman. She was prepared to use anything in her arsenal—within reason—to make him relent and see the necessity.

"If I can get to Milford, he'll take me in!"

"Milford?"

"Milford—my cousin."

"You've never mentioned a Milford."

"So? I haven't mentioned a lot of things," she said. "Milford being one of them."

He laughed humorlessly. "Go back to the Siddonses and go to bed. There's no way I'm taking you with me, Ruth. It's too dangerous. And in case you haven't thought about it, your reputation would be ruined. A man and woman, unmarried, traveling alone together . . ."

The look he gave her implied she was as green as grass. Well, Mr. Smart Aleck didn't know she'd already thought of that objection and had it covered.

"No one will ever know that I'm a woman."

"Yeah, right." Then the cad actually blew out the light and crawled back in bed. Ruth stood in the dark, fuming. How dare he. How *dare* he treat her like an unruly child!

"Let yourself out quietly," he mumbled beneath the covers. "There are people down the hall trying to sleep."

Ruth fumbled her way to the door. Why God let men like Dylan McCall inhabit the earth was beyond her. She lit a candle once she closed the door and stomped back down the stairs. She didn't bother to be quiet this time—someone could come in and carry off the hotel, and not a soul there would know.

She let herself out the front door, feeling like she was about to explode on the inside. How one man could get her so worked up and angry amazed her.

Her eyes focused on the water barrel as the heavy boots clunked down the steps. What an egotistical, self-inflated, pompous—! Her eyes lit on the bucket. Before she thought, she dipped a bucketful of water, then turned and let herself back into the hotel. The old clerk slept on as she pounded up the stairs again, lugging the heavy pail of water.

Liquid sloshed out, trailing a wet slick down the hallway. When she reached room 4, she paused to catch her breath. She wanted to have plenty of wind when he opened the door. Hefting the bucket waist high, she kicked at the door.

Dylan's gruff voice came through the wood. "Go home, Ruth, before I have to insult you."

Insult me, huh. She kicked harder. *Treat me like a child, will he?*

Voices from nearby rooms sounded. "Hey, what's going on out there?" "Whoever's kicking that door is gonna get his head knocked in!"

In a second the door flew open and an enraged Dylan appeared.

"You inconsiderate lout!" Taking a wide swing, she heaved the bucket of water, hitting him face-first. Icy tendrils streamed from his hair. Staggering backward, he muttered an expletive under his breath as Ruth turned and ran.

The clunky boots were too big for her, and she had to squeeze her toes to the front of the leather to keep them on her feet. But she'd forgotten about the water slick. Her feet flew out from beneath her about the same time a large hand clasped around her collar.

Horrified, she felt herself being lifted into a pair of steel-banded arms. "Now, Dylan . . . remember, you're a man and I'm a woman. . . ."

"A hooligan," he corrected. He was drenched from head to foot, his clothes sticking to him.

She pounded his back as he hauled her, kicking and screaming, over his shoulder and headed toward the stairway. Doors opened and candlelight glowed. Sleepy-eyed guests gathered in the hallway to watch the fracas.

Mort Carol stirred behind the counter, licking his lips. His eyes flew wide open at the sight of the marshal carrying a young, screaming woman down the staircase. The back of Mort's chair smacked the floor as he bolted up. "Here now—what in tarnation is going on? Put that little lady down!"

Dylan carried Ruth out the door and down the porch stairs and unceremoniously dumped her into the water barrel.

Ruth's indignant screams penetrated the late fall air as she hit the icy water. She surfaced, spitting water on him.

Pointing a stern finger at her, Dylan warned, "You're stepping on my last nerve, woman!"

● ● ●

Moments later Jackson appeared on the porch, wearing pants and his shirttail hanging out. "What in the—?"

Dylan's gaze moved from the half-dressed bridegroom back to Ruth. She looked like a drowned rat. Her hair hung in tangled ropes, pieces of it clinging to her face; her dress drooped on her like a wet sack, but hot resentment burned in her eyes. He almost laughed.

"It's three o'clock in the morning!" Jackson bellowed. "Don't you two have anything better to do than have a water fight?"

Dylan noticed a crowd had gathered and now stood in various stages of nightclothes, gaping at

them with wide eyes and not a few snickers. Pure
fury rose in him. This stubborn, *irrational* woman
had made a complete fool of him.

"Get away from that water barrel before you
both freeze to death!" Jackson stepped off the porch
and hauled Ruth out of the water. He propelled her
toward the hotel lobby. "Show's over, folks. Get back
to your beds, where sane people ought to be!"

Jackson stepped inside the lobby and motioned
the dripping couple up the stairway. Mort preened
his neck over the counter as he cleaned his glasses.
"Do I need to get the law?"

"We *have* the law," Jackson called over his
shoulder and then glanced at Dylan. "Although
I'm sure the government wouldn't claim him at the
moment." Wet leather boots creaked down the hallway as guests shrank back into the shadows. Doors
shut—some softly, others with distinct slams.

Glory sat up in bed, clutching a blanket to her
chest, as Jackson burst into their room with two
nocturnal visitors dripping water. The new bride's
eyes scanned Ruth's wet clothing.

Jackson sighed. "Honey, get Ruth some dry
clothes before she catches her death. I can't think for
her teeth chattering. Dylan, here. Put on a dry shirt."

Dylan would have refused the shirt Jackson
tossed at him, but his fingers were turning blue and
he couldn't feel his feet at all. Glory handed Ruth a
dry garment, then held up a blanket for her to dress
behind.

Dylan felt a twinge of guilt for disturbing the

newlyweds. Well, Ruth had disturbed him too. She had *flooded* him, and he'd have to change clothes before he went back to sleep.

Jackson sat the warring couple in straight-back chairs. Dylan knew the groom was none too happy right now. Ruth sat meekly, her teeth still chattering. She looked as innocent as a choirboy.

"I don't know what got into you two, but I've got better things to do on my wedding night than referee for you and Ruth," Jackson grumbled.

Dylan wasn't sure himself what had gotten into him. Tossing a woman into a water barrel in the middle of the night wasn't something he would normally do, but this woman got under his skin. In more ways than one—none of which he cared to analyze. On the trail to Denver City he'd noticed she was the more educated of the young women and definitely the best cook. But the spitfire could make him angrier than anyone he'd ever known. Her stubbornness, her standoffish ways, had gotten to him.

Maybe that was what startled him tonight when she'd awakened him from a sound sleep and begged him to take her to Wyoming. Wyoming! Was she that desperate or just plain crazy? The old prospector proposing in front of half the town must have really shaken her.

Of course, he couldn't even think of taking her with him. Any day the deep snows would come, and Dylan would be lucky to survive the elements himself. He couldn't take on the responsibility of a woman even if he did see Ruth's point. What woman would take to the notion of marrying a man nearly five times her age? He cast a sideways glance at Ruth. Not this woman.

Jackson's hands came to his slim hips. "I thought you were leaving at sunup."

"I plan to." In just a few hours Dylan would ride out of here and out of Ruth's life. Maybe.

Jackson paced the floor, turning to cast looks over his shoulder. "Care to tell me what this is all about?"

"He—" Ruth began.

"She—" Dylan started.

"One at a time!"

Glory sat with her hands over her mouth. Dylan couldn't tell if she was appalled, amazed, or trying not to laugh.

"This crazy woman knocked on my door fifteen minutes ago and demanded that I take her with me to Wyoming!"

"I didn't *demand*," Ruth retorted. "I asked."

"Sounded like demanding to me. Seems a prospector that's old enough to be her grandpa proposed to her tonight after you and Glory left —"

"Proposed?" Glory sat up on her knees. "Honest, Ruth? A man proposed to you? You're getting married?"

"Not really," Ruth said. "The prospector proposed, but I didn't accept."

"But Oscar still doesn't know that," Dylan said, shooting a cold look at Ruth.

Jackson focused on Ruth. "Ruth? Are you certain

you don't want to think about this? I don't know the man, but I could do some checking—"

"No," Ruth stated flatly, "I will not marry that old man. I'm going to Wyoming instead and find my cousin Milford."

When Jackson frowned, Dylan added, "She says she remembers a cousin or something in Wyoming. This is the first I've heard of it."

Ruth's chin lifted. "There was no need."

"She says she'll do anything if I'd take her with me to find this 'cousin.'"

"Not *anything*!" Ruth snapped. "I said I'd cook and wash your clothes and that's more than sufficient payment. And I do have a cousin Milford in Wyoming."

"Wyoming's a big place. Do you have this man's address?"

She shrugged. "Not with me."

Dylan was a lawman, not a chaperone. Marshaling wasn't the safest profession, and he had to travel fast. A woman would slow him down. He ate out of a can most nights. A woman wanted dishes; all he had were two tin cups. He jumped into a stream to bathe when it was convenient and let cleanliness go when it wasn't. A woman had soaps and lotions and all sorts of pretty clothes and things. A woman—

Well, a woman on the trail wasn't his idea of heaven on earth. Not even a woman like Ruth. She'd done well enough in the wagon with the other women to help on the journey from Westport, but traveling on horseback was a different matter . . . a whole different matter.

Ruth looked over at Dylan and silently mouthed, *"I would rather marry a goat than depend on you to take me anywhere."*

He shrugged. "Then marry Oscar."

"Hold it." Jackson stopped Ruth's ready retort. "Ruth, even if Dylan was inclined to take you with him—"

"Which I'm not."

Jackson's mouth firmed as his eyes silently warned Dylan not to interrupt again. This whole thing was crazy. How had he gotten into this mess? All he'd done was agree to accompany Jackson's wagonload of mail-order brides to Denver City. He didn't deserve to be humiliated by this black-haired harridan.

"Even if he agreed," Jackson said, "the two of you can't travel alone together without being married. It wouldn't do. Are you willing to marry Dylan?"

"Not on my last breath!" Ruth exploded.

Dylan's incredulous laugh burst out. "Marry Ruth?" He wasn't the marrying kind. Lawmen and marriage didn't work. Besides, Ruth was religious like Sara Dunnigan. On the wagon trail he'd seen Ruth read her Bible frequently. She'd taught Glory to read, using the Bible. He'd had a bellyful of religious fanatics.

Oh, she was fun to rile. Every word he said ignited her fiery temper. But he wasn't about to *marry* for convenience. At his age, he didn't plan to marry for any reason. If he married that woman he'd never have a moment's peace.

"I won't marry her. I wouldn't take her to a barn burning, let alone Wyoming on some wild-goose chase looking for Cousin Milford. I have a job—remember? I'm late getting there as it is."

What sane woman would ask a lawman to take her hundreds of miles to a land she didn't know, to a person who probably didn't exist? Dylan had done his good deed when he offered to help Jackson on the trail.

"And I would rather walk barefoot through hot coals than marry him," Ruth stated, her chin lifting another notch.

"Then we're agreed."

Ruth whirled to face him. "Marshal McCall—you are the most—"

"Don't start again," Jackson warned, "or I'll dump you both back in the water barrel. Seems to me, there're only two solutions. Either you stay here, Ruth, and deal with Oscar—"

"Not on your life," she breathed.

"—or you marry Dylan."

"Not on your life," Dylan said. He crossed his arms.

Having observed all of this, Glory scooted closer to the edge of the bed. "What Dylan says is true, Ruth. Winter's coming on, and you can't travel alone with an unmarried man."

"I've already thought of that, Glory—"

"Forget it, ladies." Dylan pushed out of his chair.

Damp curls were drying against his forehead. "Ruth has other choices. She doesn't have to marry Oscar. She can tell the old man no and remain with the Siddonses until spring. That was the original plan."

"I feel I can't impose on the pastor and his wife since I have received a marriage proposal," Ruth argued.

"Well, then I'd say you're in a heap of trouble, Ruthie." Dylan turned and walked toward the door, his boots squeaking with water.

Ruth crossed her arms and stared at the floor. "Fine. I wouldn't go with you now if the whole of Denver City was being swallowed by mountains."

Dylan tipped his head respectfully. "You and Oscar have a fine life together." He purposely grinned to rile her. "I can picture the happy bridegroom clicking his heels together in joy when the preacher says, 'I pronounce you man and wife.' Just be sure to keep him supplied with chewing tobacco with a spittoon by the door."

He ducked when a soggy boot sailed past his head and hit the door.

"Crazy woman," he muttered to himself as he opened the door and stalked back to his room. No way could she make the trip to Wyoming. Not in winter. She couldn't expect him to mollycoddle her. He had a job to perform and not an easy one at best. Having a woman along would be dangerous and foolhardy. Ruth needed to take care of her own problems. If that meant marrying Oscar, then so be it—though he did hate to see a young woman tie herself down to a man old enough to be . . . He switched the thought off. Nobody ever claimed life was easy or fair.

Ignoring the bitter taste the confrontation had left in his mouth, Dylan returned to his bed in hopes of getting some sleep before he had to ride out.

3

"Mary?"

Ruth gently shook the sleeping girl. Daylight would break in less than an hour, and she had to hurry. Shivering in her wet clothes, she shook Mary a little harder. She didn't want to wake the others—Mary would be the most likely one to help and the least likely to try to talk her out of what she was about to do. But Dylan McCall had left her no choice.

"Mary." Ruth grasped the young woman's shoulders more firmly.

Coughing, Mary stirred and opened her eyes sleepily. Ruth bent close to her ear and whispered, "Get up. You have to help me."

Predawn chill sheathed the bedroom. With chattering teeth, Ruth quickly reached for the towel on the washstand to dry her damp hair.

Mary's voice sounded raspy in the shadowy room. "Wha . . . what's wrong now?"

Ruth slid a sideways glance toward the three other sleeping women. Patience and Lily hadn't moved. Harper's head burrowed in her pillow, her back end protruding in the air beneath the heavy blankets.

"Ssssh." Ruth bent to lay a finger over Mary's lips. She pressed closer, whispering. "I need your help. I asked Dylan McCall to take me to Wyoming and he refused. I have no other choice but to make him take me."

"Make him?" Mary struggled to sit up. She blinked. "You can't *make* the marshal do anything—"

Harper stirred in the bed beside her.

Ruth slapped her hand across Mary's mouth and bent closer to her ear. "I'm going to trick him."

Mary coughed, the spasm racking her frail body. Ruth moved about the room as quietly as a church mouse. If the others heard and woke up, they'd try to talk her out of her plan. Mary would attempt to reason with her, but Mary would do what Ruth needed. Anxious to be about her plan, Ruth started to stuff personal articles into a knapsack.

Mary shivered as goose bumps popped out on her thin arms. Slipping out of bed, she wrapped a blanket around herself and watched Ruth's movements. "What plan? What are you talking about?"

"My plan to thwart that no-good scoundrel Dylan McCall and rescue myself from Oscar Fleming."

"Oh, Ruth!" Mary sank softly onto the side of the goose-down mattress. "You promised to think about Mr. Fleming's proposal."

"I have thought about it, Mary. I've thought

of nothing else all night. I can't—I won't—marry Oscar."

Mary's eyes followed her movements. Ruth knew what she must have been thinking. Mary was an obedient person. If Oscar had asked Mary to marry him, she would have done so out of a sense of obligation to the Siddonses.

At one time Ruth was thought to have the most common sense of anyone in the group, but Tom Wyatt's deceit had changed that. She'd been gullible enough to fall for the man's deception. Dylan McCall was about to leave and alter Ruth's life irrevocably—that is, if she didn't do something to stop him.

Mary snuggled tighter in her blanket. "What are you going to do?"

"I'm going to follow Dylan when he rides out of town at daybreak."

"Follow him!"

"*Shhh!*" Ruth clamped a hand over Mary's mouth, her eyes darting to the sleeping women. "Just for a little way. Then, when it's too late for the marshal to turn around and bring me back, he'll be forced to let me ride with him."

"Are you nuts, girl?" Harper threw the covers aside and sprang to her feet. Ringlets of tight curly hair stood up like porcupine quills. "That man will hog-tie you and haul you back here like a sack of flour!"

"*Sssssssssh!*"

Two more heads popped out from beneath the

covers. "What are you *sssssss*hing for?" Lily sat up, scratching her head. "Did you honestly think we could sleep through all this racket?"

Beside her, Patience nodded.

"Sorry," Ruth mumbled. "But I don't have a lot of time." She continued throwing things into the sack.

Yawning, Patience peered out the window. "What time is it? It's still dark."

"It's late," Ruth said. *And getting later every moment.*

"What are you going to do if the marshal decides to ride on by himself?" Harper lit the candle on the nightstand, and the room came to light. "He could, you know. Don't seem likes he's the type to let a woman trick him into anything."

"He wouldn't do that." Ruth paused. Would he? No, he wouldn't. Dylan was stubborn, but he wouldn't leave a woman in the Colorado wilderness alone and unprotected. She'd seen him be polite to other women—rarely to her, but she'd witnessed enough to know he wouldn't allow harm to befall any woman in his presence. And she planned to stick to him like honey.

"What are you going to do in Wyoming?" This came from Patience, who yawned in midsentence.

"Find my cousin Milford. Actually, I suppose Milford is a stepcousin—" Actually, Ruth didn't know how to think of Edgar Norris's kin. As relative? Distant relative? Milford was the only hope she had right now, however distant he was. "Milford lives in Pear Branch, Wyoming—or he did ten years ago. The marshal has to go through Wyoming to get to Utah. All I have to do is trail along if he refuses to help me."

Ruth didn't fool herself; it would be most difficult to locate Milford after all these years, but she would work her way through the state until she found him. There was always the possibility that he had moved, but she doubted it. The Norris family were solid folk. Edgar had spoken often of his brother's youngest son, who had made a name for himself in banking at a very early age. Once a Norris planted roots in fertile soil, that's where he stayed. Milford had written a few letters in the earlier years, but then the correspondence had ceased. Ruth figured he had married and filed the memory of his uncle's adopted daughter languishing away in a Missouri orphanage to a far corner of his mind.

"Oh, Ruth, I don't like this plan." Lily got out of bed and wrapped a robe tightly around her. "Dylan is going to be so angry when he discovers that you've followed him. It's almost winter—the weather will be dreadful soon. I know that you plan to follow him and eventually overtake him, but what if you lose sight of him out there in the mountains? You could, you know. Very easily."

The others nodded in solemn agreement.

"You could die out there, with Dylan never even aware of your presence," added Harper.

"Not to mention that a single lady would never travel with an unmarried man," Patience put in. "Why, the stares you would encounter would ruin your name, Ruth. And you're going to hurt poor Oscar's feelings."

"What name?" Ruth pitched a man's shirt in the knapsack. She favored men's warm clothing over skirts and petticoats, and had worn them often on the trail from Westport to Denver City. All the girls had. "I have no name, no family to disgrace, and forgive me, Patience, but Oscar's feelings are the least of my problems. Nobody knows me, and furthermore it wouldn't matter if they did. I will never see my accusers again once I've ridden away." She stared at the pair of male britches in her hand. "Besides, no one will know I'm a woman. That's where I need your help."

The four women frowned and exchanged puzzled looks.

"I'll dress like a boy." She looked up to meet her friends' eyes. "I only have half an hour to get ready. I need men's clothing, boots, and a hat. And a warm coat and gloves." Ruth stared at the women, whose jaws were agape now. "Will you help me? I'm intent on doing this with or without your help."

Lily snapped out of her trance first. "Ruth, you don't know the dangers—weather, a woman on her own—why, you'll be traveling with a handsome, single man. It would be very easy to fall under Marshal McCall's spell—"

"Ha!" Ruth stuck a pair of heavy stockings in the sack. "That I can promise will never happen. The man is despicable—a heathen of the worst sort. He could be the last man left on earth and I would not be the least bit tempted."

As if she even cared about a man, period. Any

man was safe with her. God had evidently pre-ordained that she was to live her life alone—or perhaps with Milford and his family. She could help with Milford's children—be a governess. No, not a governess. She would become attached to the children and she couldn't afford that—not when she knew she'd never have children of her own.

"All the more reason for caution," Lily reminded her. "If the marshal is really this awful—"

"Please." Ruth stopped what she was doing and turned to face the women with pained tolerance. She closed her eyes. "Please. You're the only family I have. If you don't help, then I'll have to do this myself, and there's so little time." She pleaded silently with each girl. If they didn't help . . .

Harper sighed. "I say you're nuts, but I'll help."

Mary slowly nodded. "I'll help—but it's against my better judgment. I love you, Ruth. I can't bear the thought of anything happening to you."

Ruth reached over to give Mary and Harper a hug.

"Count me in," Lily said. "Only I feel the same as Mary. This is crazy and dangerous, but I see you have your mind set."

"Coming all the way from Westport to Denver City was crazy and dangerous," Ruth argued. "We do what we have to do."

Patience joined the circle of hugs. "You know I would do anything for you, Ruth, but I'm still concerned about poor Oscar."

The girls burst into tears, hugging each other. When the moment passed, Ruth wiped her eyes.

"Okay. Dylan will be leaving soon. I need those men's clothes. And a horse."

"Of course," Harper groused. "A horse. And me without a magic wand."

Patience had started to dress. "You leave the horse to me. I know where I can find one."

"I'll take care of the men's clothes," Harper volunteered. "We'll get some from Pastor Siddons. Me, Lily, and Patience will make him new pants and shirts—I don't know what we'll do about the coat and gloves. We'll find something."

"I'll gather enough food for a week—will that be enough?" Mary peered at Ruth.

"I'll make it last. In a week I should be able to reveal myself to Dylan."

"Whoooee," Harper grumbled. "That's gonna be a day of reckoning. And we're gonna have to be real careful or our stay in the pastor's house will be compromised."

Ruth knew the encounter wouldn't be pleasant, but she'd face that battle when it happened. "We'll be careful, and we won't take anything that we can't replace or that we haven't earned."

The girls flew into action. Patience and Lily went after the horse. They'd take one of Tom Wyatt's mares; the girls figured he owed them that. Harper gathered warm shirts and heavy pants, tiptoeing softly about the Siddonses' bedroom as the older couple snored, unaware of the subterfuge taking place under their roof.

"We'll pay you back, sir and ma'am," the black

girl whispered as she eased out of the bedroom and closed the door. "It ain't like we're stealing or nuthin'—we're just borrowing in a pinch."

• • •

Pink was barely creasing the sky when the girls hefted a boyish-looking Ruth up into the saddle. Handing Ruth a sack of bread and cheese and a canteen of water, Mary smiled. "Be careful—our prayers go with you."

"Turn around and come back if you see this isn't going to work. Promise?" Lily grasped Ruth's hand tightly.

"Word of honor." Ruth returned the pressure. With a smile, Ruth whirled the mare and galloped off.

The women listened until the sound of hoof-beats disappeared into the mountainside. The sun broke through over the mountaintop, giving birth to a new day.

"This makes me as nervous as a long-tailed cat in a room full of rocking chairs," Harper breathed, wrapping herself tighter in a heavy shawl. Her breath came in frosty whiffs. "That girl's got David's courage."

"Yes," Patience murmured, "but this time I fear she's taken on more than a giant."

• • •

Ruth rode well to the rear of the marshal's path. Sheer elation fueled her, and she discovered a new world in the heady, brisk mountain air. The small mare was an easy ride, and she had no trouble keeping pace.

As brilliant warmth spread over the hillsides, she spotted a herd of elk feeding in a valley. The magnificent animals' young gathered close, but apparently they scented no threat as Ruth passed by on an upper ledge. Deer grazed in nearby thickets. Blue jays chattered noisily overhead. Her first day out was an adventure Ruth would never forget.

She tipped her face to the sun's rays and thanked God that she had escaped marriage to Oscar Fleming and that she would soon be reunited with family—albeit distant—she had gained the day two Sioux braves had dropped her at the orphanage after her parents died. She tried to picture Milford from the tintype the Norrises had kept on their parlor table. He'd always looked the bookish sort. His eyesight was poor, to the extent he'd worn glasses since an early age. His frail body didn't appear very manly, but he had a poet's heart, Mrs. Norris claimed. Not exactly the exciting sort of man to turn a woman's head, but a very good man. Ruth would be glad to meet Milford for the first time, and she fervently hoped he would react kindly to her unexpected visit.

That night Ruth camped early, following the marshal's lead. She could see smoke from his campfire through towering bare aspens. She did not build a fire; though she craved the warmth, the risk of attention deterred her. She ate cold cheese and bread and drank water from the canteen. Then she opened her journal and while it was still light wrote:

Day One
It has been a most wondrous day, Lord. Thank you for keeping me safe thus far. I saw elk, deer, birds, and a wild turkey just before dusk. Dylan is unaware of my presence. The weather is mild for the eighth day of November; the sky is crystalline blue. I am tired but very happy as I write this.

Sighing, Ruth repacked the journal and rolled up into her sleeping bag to read the Bible by the last rays of light.

●   ●   ●

The wind picked up as Ruth saddled up and rode out of camp the next morning. She'd been awake since long before dawn. She didn't want to lag too far behind Dylan, and she wasn't sure what time he'd leave. So she'd played it safe, waking long before he would wake up. She waited until sunlight barely streaked the sky before she set out.

Within the hour she picked up fresh horse tracks. Smiling, she settled back in the leather saddle to enjoy the day. Animals seemed to be scarce today; by midmorning she spotted a lone hawk flying low to the ground. The wind blew harder and dark clouds skidded across a pewter-colored sky. By late morning she was clinging to the pommel, trying to hang on as a gale cut across mountain passes and howled like a banshee. Nothing fell from the threatening sky, but Ruth knew she would be fighting rain or snow before nightfall.

In the middle of the afternoon, Ruth stopped to water the horse and eat. Both of her arms felt like wet sponges from gripping the saddle horn. As she climbed back on the horse and tied herself in the saddle, she silently thanked Lily for the piece of rope she had thoughtfully included. Twice she'd considered turning around and going back, but then Oscar would pop into her mind. She couldn't go back—she couldn't fail. The wind would eventually die; then things would be better.

By nightfall, Ruth untied herself and fell out of the saddle onto the hard ground. Exhaustion seized her. A heavy rain fell. In the distance she spotted the soft curl of smoke coming from Dylan's campfire. Closing her eyes, she breathed in, certain she could smell roasting meat. Had they traveled far enough for her to reveal herself? Two days of moderate riding. Was that enough to delay Dylan from his duties—so much so that he wouldn't insist on taking her back to Denver City?

She didn't know; her reasoning was clouded. Best to wait one more day—to make certain. He would not waste three whole days to take her back. Teeth chattering, she ate cheese and bread, drank from the canteen, and then hurriedly opened her journal before light gave way. Huddled beneath a dripping pine, she scribbled:

> *Today wasn't so good. The wind's been blowing*
> *so hard I could barely keep my hair attached*
> *to my head. Finally I tied myself in the saddle.*

*Then it started to rain. I couldn't see my hand
in front of my face. I held on and prayed the
horse would follow the path by instinct.*

*Dylan is still unaware that I'm following
him. Am I doing the right thing? The weather
will be better tomorrow—I'm told that weather
changes fast in these parts. I have encountered
no other traveler, but even if I did, I would be
in no danger. Lily said I looked exactly like a
boy with my denims and plaid shirt and my
hair pulled up under my hat. I feel like a man
tonight. Dirty, smelly like a plow horse. But the
bother will be worth it when I see the look on
Mr. Smart Aleck McCall's face when he realizes
he's been tricked. Ha, ha. We'll see who has the
last laugh.*

Ruth shut the rain-smeared journal and huddled
deeper into her wet coat. Her eyes followed the steady
downpour. They'd just see who had the last laugh.

• • •

Ruth awoke to fog. Thick-as-pea-soup fog. Gray
mist swirled around her like pieces of dirty lint. The
air was so thick the mist on her face threatened to
turn to a coating of ice. Her lips were cold and tight,
and the air was so heavy it was like breathing water.

This morning Ruth couldn't tell up from down;
only silence surrounded her. Even the sound of the
mare's hooves was muffled.

Peering ahead in the hope of finding some clearing in the mist, Ruth urged the animal forward. She'd been able to stay a safe distance back from Dylan until now, but in order not to lose him she'd have to ride closer today. She had to hope he didn't look back over his shoulder or hear her horse. The fog would hinder him—he couldn't possibly see her, could he? And if he did, he'd think she was a fellow traveler.

Still, with the marshal's tendency to caution if he suspected anyone on his trail, he wouldn't leave the identity to speculation. U.S. marshals were paid to be vigilant; he'd investigate. She would have to exercise caution, though common sense warned her to close the distance.

Ruth smothered a groan as she stretched her aching back in the hard saddle. Only a fool or a desperate imbecile would be out in this weather, and she and the marshal seemed to qualify on both counts. Shifting in the saddle, she flexed her numb toes in the tight boots and kept pushing forward.

The mountainous range was unfamiliar. There wasn't a clue, not a road marker, not a bent tree, nothing to guide her. Her only hope was Dylan. She needed to see him—even a speck of him—to make certain that she was riding in the right direction, but at the moment she could barely see her hand in front of her face.

Minutes seemed like hours. The mare carefully picked her way over the rocky terrain, clearly no more comfortable with walking blind than Ruth was. Leaning forward in the saddle, Ruth peered into the swirling haze until her eyes burned. Her muscles were so tense her whole body ached.

Was that faint sound ahead coming from Dylan's horse? The light pick of hoof against stone could have come from behind her as well as ahead. Fog made direction impossible to discern.

Suddenly the sound seemed right in front of her. Startled, Ruth reined in. She was too close! Dylan would hear her and turn back to investigate, and she'd be discovered! He'd take her back to Denver City and Oscar without a second thought. She recoiled at the idea. She had to be more careful. She'd never seen a man more determined to take a wife—to take *her* as his wife—than Oscar Fleming. Returning to Denver City and Oscar wasn't an option, no matter what uncertainties lay ahead.

Frightened as a snared rabbit, Ruth prodded the mare forward. Maybe she was foolish to think she could do this—foolish to think she was smart enough, cunning enough, strong enough to carry out this plan. She hadn't thought about fog so impenetrable she could neither hear nor see. She hadn't thought about there not being a clear trail. For all she knew she was going in circles. She blinked back tears.

Wyoming was north—of that she was certain—but with all the fog she couldn't tell north from east. She might as well be standing still for all the progress she was making. Tears stung her eyes. Why wouldn't the fog lift?

Fear was a hand at her throat. She couldn't breathe. Panic captured her. She was drowning—

Ruth halted the mare again and closed her eyes. "Get ahold of yourself," she repeated. "Don't panic. You never panic. Dear Lord, help me not to panic. Forgive me for being foolish. Show me the way. Please—I admit I've been a fool."

She nudged the horse forward, but the animal was as reluctant as she was to move. Only the fear of losing Dylan made her keep urging the horse along.

Ruth's fingers seemed frozen to the reins. Her legs ached and the pain in her lower back now extended to between her shoulder blades. She needed to get off this horse and walk around, gain some feeling back into her feet, ease the tension in her back and legs, but she was reluctant to lose time.

"Eat something," she murmured, refusing to surrender to the fear that threatened to paralyze her.

She reached down and fumbled for the saddlebag, then drew her hand back. The thought of food made her stomach roll. Nothing she could force down would promise to stay down until she knew she was safe, until she could pick up Dylan's trail again.

If she could find him again.

"Defeatist thoughts, Ruth. You can't stop now. You've come too far and you would never find your way back, even if you could face Oscar," she muttered to herself.

Cold seeped into every bone. If she didn't come across Dylan's trail soon, she was afraid she was going to freeze to death.

Suddenly she hit something big and solid—*smack!*

The mare's high-pitched scream pierced the air. Before Ruth could control the reins, the horse reared, throwing her from the saddle. She somersaulted into the air and landed hard, the impact of solid ground jarring her teeth.

Dazed, she rolled over once before realizing she'd been catapulted into a pile of—

She sniffed, her hand reaching out to probe the steaming, warm . . .

She clamped her eyes shut, gritting her teeth. *No! It couldn't be! This couldn't happen!* But there was no mistaking the stench. She groaned and would have flung herself down on the ground in exasperation except she was already flat on her back.

Manure. Fresh manure at that—clinging, stinking manure.

Manure meant cattle. Cattle and a manure pile meant a farm or ranch. Hope bloomed in Ruth's heart. God had heard her prayers! But why would a cow be in these wild parts? Unless . . .

Shrieking in frustration, Ruth bounded to her feet. Her screech made her already-nervous mare bolt and gallop toward the swirling haze. Slamming her fists on her hips, she yelled, "Well, if this isn't a fine howdy-do!" The animal disappeared, swallowed by the murky, gray mass.

Now what?

Flinging bits of manure off her clothing in all directions, Ruth tried to remain calm. But frustration gave way, and she screamed at the top of her lungs. She was on foot; her food, along with her blankets, was gone with the horse; and she was covered in manure!

What else could possibly happen?

She whirled when out of the fog she heard the last thing a woman in Ruth's predicament wanted to hear.

A thunderous masculine expletive that was anything but calm.

Dylan had known that he was being followed an hour after he'd left Denver City. At first he thought it might be some of those pesky rebel Utes that plagued the territory. Then he figured it was more likely someone wanting to get the drop on him. He'd waited nearly three days for the confrontation and was beginning to wonder if he was imagining things.

Suddenly, in the fog, something ran into him. Dylan was thrown from his stallion. Quickly he braced for the intruder to make his move. Instead, a woman's screams pierced the air. Tense moments passed. Gun drawn, Dylan got up slowly and took a guarded step, then another into the swirling mist. His right boot encountered something slippery and mushy. Frowning, he took another step, and his feet suddenly flew out from under him. Airborne for a split second, he dropped his gun and landed on something squashy—and warm. The stench brought tears to his eyes.

Then the kicker happened—the upheaval of the day: he saw Ruth towering above him.

Ruth was following him? Mentally groaning, Dylan wondered why that surprised him.

Instantly he dived for her, trying to gain the advantage, but she was wiry and quick. He gained his footing first but went down a second time in the slimy quagmire. Gagging from the smell, he shot back to his feet, driving for the gun.

Man and woman wallowed, rolling over and through the manure slick. Ruth broke free and crawled beyond his reach. Dylan rolled to the side, out of the path, his hand still searching for the Colt. Blood pumped from his nose.

Suddenly Ruth stood up and calmly put the gun to his temple. "Don't make a move, Mr. McCall, or I'll be forced to shoot you."

Muttering an oath, Dylan fell back when he realized that she meant it. She was desperate enough at this point to do anything.

Cold steel pressed against his temple. "Don't move a muscle or you're a dead man."

Her voice held enough conviction that Dylan decided not to test it. He'd learned long ago to pick his fights, and with a Colt positioned to blow his brains out of his nose, this wasn't one of them.

"Woman," he said calmly, "what is it going to take to get loose of you?" He couldn't see her now, but the firearm convinced him to play along. The fog would have to lift before he could gain the upper hand. Then what? Throw her to the wolves? The idea appealed to his baser instinct—but then his nobler side kicked in.

"Get up slowly," Ruth ordered as she slid the menacing gun barrel to a site between his shoulder blades. He could turn and take her; her slight weight would be no match for his. But maybe he'd let events play out, see what she wanted—as if he didn't know. Play her by the rules of poker until he turned the tables on her.

He pushed slowly to his feet. "I suppose I have to put my hands over my head?"

She cleared her throat—a nervous habit. Oh, it was Ruth—Ruthie—all right. In her most irritating mode.

"That won't be necessary."

He pictured her chin lifting a notch. She was close enough now he could make out the wool shirt, faded denims, and battered hat. Who was she trying to impersonate? A man?

The adversaries stood for a moment, reeking of cow manure. After a while, Dylan tired of the wait. She'd make a poor cardplayer.

"Okay. Now what?" He squelched the urge to yell at her—to bring to her limited attention the idiocy of what she was doing. If she had the gun, Dylan couldn't be the protector. He swallowed back pride.

So she had been the one following him for three days. What did she think? That by following him, threatening to make him late for his appointment, she'd gain her way so he'd have no other choice but to take her to her cousin's place? Foolish woman. There was nothing to prevent him from wiring ahead to inform his boss, Kurt Vaning, he'd run into trouble and wouldn't be in Utah when expected. If he did that, though, the trail on Dreck Parson and his gang would turn cold, and he was getting too close to lose the outlaw now.

Ruth had him—on a spit and roasted like a Christmas goose. His gut seethed with resentment. He turned slowly to face her, irritably shoving the gun out of his face. Her gaze met his steely one in the swirling mist. "Now what?" he repeated.

"I don't know. I didn't expect to bump into you—literally—this soon," she admitted. "I'm thinking."

After a minute, he shifted his weight to one foot. "Can you think a little faster? I'd like to get out of these clothes." The smell of manure turned his stomach.

"Okay—don't rush me." She straightened, taking a deep breath. "As you might suspect, this is the first time I've ever tried to heist anyone."

"Heist." He grumbled under his breath. For two cents he'd forget common sense and take the Colt away from her. "Heist," he muttered. Why didn't she just say *ambush*? *Bushwhack*? *Buttonhole*?

Ruth took her own sweet time thinking about the situation. Eventually she cleared her throat and explained. "I didn't want you to know I was following you—not for another day or two, but now that you do, you might as well know you're going to have to take me to Wyoming whether you like it or not."

"Oh yeah?" He shifted his weight to the other foot. "How do you figure that? I could leave your worthless hide out here and ride off." The idea was more than tempting—it lay in his brain like the thought of a steak dinner. "Someone might find you next spring. Then again—" he turned sinister now—"the buzzards would have picked your hide clean by then."

Her eyes bulged at the suggestion. She cleared her throat.

"But you won't because your conscience and duty as a U.S. marshal won't allow it, and if you turn around and take me back to Denver City, you'll be late for your appointment." She sent him a smug smile from beneath the brim of the tattered hat.

His eyes raked the man's clothing she wore. "You look ridiculous."

"Thank you. You don't look so spiffy yourself."

His hand self-consciously smoothed a bearded three-day growth. "What if I just took the gun away, shot you, and left you for the crows to eat? Seems to me that would take care of both problems."

Her eyes narrowed and she steadied the gun with both hands. "You can't do that. I won't let you." Her clasp tightened around the pearl handle.

He smiled diabolically. "Oh, but I could."

Inching closer, she pushed the barrel into the tip of his tender nose. "Just try it, mister."

He stared at her, teeth clenched. One swift move and she'd be flat on her back. But cool reasoning prevailed and made him hold off. He couldn't shoot her, could never gun down an innocent woman.

His sense of adventure began to override his

annoyance. How far would she go? He'd bide his time and find a way to scare some sense into her. His features relaxed. "Okay, you got me. What now?"

Ruth jerked her head toward his waiting horse. "Reckon we'll have to ride double until we can find my mare."

"And if we don't find your horse?"

The tip of the gun mashed the end of his nose. "Then you walk."

"To Wyoming?" Again his temper flared. If she didn't move that gun, she was a dead woman. His eyes skimmed her clothing a second time. "Why are you dressed like that?"

"If I'm dressed like a boy, no one will know that I'm a woman. My reputation won't be ruined, Mr. McCall. Not that I had one to uphold. Nobody knows me, and I'll never pass this way again. When I reach Milford and his family in Pear Branch, no one will be the wiser."

He shifted the gun barrel out of his face. "Saddle up. We have a long ride ahead of us."

She trained the pistol on his back as they walked toward the waiting animal. Dylan's horse shied as he reached for the reins. Dylan imagined the stallion wasn't fond of its own smell any better than he was. "But we should get out of these clothes first," he said.

"No time. Let's go." Ruth motioned for him to mount. Once he complied, she climbed up and slid on behind him, gun pressed to his ribs. He peevishly adjusted the barrel more to the left for comfort.

"You're not supposed to do that," she snapped. She rammed the gun back into place.

He moved it. "Do you want to lead?"

"I *could*."

"But you're *not*, so hold the gun in a more comfortable position."

She complied finally, grumbling under her breath about "remembering who was boss here."

He kicked the horse's flanks. Ruth yelled when her teeth slammed into her bottom lip. She grasped on to his coattail.

He calmly turned to peer at her over his shoulder. "Sorry—I thought you were in a hurry."

●　●　●

Ruth's mare was grazing on a hillside when they spotted her. The fog was thinner at this altitude. Dylan tied the mare to his bridle, and they rode on. Ruth insisted she ride behind him and hold the gun in place. Dylan knew the woman must be exhausted. Once or twice he'd felt her nod off, only to quickly straighten. By nightfall, his job should be easy pickings.

At the end of the long day, Dylan made camp and built a fire near a mountain stream. Though he could tell she hated the thought, Ruth suggested they take turns bathing. Clothes needed to be washed, and the manure stench had given them each a headache.

"You go first," Ruth ordered, her teeth chattering

in the cold wind as they approached the water. Tall aspens lined the bank but provided little protection from the weather.

He feigned reserve. "Modest, Ruthie?"

Her reticence was apparent as she looked away. "Keep your clothes on. You'll have to wash them and yourself at the same time. Throw your coat onto the bank." The gun came up. "And don't try any monkey business!"

"Don't worry; this will be quick. I promise, Miss—" he paused—"what *is* your last name?"

"Priggish," Ruth answered.

Silence. Then, "You're kidding. Ruth Priggish?"

She lifted the gun another notch.

He grinned. "May I call you Priggy?"

"Just get yourself and your clothes washed quickly." She clamped her eyes shut. "And don't try anything. I'm not looking, but it will only take me a split second if you try anything."

She was smarter than he thought and pretty smug about it, Dylan conceded.

Muttering something that made her blush, Dylan stepped into the water and started to lather up.

•   •   •

While the marshal splashed and cursed his heritage, Ruth, and the icy water, Ruth moved deeper downstream, listening for his location. At the edge of the stream she removed her coat and scrubbed off all the manure she could. She did the same with Dylan's coat. She could hear him, apparently adjusted to the icy water now, singing at the top of his lungs. She couldn't help smiling at his antics.

In pants and shirt, she waded into the stream, biting down hard on her swollen lip to keep from screaming. Ducking beneath the water, she surfaced quickly, holding her breath as she scrubbed her hair, body, and clothing free of manure stench.

Moments later she waded out. Her teeth chattered as she wrapped herself in a blanket she'd brought. She tiptoed back to the tree line.

"Can I come out now?" Dylan sang in a false contralto. "The big, bad marshal is freezing!" The fog was again so thick he was only a voice in the swirling mist.

"I left a blanket on the shoreline. You can wrap yourself in it. Properly!" she demanded. She heard him noisily wade out. There was a moment of silence before he appeared swathed head to foot in the blanket.

She herded him up next to the fire. They both sat there until their teeth stopped chattering. Then Dylan disappeared behind a thicket to change into dry clothes. Ruth did the same, keeping him in sight. He fashioned a makeshift clothesline from tree branches and hung their wet clothes near the campfire to dry. A few minutes later, Ruth smelled fresh coffee perking and fatback frying in a pan. Her stomach growled from hunger. Cheese and bread had been her only food for days. Would he offer to feed her? Well, she had the gun. . . .

Force proved to be unnecessary. He filled two

tin plates with fatback and buttered toast. Handing her one of the plates, he turned and poured two tin mugs of steaming coffee.

Closing her eyes, Ruth bit into the meat, deciding she had never eaten anything that tasted so good. The rich, hot coffee trickled down her throat, warming her insides.

They sat beside the campfire, eating in silence. Ruth felt guilty for tricking the marshal this way. She'd be certain to ask God's forgiveness tonight in her prayers. Yet Dylan would be a free man when he dropped her off in Wyoming. Had she stayed and married Oscar Fleming she would have been indentured to the old prospector for the rest of her life—or at least the rest of his life. In that context, what she was doing didn't seem so ugly.

The hot coffee and warm meal began to take effect. Ruth's eyes drooped. She was so tired, so tense from holding the gun on Dylan all day, frightened to death he would physically take it away and leave her here in the mountains, alone. In the distance a mountain lion screeched. Was it waiting until she slept to pounce? No matter. Sleep was out of the question—she had to stay awake and watch Dylan.

Dylan unrolled their bedrolls close to the fire. Dumping the last of his coffee on the ground, he turned and threw a couple more logs on the fire. "It's time to turn in."

She shook her head. "I'm not going to sleep. You go ahead."

"You're going to stay awake all night?"

She nodded, taking another fortifying sip of the black coffee. "I've done it before."

One time she'd sat up two nights straight taking care of Mary. She'd dozed occasionally, but she had known the moment the girl's cough worsened. She glared at the big brute climbing into the thick warmth of his sleeping roll. Her eyes stole to her own bedroll. *Oh, my . . . that does look tempting. A bath, warm food, warm blanket . . .*

She snapped back to alertness. "Just don't try anything. I'll be watching you every moment."

"Okay," he agreed. "Make sure I don't do anything to upset you." He pulled his bedroll up to his chin and turned his back toward Ruth.

Ha-ha, she thought. He was a clown too.

The campsite was quiet except for the fire popping and logs slipping lower into white ashes. Fog veiled the sky, so Ruth couldn't see the stars clearly. The night was as still as a corpse. Taking out her journal, she wrote about the day's events:

> *Dear Lord,*
> *I wasn't very nice today. But as you know, I'm desperate. I've discovered desperation doesn't make you feel any better about doing something you shouldn't. It makes you feel worse.*

A yawn made Ruth fumble for her coffee cup. The tin tipped, and the contents spilled out and seeped into the ground. Yawning again, she realized that she didn't have the energy to refill the mug.

Reaching for her Bible, she opened to the book of Isaiah. Words blurred as she tried to focus on reading about the potter and the clay. But tonight her mind wouldn't function—it refused to make the connection or find comfort in the passage.

Climbing into the comfort of her bedroll, she prayed for Mary, Patience, Lily, and Harper. She asked for kind husbands and gentle fathers for their children. Each girl was loyal and good . . . any man should be honored to marry any one of them. She prayed for Glory and Jackson. Then her mind turned toward the marshal. Now there was someone who definitely needed prayer. What, if anything, did he believe in?

Ruth yawned again, allowing her eyes to close momentarily.

Dylan's voice drifted to her. "Better go to sleep, Priggy. We have a long ride tomorrow."

"Don't call me Priggy—nobody has ever called me Priggy."

"Don't know why not. The name suits you."

She ignored the rather obvious affront.

"Better not go to sleep," he reminded her sleepily. "I'll get the upper hand if you do."

"I won't, so stop wishing. I should think you would worry about your own welfare!"

"Well, you're right again. I am. I'm very concerned about this situation."

She rolled over into a more comfortable thinking

position. Since she'd be up all night, she might as well think through her plans. Wyoming was still a long way off. She yawned, patting her mouth gently.

"Never underestimate a determined woman," she reminded the marshal.

"So they tell me."

Midnight rolled around. Ruth could hardly keep her eyes open. The wind whistled and the warmth from the fire was nice.

She shoved the gun to the middle of her bedroll—close enough to grab but far enough to keep from accidentally blowing off a toe. She prayed for the Siddonses . . . and the nice people of Denver City . . . as she drifted off to sleep.

• • •

Ruth's eyes flew open. She lifted an arm to shield her gaze against bright sunshine.

Bolting upright in her bedroll, she blinked to clear the sleep away. Why, it must be nine—ten o'clock—by the sun's position. The fog had lifted. She lunged for the gun, searching, fumbling. Ripping the blanket aside, she crawled down into the roll, clear to the bottom, searching for the Colt. Instead of finding the expected steel, her fingers encountered a piece of paper that she ripped out and read in the sunlight.

Her heart sank as she deciphered Dylan's hastily scribbled message: *Miss Priggish. Never underestimate a man who has been royally suckered.*

She crushed the maddening note in her hand, then threw it down and stepped on it. She couldn't think of a name bad enough for that lout.

"Well, at least he left my horse." Her eyes reassuringly located the mare and her saddle. "And my cheese and bread."

Relief flooded Ruth, followed quickly by irritation for falling so soundly asleep. She had no idea where she was—Dylan hadn't seen fit to share that information. She had no notion of how far they'd come or how far it was to the nearest settlement. The hard ground provided no tracks to follow, so Ruth had no idea which direction he had gone. Oh, she had a horse, bread, and cheese, but that was all . . . and the food wouldn't last forever.

Conscious of her vulnerability, she chewed on her bottom lip. She had no idea what to do now that she was truly alone. She buried her face in her hands. Now what? No matter what direction she looked there was only empty space broken by an occasional aspen grove. The purple snowcapped mountains in the distance were pretty to look at but offered no help for traveling, at least not for Ruth.

She'd never felt so alone, so hopeless. She had looked on the bright side at the orphanage, even on the trail to Denver City. But at those times there had been people around, friends who cared about her, depended on her. And on the trail, there had been Jackson, who knew where he was going.

Ruth blinked back tears and sat down. She stared at the mare. "Well, the marshal has left us in a fix," she muttered, still hoping to convince herself she was better off without him. Ruth felt a longing inside for Dylan—in spite of his orneriness—which she didn't care to identify. She straightened her shoulders. "You're a fool, Ruth." The man had refused to help her not once but twice. She didn't need to be clobbered over the head with a brick to know that he wanted no part of her.

Well, maybe she *did* need that brick. If she'd had any sense at all, she wouldn't be in this predicament.

She stared across the landscape. Now that the fog had lifted she could see how desolate the area was—wherever it was. A cloud of depression settled heavily over her. She sat with both hands covering her mouth, her eyes scanning the horizon on all sides. Nothing. Absolutely nothing. Just trees, rocks, and lonely mountain passes. Not even a rabbit whisker—let alone a human being—broke the empty expanse. Only the sound of the cold wind rattling dried grasses broke the silence.

The hard, cold truth seeped into her consciousness. She could die out here. Alone. No matter what direction she might go, chances were she wouldn't find a settlement. Hadn't someone said that was the reason outlaws went north, to avoid people and the law? The observation made sense now.

"We'll stay here," Ruth told the horse. She flicked an ear. "Maybe someone will come along. After all, Dylan was traveling this way. Surely it's a known path to somewhere." She wasn't sure that was a logical thought, but she wanted to believe it.

The mare was staked where Dylan had left her, foraging for what grass she could find. They had plenty of water—they wouldn't die of dehydration.

Ruth sat waiting, hoping, until her stomach reminded her she hadn't eaten since last night. The bread was dry and the cheese virtually tasteless, but she managed to force down the bland fare.

In late fall the evening grows dark early and quickly. At dusk a deer came out to forage and stopped to stare at her from a thicket. Ruth was grateful for that small acknowledgment of life besides herself. The animal eventually wandered off and she was alone again.

She ate the last of her bread, then drew one of the blankets about her shoulders to ward off chill. No one had come today. No one would come tomorrow. She was a fool to even hope so. If anyone had business that would bring him in this direction, he wouldn't travel this late in the year. Not unless he had to, and even an emergency would give the average man pause. The whimsical notion that another soul might pass this way held no merit.

She should have stayed in Denver City and put up with the humiliation of Oscar's public proposal and his following her around like a moon-eyed calf. The truth was a bitter pill to swallow. Marrying Oscar Fleming would have been better than this. Compromise would have been better than death, and right now death seemed likely, since she had no idea of how to get back to Denver City.

She sniffed. "Horse? Why did Dylan McCall

have to be the first man I was attracted to and the man who obviously couldn't care less what happened to me?"

Ruth decided it was time to face the truth. This was just another incident in a long string of misfortunes. She kept hoping things would change, but they never did. Even if she could have located Milford, there was no guarantee he'd have helped her.

She lay back, staring at the sky—one she hadn't seen in days. "I was only four when my parents died of cholera, horse. For some reason God spared my life. Mrs. Galeen, the orphanage mother, told me God had spared me for a reason, that he had a plan for my life."

Ruth glanced at the mare, who appeared to be listening. She smiled and continued. "I tried my best to believe that, but sometimes, particularly right now, the kindly woman's words are hard to accept. Still, God did spare me when the circumstances seemed hopeless. Mrs. Galeen told me that two Sioux braves found me crying in the wagon, my parents and two brothers dead of cholera. Instead of killing me, they took me to the orphanage. Mrs. Galeen saw them early one morning when she had risen to take care of Mary. One of the braves got off his horse, carefully cradling a wide-eyed, dirty-faced toddler, and set me, big as you please, on the orphanage steps. Then he pounded on the door and waited for Mrs. Galeen to recover from her initial fright and summon enough nerve to see what they wanted.

"Anyway, with limited vocabulary and using sign

language, the young man informed Mrs. Galeen of the deaths of my whole family. Then he quickly mounted his horse and the two braves disappeared before Mrs. Galeen could ask any questions.

"Mrs. Galeen named me Ruth—" Ruth peered at the mare. "Did you know that?" She lay back. Of course the horse couldn't have known that. Mrs. Galeen had named her after her favorite Bible character. Ruth had been adopted by Edgar and Beatrice Norris, a schoolteacher and his wife. She lived with them for several years, and they taught her to read, write, and figure her sums. But when Mrs. Norris died in childbirth, the grieving and distraught husband had returned ten-year-old Ruth to the orphanage.

Mrs. Galeen had been sympathetic to Edgar Norris's grief, but she disapproved of his choice not to keep Ruth with him when he returned East to his family. Edgar explained that he was unable to cope with a child, not even one whom he'd called his own for more than six years.

"It took me weeks to get past grieving myself," Ruth told the mare. "It was so hard to get over the death of the only real mother I'd ever known and what I then perceived in my childish mind as the betrayal by the only father I had. Mrs. Galeen, bless her kind soul, did everything possible to help me adjust. But I sought escape in books."

Ruth drew a deep sigh. "The orphanage was the fortunate recipient of any books abandoned by travelers, which afforded the shelter quite a good library of fiction, history, and the classics. I read everything and soon began reading to the younger children at bedtime, which allowed Mrs. Galeen extra time with the older ones."

Finally Ruth grew to accept that she'd lost not only one set of parents but two. "Mrs. Galeen refused to let me blame God or anyone else for my misfortune. The time came when I accepted the Lord as my Savior and friend, not as someone who caused evil but allowed it for his own purposes.

"God allows events in our lives to take place in order to make us stronger in our faith—that's what Mrs. Galeen contends. In which case I ought to be really strong. One time I told her so. But Esther Galeen had only said, 'One day you'll need to be strong, and you'll have his strength to comfort you.'"

Well, Ruth thought as she drew the blanket snugly around her shoulders, *this must be that day.* She found no comfort in the prophecy. She was lost and alone . . . and it was Dylan McCall's fault. If he hadn't just gone off and left her—

Annoyance bloomed anew. What kind of man would just go off and leave a woman alone on an empty mountainside with no help? No one but a rotten, blackhearted, just plain mean kind of man. A man with *no* heart.

"And I wanted to be strong for that man," Ruth contended. "I wanted to be the shining light in his life, to prove—in spite of an occasional bout of temper and bullheadedness—that I walk in faith not in darkness. The marshal seemed to be struggling with a limited amount of trust in the Almighty. Mare, you notice that?"

But anger couldn't drive out her fear. The silence and the darkness began to close in, and tears slid from the corners of Ruth's eyes. She laid her head on the saddle and drew the second blanket close.

"Please help me, God," she murmured. "I know I'm foolish and do things and act when I should be asking your guidance. I'm sorry. Truly, truly sorry. But in your mercy, in your forgiveness, please send someone to get me out of this."

•   •   •

She must have fallen asleep, for when she next opened her eyes, a hazy dawn surrounded her. Ruth slowly unwound from her blankets, groaning as her stiff muscles complained.

Distant thunder convinced her that she'd best take shelter from the approaching storm. Struggling with the weight of the saddle, Ruth managed to get the heavy leather over the horse that peered over her haunch with a pained expression, as if to ask what Ruth thought she was doing.

"I don't know," she muttered, tightening the cinch. "But I can't sit here and wallow in self-pity a moment longer."

By the time the mare was saddled, Ruth was trembling with exertion. She would have to find substantial food soon or she'd be too faint to ride. Urging the horse toward an outcropping of rocks,

Ruth sought cover in a small cave. She squeezed the mare through the tight opening and thanked God for safety as the skies opened up in a torrential cloudburst.

She spotted the skunk the same instant it spotted her. Lifting its tail, it sprayed the area before Ruth could flee. She turned the mare, but it was too late. Throat choking, eyes burning, she clung to the saddle, barely able to hang on to the skittish horse.

"Oh!" she managed, gagging and blinking through tearing eyes.

The horse snorted repeatedly, trying to clear her nose of the suffocating stink. Ruth clung to the bridle and tried to breathe. Wind drove the falling rain back into the cave.

Easing the horse into the rain, Ruth galloped to an aspen, dismounted, unsaddled the mare, and looped the tether rope around a rock. Then she ran under an overhanging ledge. She sank to the ground and stared at the worsening downpour. She was tired, so weary her bones ached. She stank; her clothes reeked of varmint. Her stomach ached for hot food. She wanted a real bed, not blankets on the cold ground. She wanted someone to find her, to rescue her.

She stared at the falling rain, but she didn't cry. She was long past mere tears.

Her life couldn't possibly get any worse.

5

Ruth clung miserably to the rock all night. When daylight broke harshly over the mountain range, she grudgingly opened her eyes to face a new day. Her bones felt frozen beneath the soggy ledge. The rain had stopped, but the air was damp and a chilly wind whistled through the gorge.

A noise caught her attention, and she glanced at the ridge below her. Eyes darting back and forth, she scanned the shelf. Undoubtedly there were all sorts of wildlife in these parts. She'd ridden by deer, elk . . . skunk. Her nostrils still stung from the unpleasant encounter. Late last night she'd moved farther away from the original experience and changed clothes, but the odor still lingered in the crisp mountain air.

She heard it again: a soft rustle—down below. She knew there were bears in Colorado—and mountain lions. Glory had skinned an elk once to save her and Jackson's lives when they were lost in an early blizzard.

Ruth waited, holding her breath, nervous now. *Imagination, Ruth. It's only your imagination. Out here you can imagine that you hear anything.*

She rolled to her feet and rubbed circulation into her arms. Fumbling with the knapsack, she removed the last of the cheese. Only enough rations to last the day. Then what? She didn't know what.

Crouched beneath the overhang, she ate her breakfast and pondered her actions. Actually, the marshal had every right to deny her demands, she decided. Marshal McCall had been thinking clearly. In the light of sanity Ruth realized that emotions had ruled her heart. A single man escorting a young lady across two territories would be disastrous to the lady's reputation and highly improper, however obscure Ruth considered her standing.

She took a bite of cheese.

Dylan was acting properly. It was she who had been demanding and difficult, and she would apologize if she ever crossed the marshal's path again.

Yet she wouldn't be here—stranded, alone, unprotected—if Dylan hadn't been so *infuriatingly* close-minded. Mulish pride it was. He'd behaved even more irresponsibly than Ruth—scoffing at her, playing her for a fool, biding his time until he could seize the advantage. Not to mention leaving her out here to die! She bit into the cheese again, yanking a hunk free with her teeth. A gentleman would never act as Dylan McCall had acted.

Remorse ate at her. Why had she fallen asleep and allowed him to escape? She was certain she had been watching the campfire flames lick at the burning wood, totally attentive.

She ripped off another bite of cheese.

Next thing she knew, Mr. McCall had fled like the rogue he was and left her with an embarrassing note—and egg on her face!

Springing to her feet, Ruth flung the last bit of cheese into the wind. Apologize to *him*? Never! Wild horses couldn't drag an apology out of her. If an act of contrition was in order, Marshal McCall should do the apologizing. She just ought to write the United States government and inform them exactly what kind of man they employed! And she would, the moment she could get her hands on suitable writing paper—not a page from a journal.

She started as a mountain lion suddenly appeared on the ridge below. The cat stood for a moment, green eyes assessing her. Then he lunged toward her, his sleek body sailing through the air.

With a high-pitched squeal, the mare bolted and scrambled over the rocky shelf. Ruth froze. She could feel her heart beating in her chest like a trapped sparrow.

The cat landed not twenty feet in front of her. It didn't move; nor did she. Eternity passed while beast and woman faced off.

Ruth's life flashed before her eyes. Early child hood—Papa bouncing her on his knee; Momma, beautiful Momma, thrashing about, pale and hot in the back of the wagon.

Years in the orphanage when she sat at the window and watched the road for any sign of Edgar Norris. He'd promised to come back; he'd said he needed her to help him begin a new life without

Beatrice. But he'd ridden off. Ruth had waved and waved until she could no longer see the schoolteacher's slumped form in the saddle.

Other images raced by: the hot, dusty journey across Missouri and Kansas. Patience, Lily, Harper, Mary, and Glory—the only family she knew—laughing across the campfire as the girls cooked and washed dishes after the evening meal. Ruth didn't want to die—she didn't want to heap even more heartbreak on the girls—even if the women might never know her fate.

Ruth suddenly straightened, stretching taller than her five feet two inches. She was too young to die, but die she would before she'd run. She glared back at the cat, pasting her most determined look on her face.

Then as suddenly as he'd appeared, the animal turned and softly padded away. It took a moment for the act to register. Ruth dropped to her knees in relief and gratitude and burst into tears. But still, her resentment toward Dylan was so strong she felt faint.

After a while she harnessed her emotions. Picking up the knapsack and the saddle, she set off in search of the horse. The mare hadn't wandered far; she grazed in a small valley about a quarter mile from camp. Ruth threw the heavy saddle onto the ground and collapsed in a heap on the leather. Her arms ached from dragging the burdensome load, and her heartbeat had only now slowed to normal. However could she survive? She was a woman alone in the wilderness. A woman without a man's protection—curse that Dylan McCall's rotten hide.

Later she rose slowly and dampened the tip of her finger to test the wind. Should she ride back east, where she knew Oscar Fleming waited, or ride northwest, where her future was less certain?

She saddled the horse and turned northwest. As long as she kept her bearings and watched the sun, she should reach—what, Mexico? In a year? No, Mexico was south. Maybe she'd wander into Alaska—she had no idea where she was going, but she must keep going. She would have to work along the way, but she was capable of earning her keep. She knew how to cook, clean, sew—do whatever a new start required.

That night, as she warmed herself over a small campfire, Ruth decided God was taking care of her after all. She'd made it this far without any real harm. It was still possible she would find Cousin Milford. Then again, the effort might surely prove as futile as her demands on the marshal. Wyoming was a large territory. She hadn't had contact with Milford since his last letter five years ago; he could be dead for all she knew. She had to stop this wishful thinking and concentrate on reality.

Turning a page in her journal, she wrote:

Dear God,
Though I must try your patience, please forgive me. I know that you keep your promises and I unthinkingly break mine. Forgive me for my uncharitable feelings toward Dylan McCall. He must surely

feel very proud of himself tonight. But his
thoughts don't matter. You have protected
me from harm as surely as you protected
Daniel, who continued to worship you
morning, noon, and night, even when King
Darius sadly agreed to throw him to a pack
of starving lions. I shall continue to worship
you, too, and I give you praise and thanks. I
am very tired tonight, but because of you, my
hope remains intact.

●　●　●

The days started to blur. Ruth rode backcountry,
wandering aimlessly at times. When the sun shone,
she studied the cooling sphere, as its warmth grew
more distant from the earth. Each rustle, each unex-
plained crackle, sent her hopes spiraling. Dylan. He
had come back for her!

But when a squirrel or chipmunk scurried past,
storing nuts for the winter, her spirits plummeted.
She might never reach a town or a mining community. The prospect that she could very well die here
among scented pines and industrious squirrels grew
more probable with each passing hour.

Wind whispered through brittle branches. Each
morning Ruth noticed evidence of fresh snowfall on
distant peaks as she read her Bible. The air had a bitter bite now, yet she marveled at sights she'd never
appreciated. Everywhere she looked she saw evidence
of God's hand. Breathtaking land was dotted with

pine stands so tall and thick that daylight couldn't penetrate the ground. Overhead the sky stretched wide, providing an endless canopy. When the sun shone, it glowed with a blinding radiance. Ruth had heard stories about miners going mad in the solitude, and she could understand why. Out here with no one but the horse for company, she was filled with loneliness deeper than she'd ever experienced. Other times, the solitude was her friend, and she communed closer with God than she'd ever thought possible.

Nights she camped earlier and earlier, eating what she could find—bitter berries or an occasional trout she managed to snag from an icy stream.

* * *

Nearing noon on the fourth day, she came upon a sight that made her stop the horse dead in its tracks. An old mining road cut through a stand of pines. A canvas wagon pelted with arrows stood ablaze in the middle of the path. From her vantage point, she was able to make out two sprawled forms—men, she thought—lying beside the wreckage. Both dead, from the looks of it.

Shuddering, she eased the mare a safe distance around to pass. She said a silent prayer for the poor unfortunate souls. Indian attacks were less frequent now, but she'd heard that certain rebel bands still carried a deadly grudge. Fear rose like bile to the back of her throat when she realized the attack must have taken place not too long before she came upon the devastation. Her eyes scanned the area. Were the savages still around? Everything in her said, *Run! Don't go near the butchery!*

She swallowed back panic as the horse traveled slowly past the gruesome scene. Ruth's conscience nagged her. What sort of person refused to help a fellow human being? Though both men appeared lifeless, what if they weren't? What if a speck of breath remained and she rode past?

The poor souls are dead, Ruth. Don't be foolish. Ride on.

But one could be alive, and it wasn't as if she couldn't spare a moment. Maybe somewhere a distraught wife or anxious child prayed for a husband or father, and worried eyes scanned the horizon looking for him.

Pensively she slowed the horse. She knew little about nursing, but she might hold the dying man's hand and pray with him until he drew his last breath.

Every instinct screamed for her to be rid of the obligation. Waves of apprehension rolled over her at the gory sight adjoining the flaming wagon. But words of Jesus rose unbidden to her mind: *"Inasmuch as ye have done it unto one of the least of these my brethren, ye have done it unto me."* The horse stopped and Ruth studied the situation. The savages could be lying in wait for yet another unsuspecting victim. *I'm afraid, Lord. I'm a woman alone,* she reminded him. *I don't have a gun.*

She listened for God's answer in the swaying pines.

What if one of the victims was alive? What if by a simple act of compassion she could save a life? Fear so thick she could taste it lay on her tongue. Then anger broke the surface. This was all Dylan's fault! How was the marshal going to feel if a prospector or some kind stranger found her arrow-riddled carcass picked clean by buzzards? Would he be so proud of his cowardly actions then?

And you, God. Why would you put me at the mercy of such a despicable man! Her bitterness smoldered, working her into an anxious state.

Clucking softly, she nudged the mare closer, aware that her hands were trembling. Well, why not? What hands wouldn't tremble at the sight before her? Even fearless Harper wouldn't think twice about kicking the horse into a gallop. Her eyes focused on the task, Ruth urged her skittish mare forward. *You can do this, Ruth.* Only a heathen would ignore the need. She could at least see if there was a breath of life left in either body. If both victims were dead, she'd set the horse into a gallop and never look back.

The sight before her strung her nerves tight. The only sound was the snap and crackle of the flames eating at the white canvas and Prussian blue wagon body. Whoever had committed this carnage was barbaric. Even the horses had been slaughtered, left lying in their tracks. Dread that she'd suffer the same fate warred with Ruth's sense of Christian duty. No. There was no reason for the savages who'd done this to come back, she told herself. Every living thing was dead, and the wagon would soon be reduced to ash. Whoever had committed this horrible deed had meant to leave no witnesses or anything of value behind.

Ruth girded up her courage and slid off the horse. Holding the reins tightly, she surveyed the scene carefully. Nothing. Not one sign of life in the motionless bodies that lay in the dust.

Her stomach pitched. So *much* blood. No one could survive after losing that much blood. One man lay faceup. An arrow jutted from his chest. No sign of life there. The second man lay facedown. She approached slowly, trying to determine if she could see even the hint of a rise and fall of his back to indicate life, hoping against hope that there was. Two long arrows protruded from his left shoulder.

Ruth whirled when she heard something above the roaring fire that was now making strong headway with the wagon canvas. A thin, high-pitched wail filtered through the hot inferno. What was that?

The cry came again, angry this time. Then it struck her. A baby! A *baby* was in that wagon!

Ruth dropped the reins and raced toward the fire. Heat radiated from the dancing flames, scorching her face. Black smoke stung her eyes, but she forced herself to rip away the back opening. The wagon was tall, and her gaze barely cleared the gate as she peered into the black pit. Flames had begun at the front of the wagon, but now burning scraps of canvas swirled upward over the frame and rained down to set fire to anything in their path.

A baby's cry came to her, weaker this time.

Concern for personal safety fled as Ruth stepped on a wheel spoke and heaved her slight weight into the burning wagon bed. The wail intensified—and then she saw it. A tiny hand waving above a make-shift bed secured against one side of the conveyance.

Horror filled Ruth. *Hurry. Hurry!*

Swallowing back dread, she fought her way through thick smoke. *Hurry! Hurry!* Coughing, her lungs burning, she refused to acknowledge the lick-ing flames. The child's cough and strangled screams tore at her heart.

She snatched up the infant and the blankets around it and stumbled her way blindly back through the wagon. Bits of burning canvas filled the air, burning holes in her shirt, but Ruth ignored the pain and clutched the screaming infant to her chest. With one hand grasping the wagon frame, she hurled a leg over the tailgate. In her haste, her foot caught and she sprawled out of the wagon, but she kept a firm hold on the child. Her breath was knocked out in a whoosh, and for a moment everything turned black. She staggered to her knees, then to her feet, and ran away from the wagon, now fully engulfed in flames. Ruth sprawled back to the ground and groaned audibly, now acutely aware of burns on her shoulders, arms, and hands. But she'd made it out alive, and the baby was safe.

The baby snuffed and grasped Ruth's hair with

its tiny hands. Balancing the infant on her lap, Ruth drew back the blanket.

A round, smoke-smudged face dominated by large brown eyes peered up at her. Tears formed dirty rivulets down its cheeks, and its pug nose was running. Absently Ruth wiped the moisture with a corner of the blanket.

Serious dark eyes studied Ruth, and then a short stub of a thumb popped into a rosebud mouth. A thatch of straight, black-as-coal hair fell over the rounded forehead.

"Oh, my," Ruth murmured.

The baby looked to be about six or seven months old. Just big enough to sit up alone and perhaps begin to crawl. Ruth studied the little chubby hands, the fingers wrapped around her thumb. Perfect little nails and smoke-smudged, brown skin.

"Why, you're an Indian baby," Ruth whispered. "What were two grown men and an Indian baby doing out here alone?" The gruesome discovery didn't make sense, but Ruth was so exhausted she could hardly think. What were they doing here? Unless . . . unless the two men had stolen the baby. But why? Why would two men steal an infant? That didn't make any sense. Still, here were two white men, probably both dead, and an Indian baby. Had the Indians followed and massacred the thieves? But if that was the case, why didn't the Indians take the baby with them? Nothing made sense here, but the fact remained that an infant survived, and the child was now her responsibility.

Ruth sighed, gazing down at the child, whose eyes were beginning to droop with sleepiness. Behind them, flames destroyed the wagon. "What am I going to do with you?"

The baby peered up at her as if to say, "I thought you might know."

Something twisted inside Ruth. A baby. Knowing she could never have children of her own, Ruth had carefully pushed all thoughts of a baby to a dark corner of her mind and safely locked the door. God didn't intend for her to have children, nor a young husband. . . . The two naturally went together.

But she wouldn't think about that—not now. If she didn't think about it, then it wouldn't hurt. *You cannot care about this baby; it isn't your child. It belongs to someone else. Don't care about it; don't get attached to it. Just take care of it until you can get it to someone.*

Her eyes searched the area. Now what to do? What to do about those two men? Could she just leave them out here like this? She had nothing with which to dig graves. She could say a few words over them, but that was all she could do.

Immediately a host of new problems presented themselves. Food. The baby was probably hungry, and she had no food or milk to feed it. She could barely feed herself. Shelter. Ruth struggled with a flooding sense of urgency to leave the scene of massacre as quickly as possible. Refusing to acknowledge minor burns that now were quite painful, Ruth made her tired mind think logically. What should she do first?

Holding the baby close, she turned back to survey the scene. The wagon was nearly gone. Even as she stared, the wagon bed burned through and fell to the ground, taking the remainder of the canvas with it as the wheels fell inward. Soon all that would be left were ashes the wind would blow away.

What had two men been doing with a baby? Would anyone miss the thieves? Was someone nearby waiting for their return? Was this baby's mother frantically pacing a tent and wringing her hands in despair? Or had the mother died during a battle and that's why these men had the child? There were a thousand questions and no answers.

Ruth drew a deep breath as she studied the two men—one obviously dead, the other surely—

No. Ruth felt brief hope. No. The one lying on his face had moved, hadn't he? She shook the notion away. Maybe she only *wished* he had moved. Then she wouldn't be alone. His bloodstained shirt was a stark reminder that no one could survive such grave injuries. She stared harder. But there it was again . . . the slight, almost imperceptible movement that meant . . . he was alive?

Ruth carefully set the baby aside and stood up, her eyes fixed on the wounded man. She wondered what, if anything, she should do. She possessed no experience with such dreadful wounds. A few times she had helped Mrs. Galeen dress a cut finger or bandage a scrape, but certainly nothing this serious. Two arrows stuck out of the stranger's left shoulder blade. Blood pooled near his waist. Perhaps he wouldn't welcome her help; perhaps she should just leave and allow the poor creature to die in peace.

A man who would steal a child could hardly be worth saving, but the Good Book said that each man was a creation of God and therefore worthy of attention. So this man was actually, in a way, a lost brother. Must she lay claim to him? Jesus' story of the Good Samaritan came to her mind. But the Samaritan had an inn to take the man to; Ruth didn't even know where she was.

She edged forward, hands clenched at her side. She didn't have herbs or healing tonics. She couldn't supply blood. But she could pray with the poor soul—that she could do. Jesus promised the thief on the cross, when the miscreant petitioned the Lord for salvation, that that very day he would be in heaven.

The baby started to cry—a reedy, pitiful appeal. Ruth shushed the child under her breath. "Quiet, baby. *Shush*."

Overhead a mountain jay circled, its shrill cry blending with the baby's. Wind whistled through the passes and a threatening sky lowered.

Cautiously approaching the inert man, Ruth knelt in the dirt and laid her hand on his back, wincing as her hand encountered warm, sticky, life-sustaining blood. Her heart went out to the stranger though she knew he must surely be evil. But life was precious—too precious to waste in pursuit of wickedness. She said a silent prayer for his soul.

At her touch, he moaned and she sharply drew back. So he *was* alive!

She sat back on her heels and thought, trying not to look at him. The sight made her squeamish, and she couldn't afford to faint now. The arrows had to come out. Her stomach heaved at the mere thought of what that would entail. He needed to be rolled to his back, and that wasn't possible with the arrows still protruding. If he lived—and that was optimistic thinking at this point—it would be more merciful to remove the weapons while he was unconscious.

Stripping out of her coat, she laid it aside and rolled up her sleeves. The baby fretted, needing attention.

"I'll be there in a moment," she said, her eyes fixed on the task ahead. Bracing a boot on the injured man's back, she leaned over and pulled, jerking the first arrow out cleanly.

Sweat pooled on her forehead as she took a step back to view her work. A tiny stream of blood seeped out of the open wound. Not bad—he wouldn't bleed to death—at least not from that particular wound.

Biting her lower lip, she braced her boot on the man's right shoulder, then grasped the second arrow in both hands and yanked. The stubborn projectile had imbedded deep. She got a firmer grip and pulled, gritting her teeth as the flint tip refused to budge. Tightening the hold on the arrow's shaft, she strained, pulling now with all her might.

A scream rent the air as the man drifted close to consciousness.

Sweat rolled from Ruth's hairline. She bit her lip and pulled harder, the man's pain barely penetrating her numb senses. The baby started to wail louder. Ruth felt like crying herself, but she couldn't let up now. She tensed, pulling, ignoring the man's screams of agony.

"Come on," she pleaded, then tightened her hold again and pulled with all her strength. Sweat dripped into her eyes now. Only adrenaline kept her focused. The baby's howls fused with the injured man's voice. On the fifth try, the stubborn arrow gave way, propelling Ruth backward. She landed hard on her backside, her teeth slamming into her upper lip. She tasted blood. Her head was spinning.

The arrow rested in her hand, its pointed head still attached to the shaft. This was good, she knew. She wouldn't have to dig any part of the arrow out—she doubted the man could survive such torture.

Getting to her feet, she returned to the sprawled form and bent close, trying to detect life. Surprisingly his back rose and fell laboriously. The second gaping wound pumped like a geyser. She ripped a strip off his shirttail and carefully packed the most severe wound, oblivious to her burns. It wasn't an ideal bandage, but she'd done all she could to try and save his life.

Confident she'd done all that she could do, she stepped to the other man and checked for a pulse. The unshaven man looked old enough to be her grandfather, his faded blue eyes staring up at her sightlessly.

"May God have mercy on your soul," she whispered before closing his lids. Straining, she lifted the limp body to strip off his jacket.

Ruth returned to the squalling infant and tried to quiet it. The child alternately sucked its fist and screamed, thin arms thrashing the air. The baby was hungry. Responsibility felt like a wad of cotton in the back of Ruth's throat. How would she feed a child? She had no cow—nothing. The wagon had been reduced to smoldering rubble, its contents destroyed.

She picked up the child and walked, jiggling it up and down. Her mind raced. She was suddenly responsible for two lives, and she had no idea how to help either one. The injured man remained face-down in the dirt, as still as lake water. And the baby had worked itself into a hysterical fervor.

Lifting her face toward the sky, she called out, "What do I do? Help me!"

When no answer came readily, Ruth took the child and sat down on a rock. Gently prying the baby's mouth open, she probed for teeth. Her heart sank when she encountered two rows of smooth pink gums. Well, so much for berries and fish. Her eyes scanned the area. Black smoke was boiling up from the charred, boatlike remains of the wagon. She got up and scavenged through smoldering debris, searching for anything usable. How had the men fed the baby? Perhaps they hadn't meant to feed it.

Horror made her catch her breath. What if they'd intended to do the child harm? Let the poor thing starve to death as some sort of horrible reprisal? She shook the ugly thoughts away. *Concentrate, Ruth. You have to find food for the child.*

Hope surfaced as a new thought beset her. Maybe the men planned to take the child to a nearby community. If so, the town couldn't be far. Relief flooded her and she carefully held the baby, taking care not to cradle it. If both men died, she'd take the baby and ride to the nearest town—settlement—whatever.

Returning to the sprawled form, she bent down and peered at his bloodstained back. She could detect only the faintest rise and fall now, but he was still clinging to life.

Her eyes fell on his boots and she frowned. They looked vaguely familiar—but she supposed all men's boots were similar. These looked new and made of expensive leather.

Her thoughts turned to the job ahead. She wasn't strong enough to bury either man by herself, and it wouldn't seem fitting to bury one and not the other. She would be forced to leave both victims and pray that a stronger stranger would take pity and bury them before the vultures had their day.

Laying the baby on the ground, she turned and took the younger man's shoulder and gently tugged, trying to roll him to his back. He was so large, his deadweight was impossible for her mismatched strength.

Straddling his shoulder blades, she grasped his right arm and strained, managing to get his lifeless form rocking. She got a firmer grip and rocked until she managed to flip him to his side. She gave him a final heave, and he flopped over on his back. Task accomplished, she paused to take a deep breath and assure the baby she was nearly finished. "Maybe God will even provide a cow along the way," she encouraged.

She turned, gearing up to put a face to the injured man, when her jaw dropped. For a moment she forgot to breathe. Lying before her, bleeding to death, was none other than Marshal Dylan McCall!

Her breath caught in a short gasp before she fell to her knees and began ripping the hem of her shirt into narrow strips. Dylan! *Dear God, don't let Dylan die!*

The smoking water barrel from the wagon still contained a few precious drops. Ruth dashed the cloth strips into the dampness and rushed back to Dylan.

Rolling the law officer to his side, she packed the damp cloths in the worst wound, all the while incoherently praying that her pitiful effort would be enough.

As she watched life drain out of the impossibly stubborn Marshal McCall, her thoughts screamed for answers. *What* was the marshal doing with an Indian baby and a man old enough to be his grandfather? If the thought of Dylan's dying wasn't enough, the realization that she might never know the answer to this crazy puzzle was almost as unsettling.

An exhausted Ruth studied Dylan, who hadn't moved in over two hours. Only through God's grace had she managed to drag him away from the carnage to the small fire she'd built.

Darkness closed around the woman, injured man, and child. Fifty yards away the smoking rubble burned low. She'd gathered enough firewood to last the night, then dragged the older man's body farther away—far enough that she could no longer see him.

Over and over, Ruth mashed bits of dry berries into the little girl's gums, but she only spat the bitter fare out and cried harder. "I know it isn't milk, but you have to cooperate," Ruth cried in frustration. "We're both making sacrifices here." She'd been at this process for over an hour, and she was crying as hard as the baby. She couldn't get enough of the sustenance into the child to ease her hunger.

She got up and walked the baby around the fire, jiggling, jostling. For the first time in her life she was actually thankful that God had spared her from motherhood. She definitely would have been an abject failure! As darkness fell, a cold chill settled over the campsite. She took the coat from the dead man and laid it over Dylan. She was cold; the baby was chilled and crying. She sat down, staring at the campsite. She would have sworn hell had more flames—but then she'd been wrong about other things, too.

In the wee hours of morning, Ruth couldn't take the child's agony any longer. She decided to try nursing her. She had no idea if she could sustain the infant until she could find a source of food, but she was down to her last option. The child hungrily suckled. Ruth's eyes smarted at the infant's vigor. Nursing hurt! After a while, she settled back, listening to the blissful silence. Whatever fluids the child was getting, the effort had worked, for now.

Ruth rested against a rock and closed her eyes as exhaustion overcame her. Dylan couldn't die— the idea was simply too horrific. Though their wills clashed, she didn't wish him harm. The thought of his dying almost stopped her heart. She was afraid, so terribly afraid to check his reedy pulse. She had no idea what he was doing out here with a baby and an old man, but he must have had his reasons. Jackson thought highly of the marshal; Dylan must possess some redeeming features. Instantly his smile came to mind, his teasing voice, the way he'd helped protect the wagon train of girls on the trail. . . . Just because he got under her skin was no reason not to see the good in this man.

Her gaze turned back to check on the sleeping

man, and she felt something inside her soften. This insane, intense notion that strong men—particularly men like Edgar Norris and Dylan McCall—would take care of women wore on her. She didn't like the direction her thoughts were taking. She felt almost pity for the marshal . . . perhaps it was just deep compassion.

She gazed down at the now sleeping baby warmly cuddled against her bosom and fought back a burgeoning wave of pride. She had to be careful about this; the baby was an unwanted responsibility, just like Dylan. She couldn't let herself fall in love with the black-haired cherub.

* * *

The sound of wind first penetrated Dylan's awareness. The wind was rising, howling through the passes. Recoiling from the feverish pain in his left shoulder, he realized he was lying in the dirt. What was he doing on the ground? His brain refused to function, and when it did, he was ambushed by images—the wagon, the old man. Comanches. And then came the pain. Searing, blinding pain.

He lay with his eyes closed, listening. Where was he? He heard the wind—and a woman's soft murmur . . . sounds, not words. Who? What?

Summoning the courage, he slowly opened his eyes and saw sky. It was early morning and he was cold—very cold. There was a blanket—no, a man's coat—over him. Then he saw her.

Ruth.

Ruth sat across the fire, bent over something small she held in her arms. He blinked to clear the haze from his sight. A tiny hand—a baby. Ruth was holding an infant.

She glanced up and saw him, and relief momentarily crossed her face. "You're awake," she said softly. She laid the infant on the ground and moved around the fire to kneel beside him. Her touch was gentle, almost caring, as she lightly brushed the backs of her fingers along his forehead.

"Your fever isn't as high. Would you like a drink of water?"

His throat was a hot, dry bed of pain. He nodded.

She reached for the canteen and took off the lid. "Is the pain bad? I'm sorry; I don't have anything to treat the injuries—I tried."

"Water," he whispered.

"I know. Here. Drink." She lifted his head and allowed only tiny bursts of relief to fill his parched throat. "Careful. You haven't had anything to drink or eat in a while. Slowly . . . slowly," she encouraged. He hungrily lapped at the moisture trickling into his mouth.

"I found a spring yesterday—there, over that rise," she said, pointing to the east.

He laid his head back, warring with the threat of losing consciousness again.

"There," Ruth said in a hushed voice. "You should feel better now. You may have more in a few minutes." She twisted the lid back on the canteen and set the container aside. Bending close, she adjusted the coat more tightly against his neck. He watched her movements, wanting to ask why . . . when . . . but pain stole the effort.

It was dark when he opened his eyes again. Ruth was holding a baby. How and why was Ruth with a baby? His thoughts refused to come together.

"How did you get here?" he croaked.

She jumped, apparently startled by his voice. When she recovered, she modestly turned so that her back was to him. "I could ask you the same thing. I saw smoke and found you and another man full of arrows and the wagon on fire. How did you happen to be here?"

Words refused to form. It hurt to speak. Finally he found his voice. "I . . . heard the confusion . . . made my way closer. Comanches . . . had the old man surrounded. He was under . . . wagon, behind the wheel . . . holding them off with a rifle. I started shooting from . . . behind a rise. I surprised them, but . . . too many. By the time I worked . . . close, they overrode us." His fevered eyes moved to the bundle she was holding. "Where . . . did you get . . . baby?"

Surprise marked her features. "Here. It was in the wagon. Those savages set the wagon on fire with the baby inside it."

He closed his eyes briefly. "I didn't know. I didn't know there was a baby."

The blanket fell away from the infant's head. Black hair, shiny as a crow's wing, registered with his dulled senses.

Ruth changed the infant's diaper, fastening at the baby's hips the strips of cloth she'd made from the dead man's shirt. She spoke in soothing tones as the infant protested the cold intrusion.

Dylan closed his eyes, pushing pain away. Sometimes he clung to consciousness by a thread; other times he felt almost clearheaded.

In one lucid moment, he looked at Ruth again. Her hair was in tangles; her clothes had holes burned in them. She looked very different from the girl he'd met on the way to Denver City—older, more tired. Very different from the scared girl he'd backtracked and kept an eye on for the past several days. This Ruth was different from the spitfire he'd left on the trail; this Ruth was tender, warm, and caring.

Though he'd been so blindingly furious at her, he hadn't ridden far before he realized he couldn't leave her alone. He'd circled back each morning to make sure she was traveling in the right direction. She had piqued his exasperation even more by staying put the first day. She'd delayed him so long he wondered if he'd ever reach his destination. She'd stall, but then the determination that drove Ruth Priggish marched out like ants at a church picnic, and she was off again. He'd made sure he was riding far enough ahead that she couldn't detect him. He wanted her to stew in her own gravy—make her think that she was lost and alone and had no way out. Her reckless behavior warranted a few anxious days, but he'd known all along he'd be the one to see her safely to Wyoming—on his terms.

Now here they both were: Dylan with two holes in his shoulder; Ruth sitting there in a charred shirt and scorched trousers, nursing a Comanche baby. He closed his eyes and wished that he had the strength to ask how she'd fallen into this one, but he didn't. Maybe later . . .

The answer was sure to confuse him.

•   •   •

Dylan next woke to find the fire blazing and Ruth bustling about the campsite, talking to the baby. Somehow he had lived through another night. Because of Ruth's prayers? He doubted it.

His smothered groan drew Ruth's attention, and she quickly set the child back on its blanket and returned to his side. "Would you like more water? I know you must be hungry. So am I. When you feel well enough to keep an eye on the baby, I'll search for food." Her eye fell on the rifle. "Perhaps I can shoot something . . ." She tipped the canteen to his dry lips. "I'm sorry I can do so little, but I have nothing to work with."

"Is the baby all right?" Dylan asked between drops.

"As well as she can be under the circumstances." Ruth cocked her head to one side in query. "We need to find a town, to find suitable food for her."

He weakly pushed the water aside. "Sulphur Springs . . . we can't be too far."

Her face brightened. "There's a town nearby?"

"Not nearby, but within fifteen, twenty miles." He shifted and then closed his eyes as the world spun. "Three—maybe four days' ride."

She got up and threw another stick on the fire. "You should be happy I came along. Otherwise, you'd be dead."

"You're lucky you're not dead as well."

Comanches were a fierce lot, and the band that attacked the wagon had been bent on destruction. Dylan's blood ran cold when he thought of Ruth and the child unprotected. He was as weak as a newborn—there was nothing he could do to help her or the baby in his present condition.

"I hope you've . . . consulted your God . . . about our state."

Ruth glanced over as she picked up the baby. "He knows our state."

"Yeah?" Dylan closed his eyes, trying to picture a man big enough to manage the universe and have time left over to care about his predicament. His sense of logic fell short.

*   *   *

As Ruth spent the next day searching for berries and nuts in the Colorado wilds to feed her newfound family, she couldn't help but think about Thanksgiving. She wondered if Patience, Mary, Harper, and Lily had thought about her as they gathered around the Siddonses' bountiful harvest table to return thanks.

Ruth concentrated on what she could give thanks for. Though it was approaching the end of November, the weather was holding . . . Dylan and the baby were still alive, and . . . and there was the hope that God had not abandoned them. That's all she could think of.

She made frequent trips to the spring to carry water back to camp. Despite Ruth's best efforts to produce some kind of nourishment for the child, she cried endlessly.

Dylan grew stronger, but when Ruth plopped the baby next to him later that morning, doubt filled his eyes.

"You watch her while I hunt for food."

Without waiting for an answer, she walked away, praying the baby wouldn't need anything while she was gone. But she had to get away from both the man and the child. She'd grown to care about the baby, and that wouldn't do. She couldn't care about her—or Dylan. When the marshal gained sufficient strength to travel, they would move on to Sulphur Springs. There Ruth would turn the child over to the sheriff, who would find a suitable home for her. A good home. Some place where the little girl would have a mother and a father and grow up graceful and lovely.

Ruth marched toward the thicket with the rifle under her arm. She wasn't going to nurse the child today; she was going to shoot something and cook it. Later she returned with a small bird and a lighter attitude. She would survive—with God's help and Dylan's gun.

• • •

Ruth awoke early the next morning. The feel of snow was in the air. She looked over at Dylan; he was getting up slowly, testing his strength. He looked stronger today.

"We have to move on," he said.

She set the baby aside and went to him. "Yes, we do. We need food. Real food. What little I provide for the baby isn't enough." She frowned. "But are you ready—are you capable of traveling this soon?"

"If Mary can do what she does, I can match her." Dylan's smile at the mention of Mary's name caused a twist of jealousy inside Ruth. Why, Dylan McCall had a soft spot for Mary!

"I'm not sure how far Sulphur Springs is," he admitted. "But the weather isn't going to hold any longer—we have to get you and the baby to shelter soon."

Ruth already knew time was now of the essence. Each day got colder and more miserable. They could easily freeze to death in this climate if hunger didn't take them first. Not to mention Dylan's injuries.

"I haven't seen any sign of human life for over two weeks," she conceded. "Other than you and the baby."

"Houses are few and far between up here. It's not likely we'll see anyone."

Her heart fell. What were they going to do?

"Sulphur Springs is a mining community— almost defunct now. I rode through about a year ago, and the veins were drying up. A few families should still be around, though. If I remember right, the community's less than twenty miles from here." He turned to study the sun. "To the west. If we start now, we should make it in a few days."

"If your strength is able to hold out." With pity, Ruth watched the baby try to pick up a dry leaf. After the first few days of nearly inconsolable crying, she was mostly quiet now. Probably getting weak. She needed food, milk. Ruth's hunger was never satisfied, and Dylan needed better fare in order to gain his strength. The few wild game she'd managed to kill hardly sustained them. They were in trouble—real trouble. Moving on was their only hope.

The baby deserved to grow up and have a good life. Ruth deserved . . . well, nothing, actually. She was fortunate God had let her come this far. "Then let's get started," Ruth said.

They only had Ruth's mare, and Dylan would have to ride. The stench of dead horses filled the air, but Ruth knew she had to get Dylan's saddlebag off his horse to take with them.

Working with grim determination, she stripped the saddle off, tugging at the cinch until the belly strap came loose. They couldn't take the saddle with them, but she could hide it somewhere so at some point he might be able to come back for it. A good saddle was nothing to be sneezed at even if it was government issue.

Once she had both saddlebags and bedrolls on her horse, Ruth helped Dylan to his feet. Pain etched his craggy features, and she silently applauded his bravery.

They had to move. Dylan knew it; she knew it, but knowing it didn't make his injuries any less painful.

Dylan slumped in the saddle, his face pale, his mouth thin with pain. Ruth carried the baby, whose eyes were wide with question. She wished she could set her on the horse in front of Dylan, but he was too weak to balance her. If she had a sling or a carrying board . . . but she had neither. Maybe given another day she could depend on Dylan not to lose consciousness and fall off the horse or on the baby. Then he could help.

When Ruth had her charges prepared to travel, she drew a deep breath and tucked a warm blanket around Dylan's waist. "West, did you say?"

"Head straight toward those mountains," he grunted. He held on to the saddle horn.

"Okay." Ruth straightened her shoulders and set off. She held the baby in one arm and led the horse, praying with every step. *You must be with us, Lord. How else would we have made it this far?*

What a sight they must be. A seriously wounded U.S. marshal, who might at any moment die from his injuries. A baby, who needed to be fed and cared for. A young woman, who felt grimy and whose clothes were full of burn holes, suffering from still-painful burns on her shoulders, arms, and hands. Ruth realized she must look at least as bad as Dylan. What she wouldn't give for a bath, hot food, and clean clothes. She was sick of pants and boots and half-raw meat.

Sulphur Springs meant new hope. The Comanches had stripped nearly everything of value from the wagon and from the two men, so the travelers were penniless. All they had left was Dylan's badge, which might convince a merchant to advance them credit, should they reach the community. Ruth's mind examined all the possibilities as she mechanically put one foot in front of the other. A town. She put her mind to imagining a town over the next rise.

But by late afternoon she was just hoping for shelter. Somewhere—anywhere—warm where she could rest her aching feet. Snow had started to fall, making travel even more laborious. Head bent, Dylan gripped the saddle horn, speaking only when spoken to.

Ruth wondered if her life would end this day— here, on a snowy, windswept mountainside. *Ironic,* she thought as she trudged through a narrow pass. If her life was over this day, wasn't it odd that God had chosen to let her die with a man she could easily love under different circumstances and a baby she could deeply love if she allowed herself—two precious fundamentals she was most certain never to achieve in life?

Odd? Or was it God? she wondered with overpowering gratitude. Just when she thought she knew what God was up to, he proved her wrong once again.

• • •

A day later, Dylan motioned for Ruth to mount the horse in front of him. By now she looked tired enough to drop, and she was limping. She didn't argue. Two adults and a baby on the horse was a tight fit, but Dylan figured there was little choice. "The mare can carry us," he told her.

He cut the animal off the traveled path to save distance and rode through thicket until Ruth complained that the brambles were cutting her legs. The thick trousers did little to protect her from the prickly briars. Her disguise was adequate; only the most discerning traveler would notice that she was a woman. Dylan alone knew that feminine beauty lay beneath the wool and denim. Had he been half the man he was a week ago, the lady might be in trouble. . . . He must be getting better.

The baby's cries were weaker this morning. He had to find a cow or goat, and soon. Despite Ruth's efforts to feed the baby, it didn't look as if she could nourish her herself. Sulphur Springs was still a few days' ride away. Would they make it through the endless miles of trees and falling snow?

With each jounce in the saddle, Dylan sensed the wounds in his shoulder give way. He'd lost a lot of blood. He felt the warm stickiness seep through his shirt fabric.

He was late for his appointment with Kurt Vaning, but surely his boss would know he had a good excuse. Trouble was common in these parts this time of the year. Kurt wouldn't start to worry for a few weeks if Dylan still didn't show up, but the assignment would go to another marshal. That Dylan resented. He'd been on Dreck Parson's trail for months. He wanted to be the one to haul the outlaw in for justice. Now that wasn't going to happen.

"The baby is so hungry," Ruth said. The three fit in the saddle snugly: woman, man, child—and supplies. Dylan felt uncomfortable with the close proximity. Despite his earlier assurance to Ruth, he doubted the animal could take the load for much longer.

"The first thing we do when we reach Sulphur Springs is get you to a doctor," Ruth said.

"The first thing we do is get the baby milk."

"Fine. I'll get the milk while you see a doctor." Worry tinged her voice as the sharp wind caught it and flung the words over her shoulder.

"What about you?" Dylan asked.

"What about me? I'm fine."

"No, you're not fine. I see the way you favor your shoulders—you have some burns, don't you?"

"Nothing serious," she contended. "Nothing worth even mentioning."

Dylan bet otherwise. If she had climbed around in a burning wagon searching for the child, the wounds had to be more than minor. But she had not complained once.

"We'll both see the doctor in Sulphur Springs," he said.

"If it's a small community, they might not have one."

"They'll have someone who can help." He cut the mare back to the path, which was deepening with snow.

He'd see a doctor about his wounds and make sure Ruth and the baby were okay. They'd rest up a few days, ask around about couples interested in taking a child. He'd have to send a wire to Kurt . . . then what? What would he do with Ruth? Take her with him? Over his best judgment, he'd gotten close to the pretty nursemaid the past few days. The strange bond hammered a dent in his plans to leave her and ride on once he was stronger.

He cleared his throat. "Be on the lookout for a cow or goat."

They were all hungry. Ruth hadn't complained, but he knew she hadn't eaten a decent meal in more than a week. Only what she could run down, pick, or accidentally kill with his rifle. But she wasn't a whiner. That both surprised and relieved him. If she'd been a complainer on top of a nuisance, he would have ridden over the first cliff.

He felt her nod in agreement as she shifted the baby in her arms. He noticed that she never held the infant close. She kept the little girl at bay, almost as if she feared intimacy. A slow smile started at the corners of his mouth. He couldn't imagine this strong-willed woman fearing the devil himself. But a tiny baby had her on edge. Why? Didn't most women take to mothering?

Toward dusk, Ruth and Dylan dismounted and walked. Dylan offered to carry the crying baby, but Ruth refused. "You can't carry a child."

She walked ahead, breaking a path for him, her flushed features marked with grit. When they spotted a cow grazing on the side of the road, they stopped and stared. Some farmer had a fence down, and the last of the fall grass poking up near the roadside had proved too tempting.

Their breaths came in foggy vapors. "Am I dreaming?" Ruth murmured.

"If you are, I am too." Dylan noticed the cow's bag, tight with milk.

The cow lifted her head and met their stunned eyes as she chewed her cud.

"I'll get her," Ruth said without moving her lips.

"I'll get her," he insisted. He wasn't an invalid, though he was close.

Before the matter was settled, Ruth handed him the baby and slowly approached the cow. "Here, Bossie."

"Bossie?" Dylan shook his head. "Now you've insulted her."

"What's wrong with the name Bossie? I knew a lovely woman named Bossie who brought fresh vegetables to the orphanage every week during the summer." Ruth crept toward the cow.

The animal mooed, startling the baby, who started crying.

Ruth approached the animal cautiously. At least she had enough sense to know that if the cow bolted, they wouldn't see it again. She walked slowly, speaking softly under her breath.

"Good Bossie. Good girl. We just need to borrow a little milk—you have lots to spare, don't you?" She peered around the cow's fat sides, eyeing the bulging treasure. "Well, look at that. You sure do. How about that—and I suppose a nice cow like yourself wouldn't have strong objections to sharing a quart or two—would you? Thank you, I thought not. You're very kind."

Dylan frowned, focusing on Bossie's udder, swollen with rich, creamy, life-giving substance. "Go easy," he warned.

Ruth turned to look at him. "Do I look like I want to scare her?"

"Just go easy—don't make her bolt."

She eased close enough to reach out and hook her arms around the cow's neck. For a moment Dylan wondered if Ruth planned to ride it to the ground. The animal seemed tame enough. She chewed contentedly, bawling occasionally as if trying to carry on a conversation with the strange-looking creature who had her by the collar.

"Give me your hat," Ruth called over her shoulder.

Dylan carefully shifted the baby into his left arm and removed his hat. Ruth took it, and seconds later she knelt and buried her face in Bossie's side, her fingers probing for teats. "Do you just pull these things?"

"You've never milked a cow?"

She shook her head. "You will discover, Mr. McCall, I have not done a whole lot of things."

Dylan slowly walked over and handed her the baby. "I'll milk."

She stepped back and within minutes the crown of his hat overflowed with warm, foamy milk. Ruth surveyed the bounty, grinning. "How do we get it down the baby?"

"Tear a piece of fabric from your shirt—" Dylan frowned when he noticed the already-tattered sleeve hem as she quickly shimmied out of her coat.

In seconds Dylan had fashioned a makeshift bottle by tying a knot in one end of the material and pouring warm milk into the fabric. "It's not the cleanest, but it will have to do."

He put the end of the fabric into the baby's mouth and squeezed. The baby gulped hungrily. The milk seeped out almost as fast as Ruth poured it in. It took over half an hour to get enough milk down the child to fill her hungry stomach. For the first time in days, the child curled into a tight ball and fell sound asleep in Ruth's arms.

A proud Dylan and Ruth looked on, their faces glowing.

Dylan spoke first. "She's kind of cute, isn't she?"

Ruth quickly looked away. "I . . . I hadn't noticed."

That night when Ruth took off her boots, Dylan's eyes fixed on her bleeding feet. Large, angry blisters covered her toes and heels. He felt a flash of anger. "Why didn't you say something?"

She looked up to meet his eyes. When she looked at him that way, something inside him moved—something he didn't like. "Would it have made a difference? We have no choice but to walk."

He got up slowly, favoring his wounds, and got a knife out of his saddlebag. "You could have ridden."

"And let you walk?" Her chin lifted with stubborn pride. "I'm capable of holding my own. I don't plan to be any trouble—I only want to reach Wyoming and my cousin Milford."

He returned to the fire and picked up her left boot and cut the toe out. She gasped. "What are you doing? That's my only shoe, and it's snowing!"

"Those are your only toes and heels," he reminded her, severing the toe from the right boot. "Put on more socks." He repeated the procedure on the heels of both boots. Ruth watched, her eyes set in horror.

He set the boots close to the fire, then carefully dropped back down on his sleeping roll. "Tomorrow you ride."

Jaw agape, Ruth's eyes moved from her butchered boots to Dylan on the other side of the fire. She closed her mouth, her eyes narrowed as she handed him the sleeping infant.

Without another word, he tipped the milk-soaked brim of his hat over his face, drew the sleeping baby closer in his arms, and promptly went to sleep.

7

After they milked the cow and fed the baby again, Dylan began to tie the cow to the horse to take it with them.

"What are you doing?" Ruth asked.

"Taking the cow; what does it look like?"

"We can't," Ruth said, chin jutting out. "We don't know whose it is. We can't take it without permission. Stealing isn't going to help the situation."

"Dying is going to improve it?"

"Dying would not be the worst thing that could happen—though I'm not ready to go yet," she admitted. "God will provide food for us and the baby without us stealing."

Dylan ignored Ruth's optimism and made her and the baby ride while he walked this morning. He was in no mood for an argument after grudgingly leaving Bossie behind. His strength was waning; he could feel his limited energy stretched to the limits. Each night he took off his blood-soaked shirt and Ruth washed it and hung it over the fire to dry. Though she said nothing, the unspoken fear he saw in her eyes disturbed him. She was afraid he would die and leave her and the child out here alone. The same fear hampered his concentration.

"If anything happens to me," he told her as he walked the mare up an incline, "you head straight northwest. Sulphur Springs is that direction—I'm not sure how far, but I know it's there. Someone will help you and the baby."

Ruth fixed her eyes straight ahead, her chin set with determination. "Nothing's going to happen to you. I've already talked to the Lord about your condition."

"Yeah, well . . ." He absently rubbed his burning shoulder. "I hope he feels better about the situation than I do."

"He's given me no reason to be discouraged at this point." She locked gazes with him. "Do you know him?"

Dylan shook his head. Did he know God? They'd never officially met—not the God Sara Dunnigan had claimed to know. "I never talk religion or politics, especially with a woman or on an empty stomach."

Ruth's small teeth worried her bottom lip. She was pretty when she was upset; yet he grudgingly admired her for holding her tongue when he knew she wanted to spout off. Her concerns were warranted, but he saw no reason to give them new light. Either they made it or they didn't. He hoped for the best but mentally prepared for the worst. They couldn't make it long in this kind of weather. They either ran into help soon or . . . the *or* bothered him the most.

He wasn't ready to die yet either—he had a lot of living to do. And he wasn't as sure about the here-after as Ruth professed to be—but then he didn't read the Bible like Ruth did. Dylan didn't depend on God to look after him; he figured God gave him the brains and experience to take care of himself. Though he had to admit, in his current straits, he sure could use a little extra help. . . .

Later that morning, Ruth sat up straighter and pointed. A nanny goat was grazing in the ditch, oblivious to the travelers. When the animal spotted the horse and couple, it bolted. Its thin, reedy voice shattered the silence. *Blaaaaa. Blaaaaaaaaaa.*

Dylan was closest to the fence line. Automatic reflex sent him spiraling though a deep snowbank in pursuit. Ruth clamped her hands over her mouth as man and goat burst through the thicket. Dylan heard Ruth yelling to "come back!" her voice edgy as he pursued the life-giving source. But all he could think about was milk for the baby. And silence from the infant's constant crying—peace and quiet.

Yet Ruth's fear registered as he felt his wounds tear open; only pure desperation kept him going. The pesky animal darted in and out, disoriented by the chase. It spun and dashed back toward the road. Dylan slipped on icy grass, then regained his footing and lunged. The animal slid through the thicket and bounded back up the snowbank.

Dylan was hot on the trail now. With a flying

leap, he managed to snag the nanny by the left back leg and hold on. The goat went down, bleating desperately. Dylan reeled the creature in, fell across the animal, and pinned its bleating carcass to the ground.

Ruth was off the horse in a split second, running toward him with the crying infant in her arms. "You *fool*!" she accused, dropping to her knees in the snow beside the sprawled marshal. Anxious tears filled her eyes as he looked up and gave her a goofy grin.

"Got more milk," he announced. And then he promptly passed out.

• • •

Ruth was bent over a book when Dylan opened his eyes. Firelight shed a rosy glow on her pretty features as she intently scribbled in her book. He'd give a month's pay to see what she'd written. The baby lay next to her, sleeping soundly. He averted his head slightly to focus on the goat firmly secured to a low branch near a stream of running water. How had she gotten him, the goat, and the baby here?

"It wasn't easy," she said as though she had read his thoughts. Closing the journal, she set it aside and came around the fire to kneel beside him. He was in his bedroll, his bloody shirt washed and draped on a stick hanging near the fire.

"I put a rope around the goat's neck and tied it to a tree," she said as she tucked the blanket closer around him. "I dragged you here—by the way, you could stand to lose a few pounds—but the packed snow helped. Then I put the baby in your arms and went back for the goat, which has a worse disposition than I have."

He grimaced. He knew he'd lost so much blood he was reaching the critical stage. "Impossible."

She shook her head before her features sobered. "You scare me like that again, and I'll have to beat you."

Was that real worry he saw in her eyes? The thought brought a warm, irrational sentiment. Ruthie was worried about him—really *worried* about him. He wasn't sure if that was good or if it only complicated the situation, but he liked the feeling. For the moment, he decided he liked it more than he resented it. It had been a long time since anyone had worried or cared about him. He'd forgotten how first-rate that could make a man feel.

Struggling to sit up, his effort failing, he dropped weakly back to the bedroll. "How long have I been out?"

"Most of the afternoon." She rose and turned to stir the contents of something bubbling over the fire in a makeshift pot. The scented air set off an ache in his empty stomach.

"What are you cooking?"

"I found oatmeal in your saddlebag, and I mixed it with goat's milk. The fare would taste better with sugar or honey, but it isn't bad now."

She dipped a small amount of the bubbling mixture into a tin cup and knelt to spoon-feed him.

"Rather good, actually," he affirmed. The oatmeal was steaming hot, so she spooned slowly.

Dylan took the nourishment, his eyes meeting Ruth's. She was a far cry from Sara, the coldhearted female who had raised him. Sara was so full of religion it ran out of her pores and tainted everything it touched. He'd hated Sara Dunnigan and everything she represented until the welcomed day she was lowered into her grave. Dylan figured every religious woman possessed Sara's hostility, her narrowminded views, and her judgmental nature.

Until he met Ruth.

Ruth puzzled him. She claimed to know the same Lord Sara had touted to serve. But that wasn't possible; the two higher powers were direct opposites. The God Ruth believed in seemed to care about individuals. Sara's Lord was a mean tyrant who demanded ritualistic worship. Sara had taken glee in those going to hell; Ruth seemed to care genuinely about others' souls and the threat of eternal damnation. Which woman was right?

Which woman served the true divine being, if there was a God? Something basic in Dylan wanted to lean toward Ruth's belief—that whoever had created him watched over him. But a man's thoughts didn't often consider how he'd gotten here—only why.

During his years with Sara after his parents died, he had thrown his head back and yelled the question, trying to prove to himself that no one was up there listening. And to his knowledge, nobody was up there. Nobody had cared about him; nobody had come to save him from "Sister Sara's" wrath. Once, when he was very young, he'd caught the woman praying out loud, lying facedown on the floor, arms extended, petitioning the Lord to give her strength to raise the awful burden he'd sent upon her. Dylan didn't know what a "burden" was at the time—only that he was one and Sara hated him.

He shook the thought to one side as he swallowed one last bite of oatmeal and moved the spoon aside. "Can you get the map out of my saddlebag?"

Ruth nodded, wiping his mouth gently. He gave her a don't-do-that look as she got up and headed for his saddlebag.

Over firelight, they bent their heads close, and he showed her the exact spot on the map marked Sulphur Springs.

"It looks to be still some distance away," Ruth said softly.

"At least another eight miles, best I can figure." He realized they hadn't come as far as he'd hoped.

He saw her eyes darken at the news, but she kept a stiff upper lip. "Then we're practically there."

For the first time, Dylan realized he wasn't going to rise to the occasion. He'd lost so much blood that he could no longer walk. The baby still lay in his arms, satiated with goat's milk for now, but how long would that last? As long as Ruth could hold on to the goat, they would have nourishment for the baby. But their survival was up to Ruth now—a young woman, a girl who had never been in rough country or even knew how to shoot a gun properly. Some higher power had to be watching over her.

Yeah—and there must be an all-knowing, all-caring God looking after him too. *McCall, get your head screwed on properly.*

Mentally groaning, he dropped his head back to the bedroll. The baby sighed and snuggled deeper into his warmth. If Ruth's God was listening, Dylan told him he'd better have a plan, because at this point Dylan had run out of options.

• • •

In the gray, still dawn, the small group hit the trail early. Ruth studied the map, nodding as Dylan pointed out the way.

"Stay to the road. The ruts will be deep, but we'll have better footing," he said.

The baby lay in Dylan's arms, contented now. Ruth walked, leading the mare with the marshal and the infant riding.

Taking charge gave her a sense of belonging—of being needed. It wasn't often that a man like Dylan needed anything or anyone, and she was proud to serve. The goat trailed, balking occasionally as the mare dragged the tenacious milk source through mounting snowdrifts. Cotton-ball-size flakes swirled around Ruth's face as she trudged on, holding the collar of her coat over her mouth. Icicles formed on her eyelashes. Hard as she tried to be optimistic, her spirits began to sag.

Her burns had scabbed over but they itched now. Her clothing was in tatters. She didn't think she would ever be able to get a comb through her hair. Her feet hurt so badly she wanted to cry. Every step was agony, pain radiating from toe to knee. Even with the toes and heels cut out of her boots, the blisters were still raw and bleeding. The toes of her socks were stiff and wet—it wouldn't be long before she lost feeling. She actually looked forward to the numbness that would surely come after walking long hours in the snow. She could make it until then. She had to. At least the baby was fine, tucked in a snug pouch inside Dylan's coat lining, cocooned in the warmth of his body.

She alternated between praying that they would find someone to take the child soon and begging the Lord to let the baby remain with her for a while longer. Death didn't seem so frightening; at times she resolved to meet her fate without regret. Dying was merely a transition—not one she welcomed, but neither did she fear it.

She wanted Dylan and the baby to live, though. No matter how hard she'd tried not to—and she had tried her very hardest—she was starting to love both the child and the marshal. Maternal feelings were seeping out of every pore, and she didn't know how much longer she could bear the feeling. What if she were to slip and allow Dylan the briefest glimpse into her thoughts? Would he think she had lost her mind? He clearly wasn't a man destined for marriage, not to a woman so clearly his opposite. Then there was the matter of their difference in faith. She didn't know where he stood in terms of belief in God, but his answer to her question about God offered little encouragement. No way could she let herself fall any further in love with the marshal.

Conversation had now ceased. They were too weary to attempt to converse above the icy wind that snatched their words and flung them away. At dusk they dropped onto the ground, and she dealt with the child who was too tired, too cold, and too hungry to do much more than whimper. Ruth knew the same could be said about her and Dylan—they were too tired to exist. They lay down without a simple good night and fell into an exhausted sleep.

At dawn, they got up and continued on. Ruth laboriously put one foot in front of the other and climbed each rise. She could hear Dylan's labored breathing as he rode the horse and carried the baby. At times she was forced to rest her hands on her knees for support. At the top of each hill she stopped to catch her breath.

Suddenly she saw what looked like a trail below them. Recent wheel tracks showed in the snow-packed ruts. She yelled back at Dylan. "Is that what I think it is?"

Dylan opened his eyes and focused on the scene below. Snow had tapered into swirling, barely perceptible flakes. "It's a road." His mouth thinned. "I don't know—could be the one to Sulphur Springs, Ruth. Maybe not."

Elation filled her, and tears brimmed in her eyes.

She would take the chance. Grabbing the mare's reins, she started down the incline, stumbling, falling twice before she reached the road. Her mind whirled. Food, shelter. Tonight they would sleep in a warm room and have hot food and coffee in their bellies.

Her eyes searched the distance for signs of life—anything that moved. Panic crowded her throat. What if this wasn't the road? What if nobody lived for miles around? What if the miners had all gone and Sulphur Springs was nothing more than a deserted camp now? But the tracks indicated recent passage.

Please, God. Let someone come to help us. We're going to die out here if you don't help us.

"Do you hear that?" Dylan's voice rose over the wind.

Ruth stopped in her tracks and listened carefully. "Is that a wagon?" she whispered. It sounded like wagon wheels churning through packed snow. There it was—the unmistakable creak. Turning wheels . . .

Before her eyes a wagon pulled by a team topped a rise in the road. Tears blinded her now, and she bit back a smile. It *was* a wagon! *Thank you, God.*

Dylan lifted his fingers weakly to his lips and gave a shrill whistle. The sound ricocheted over the snowy mountainsides. When the male figure in the wagon spotted the travelers, he stood up, gaping in surprise. "Helllooo!" the stranger called.

"Helllooo!" Ruth called back. She cupped her hands to her mouth. "Can you help us?"

The buckboard rattled closer, and Ruth turned back to grin at Dylan. "It's okay—we made it! Hold on . . . in a very short while we'll have food and a warm fire . . ." Her voice trailed off as she viewed the marshal's ashen features. Help had come none too soon—but it had come and Ruth was grateful.

The buckboard rattled to a stop and the man set the brake. He stared at the frozen strangers. "Surprised to see travelers on a mornin' like this— what are you doing out in this weather?" The grisly-looking old man was bundled in heavy buffalo robes; a fur hat sat atop his head.

Ruth drew back, intuition warning her not to move closer.

"Coming from Denver City," Dylan told him. "Ran into some Indian trouble some miles back."

"Indians, you say?" The old man's eyes narrowed. "Trouble's been scarce lately." His gaze swept the mangy travelers. Ruth imagined they looked more like a couple of scarecrows than human beings.

"We're trying to reach Sulphur Springs." Ruth edged forward.

The man nodded. "Town's still five . . . six miles away," he said, gesturing over his shoulder with his thumb in the direction he'd come.

Dylan shifted in the saddle. "We're without food, and we've traveled by foot and mare for days. Can you help us? We need shelter for the night, a hot meal, food for the child."

The man peered at them. "Got a baby there, I see."

"Yes. The child needs shelter," Ruth said.

The man, who looked to be in his sixties, eyed the couple. Ruth wasn't sure he was buying their story. Finally he reached for the reins. "Well, climb aboard. Name's Nehemiah Ford. The missus and I have a place not too far from here. Got some cattle, some horses; do a little farmin'. You can stay the night. I reckon the missus can rustle up some grub for ya and the babe."

"Thank you, God," Ruth breathed aloud.

Dylan nodded. "Name's Dylan McCall, and this is Ruth."

"'Pears you're Christian folk," the man said, staring at Ruth's trousers. She thought an explanation of why she was dressed like a boy might be in order, but then the response wouldn't help the cause. Some things were best left a mystery.

"Yes, sir, we're Christian," Ruth said, noting that Dylan neither agreed nor disagreed. Perhaps he was making some progress spiritually.

The marshal dismounted and helped Ruth into the wagon bed. He handed her the baby, then secured the horse and goat and climbed in himself. The wagon was piled high with supplies—two fifty-pound sacks of flour, two of sugar, cans of sorghum, other canned goods, as well as sacks of corn that would probably do for both horses and chickens, if the old man was indeed a farmer, Ruth thought. Somehow nothing rang true about Nehemiah Ford.

"Hi-up," Nehemiah called to the team, slapping their rumps with the reins.

The wagon lurched forward, and Ruth and Dylan leaned gratefully back against the sacks and rested.

The buckboard rattled as it plowed through the deep snow. Ruth closed her eyes, exhausted. When Dylan nudged her shoulder, she opened her eyes to the welcome sight of a tightly constructed cabin with smoke curling from the chimney. Her gaze followed to the right side of the house to another structure, quite clearly serving as a barn with a small corral beside it. The corral was empty, but a dozen or so chickens pecked in the snowy barnyard. Ruth's mouth watered. Fried chicken. Or maybe even an egg or two.

Nehemiah Ford drew the wagon to a halt and set the brake. The front door opened and a short, heavyset woman appeared, wiping her hands on a cloth. Her dark eyes landed suspiciously on her husband's two passengers.

Nehemiah jumped down from the wagon seat and looped the reins over the brake handle. "Got company," he announced. Then he spoke Indian, something Ruth didn't understand. Ruth slid from the wagon bed, wincing when her tender feet touched ground. The baby awoke in a fretful mood. She was so hungry, Ruth thought. She spotted a lone cow standing near the fence line and breathed a sigh of relief. It looked to have sufficient milk.

The woman stood back from the door as Dylan handed the baby to Ruth; they trooped in and gravitated to the fire. Nehemiah hung his hat on a peg by the door and went immediately to the stove to pour a cup of coffee from a huge black pot.

"This here's my wife, Ulele. She's full-blooded Cherokee. She don't speak much English, only 'sit' and 'go' and a few other phrases." He took a sip of the scalding coffee, his gaze on Ruth. "You look plumb tuckered out. Why don't you give the baby to Ulele? She'll take care of the young'un whilst you catch yore breath."

Ruth was reluctant to surrender the child to a stranger, but if the old woman could help, she would be grateful.

The woman pointed to a chair by the fire. "Sit." The guttural command was low, but the authority coming from the woman with thickened features was unmistakable.

Ruth and Dylan sat at the table before the fire. Ulele held the child in the crook of her arm, her velvet-brown eyes evaluating the infant. The two looked as if they belonged together, each dark-skinned, each with coal black hair and a prominent nose. The baby seemed fascinated by the woman and immediately quieted down. Chubby hands reached out to touch the woman's face, patting it with exploring hands that were grimy from travel.

"Gonna see to the team," Nehemiah said. "Ulele will get ya somethin' to eat. Real lucky I came along. Ordinarily I buy supplies in the early fall. But I been feelin' poorly and couldn't get to town until yesterday."

"Can I help?" Dylan slowly moved from the fire.

The old man's eyes noted his condition. "Not this time. Looks to me like yore in bad shape."

Dylan sank gratefully back into the chair. "I'll be fine once I get warm."

Ruth's heart broke as she watched Dylan's valiant effort at normalcy. It would take more than a simple fire to help him. "He was injured almost two weeks ago now—gravely injured. We haven't had the necessary medicine to treat his wounds," she explained.

"Well, the missus can help. Woman, git yore healing herbs—this man needs help once he's et and got the chill outta his bones."

Ulele wordlessly shuffled off to the bedroom, carrying the baby on her hip.

"Whilst she's getting her herbs, I'll stow the supplies and get the horses in the barn." With that, the old man went back outside and started hauling in sacks of flour to store against the back wall before he drove the wagon to the barn.

Ulele returned with a small wooden box and set it on the hearth. While Ruth watched, the stout woman, still holding the baby, put bowls and cups on the table and dipped brown beans and some kind of meat from a kettle on the stove.

Ruth's stomach cramped from lack of food. She wasn't able to wait for the food to cool. She snatched up a bowl and eagerly spooned beans into her mouth.

Ulele filled a fourth bowl, then sat at the end of the table opposite Ruth. She picked a piece of meat out of the dish and chewed it. Then, before

Ruth's astounded gaze, she removed the piece from her mouth and popped it between the child's lips.

Ruth's stomach heaved as Dylan leaned over and whispered, "That's how squaws feed their infants, chewing the food first so the child can swallow it."

"But—"

His warning look made her clamp her lips together. *Simple milk would have done.*

Ruth couldn't bear to watch the woman feed the starving infant. Maybe it was common practice for Indian mothers to chew the food prior to feeding, but she couldn't imagine that it was healthy, even if the baby seemed to accept it. Though she'd been famished earlier, Ruth couldn't eat the food in front of her. But she noticed Dylan had no problem. When he had cleaned his bowl, she nudged hers toward him.

He glanced up, concern darkening his face. "You've got to eat."

"I can't right now," she murmured. She averted her eyes as Ulele spat beans into the child's mouth.

In a short while Nehemiah returned from the barn and sat down across from Dylan. Ignoring his wife, the man quickly devoured his meal, like a hog emptying a trough, not even noticing its content.

"What are your plans?" He studied Dylan as he pushed back a few minutes later.

Dylan drained the last of his coffee and set the mug back on the table. "I'm a U.S. marshal. I was on my way to Utah when I ran into trouble." He glanced at Ruth. "We're trying to reach Sulphur

Springs, where I can wire my boss and inform him that I'll be late for my assignment and, I hope, get credit for clothes and supplies. Right now we're at a bit of a disadvantage. We have no money and only one horse."

Ruth held her breath while the old man appraised Dylan. Would knowing that Dylan was a marshal make the man more likely to help? She knew that sometimes men who were running from the law came to this desolate area to make homes and were never heard from again, and this old man and his wife were strange. Both looked as if they could be running from anything, or was it only her imagination running amok again? Ruth couldn't be sure. Lately she couldn't think straight. At least these people had been kind enough to take two frozen strangers and a baby into their home.

"A marshal, huh?"

"Yes, sir."

After a while, Nehemiah leaned back and said quietly, "Well, I got a proposition for you, Marshal. I got some work to be done around here before winter sets in. Don't look like I'm gonna get it done myself. Say you work for me a few days, earn a couple of horses, some supplies—even a bit of cash money? Maybe a week or so, depending on how fast you work." He glanced at Ruth. "My woman here, she can use an extra hand, and yore wife looks like she could stand some help with the baby."

Ruth held her breath. Should they tell the Fords how they came to have an Indian baby? She wasn't sure how much they could trust these two peculiar people, though it seemed they must.

Dylan glanced at her, his ready answer evident in his eyes. It appeared the good Lord had just laid a miracle at their doorstep—the perfect solution to their problem. With the weather so bad, they couldn't move on—at least Ruth hoped the Fords wouldn't expect them to leave until the storm broke.

But Dylan couldn't work; he could barely hold his head up, so Ruth was surprised at the old man's offer. "You're not well enough to work," she reminded the marshal softly.

Dylan glanced at the Fords, then back at her. Lowering his voice, he said calmly, "I'm sure Mr. Ford understands my condition, but I can work some, Ruth. A good night's rest, solid food—I'll be better in the morning." His eyes silently urged her. "So will you. Your feet are raw. You can't go another step. Think of the baby—we're lucky she's made it this far without enough milk or warm clothing. We'll be better off here for the time being."

Ruth knew he was right, though she was still leery of the terms. The offer seemed odd—couldn't the old man see that Dylan was in no condition for physical labor?

Dylan's jaw firmed. "I don't see that we've got any other choice. We either stay here a few days or we start walking again. We can't walk a mile, much less another five, to reach Sulphur Springs."

"Shame you didn't come along earlier," Nehemiah

observed. "You coulda rode into town with me, but I won't be going back till spring now."

Of course Dylan was right; he always thought more clearly than she did. But Ruth still didn't like the circumstances. Yet the child was warm and had something other than milk in her tummy—albeit nauseatingly so—and she wasn't crying so much.

"All right," Ruth reluctantly agreed. "But I still don't know how you're going to be of much help to Nehemiah." She would try to do more than her share to help Ulele as a trade-off.

"I'll do what has to be done. We don't have a choice," Dylan said.

Admiration swelled within Ruth for the marshal's continuing concern for her and for the baby. He'd never once grumbled about taking care of the infant, though he had to wonder why she wasn't tending to the child more. Still, he hadn't asked. He'd kept pushing on when she knew he was too weak to walk and in terrible pain. Dylan McCall was, she had to admit, a man of true grit.

"We'll stay," she agreed. Not that she'd ever had any real say in the matter. The set look on Dylan's face told her he was only being polite; they would stay no matter what she felt.

"We'll be glad to work for you," Dylan told Nehemiah.

The old man nodded. "We'll start at daylight then. You two can put your bedrolls over there in the corner."

The accommodations weren't the best, but at

least the weary travelers were inside and warm. Ruth managed to eat a piece of buttered bread with her coffee so her stomach didn't growl. Her eyes were growing heavy when Ulele motioned toward her feet.

"Go," she said.

Ruth didn't understand.

"I think she wants you to take off your boots," Dylan said.

"Why?"

"The missus is good with herbs and such," Nehemiah said. "She can do something for those feet of yours, as well as for Dylan's back."

Ruth was still apprehensive. Dylan bent and began unlacing her boots.

She drew back. "I can do that."

"Don't look," he advised her. Ruth met his gaze and realized that her feet were in worse condition than she thought.

She gritted her teeth and closed her eyes against the pain as Dylan gently worked off each boot. Her stockings were worn through, her broken blisters raw and bleeding.

Ulele shook her head when she saw the damage.

Dylan's face clouded and he swore under his breath.

"Don't," Ruth whispered, stifling back a groan. "I can just imagine what your shoulder looks like now."

Ulele brought a small tub with warm water and motioned for Ruth to immerse her feet. Ruth couldn't hold back the moan this time as she very gingerly put her toes into the pan.

While Ruth soaked her feet, Ulele motioned for Dylan to remove his shirt. Ruth winced as he pulled the fabric loose from the wounds that were raw and puffy. Tonight it looked like infection had set in again; from Ulele's grunt the woman agreed.

The stern Cherokee mixed a batch of vile-smelling herbs, forming a poultice, which she applied to Dylan's shoulder. He hissed in a breath and then relaxed after a few minutes. Ruth wished that she could be the one to administer the care but she didn't intercede. Her sudden envy puzzled her.

"Feels good," Dylan conceded, smiling at Ulele.

"The herbs draw out the poison," Nehemiah said. "The missus is a fair hand at doctorin'."

A few minutes later Ulele threw down a clean rag and indicated that Ruth was to put her feet on it. She then handed Ruth a small tin of some kind of foul-smelling cream.

"Smells like polecat," Nehemiah conceded, "but it's good for raw skin."

Ruth carefully dried her feet and applied the cream. After she'd warmed the salve in her hand, it was easier to spread on the sores. Within a few minutes the wounds didn't hurt so much. Whatever Ulele put in the concoction seemed to be working. She sent the old woman a smile of appreciation.

That night, bedded down on the opposite side of the room from Dylan, Ruth listened to Nehemiah's snores rolling from the bedroom. She stared at the glow of the banked fire in the stove. Ulele had taken to the baby, so Ruth was momentarily free of the responsibility. She wasn't sure how she felt about that. While she didn't want to become attached to the child, she missed her. She missed the cute smile and the way she clasped on to her finger and held tight. Ulele had taken a drawer from a dresser that stood in a corner and made the baby a makeshift bed, where the child was now sleeping peacefully with a full stomach.

"What are you thinking about?" Dylan whispered.

"About how different this is from last night," she whispered back. "How is your shoulder feeling?"

"Better. Whatever that old woman put in the poultice, it seems to be working. How are your feet?"

"Better as well." She hesitated to voice her thought. Deep down she felt guilty for sometimes, in her lowest moments the past few days, secretly blaming God for letting them get into such a life-threatening situation, though part of her knew it was their own fault. "Dylan?"

"Yes?"

"I . . . wanted to take care of your wounds myself, but I didn't want to ask Ulele."

It was quiet from his corner, then, "You did?"

"Yes. Would . . . would you have minded?" She held her breath, praying that he wouldn't.

"No, I wouldn't have minded."

She smiled. "Then I will tomorrow."

The fire popped as she grew drowsy. The heat felt

wonderful. She could hear the howling wind battering the thick front door. "God was good to lead us to Nehemiah," she murmured.

Dylan was silent and Ruth wondered if he agreed. Certainly he must—they were sleeping by a warm fire; the baby had milk and food in her tummy. Ruth's feet were better; Ulele had given Dylan something in a glass to make him sleep better. Perhaps his silence indicated the herb had worked and he was resting comfortably. She closed her eyes, praying it was so. For so long she had watched his agony.

Turning on her side, she tried to see his face, but the room was dark. "Dylan?"

"Yes?" he said quietly.

"Oh . . . I thought you were asleep."

"Not yet."

"You're so quiet." She bit her lower lip. "You do agree that we're better off tonight, don't you? Nehemiah and Ulele are sort of like our own personal angels." Everyone had angels; the Good Book said so.

"Angels?" He chuckled and for the first time in a long while he sounded like the old Marshal McCall. "Go to sleep, Ruth."

Snuggling deeper into her bedroll, Ruth closed her eyes. He could be such a riddle: one moment all tender, a complete gentleman, compassionate to her and the baby's needs. The next moment he could be as mysterious as God's workings.

Right now, the chuckle didn't reassure her.

8

Ulele Ford was a dictator.

Ruth was firmly convinced the woman was a tyrant as she cleaned the old shack from top to bottom. She scrubbed floors down on her knees. Since she'd been here, she'd hauled heavy water buckets up from the creek, cooked three meals a day, and washed the old couple's clothes in the icy stream. The whole while, Ulele sat in the rocker and talked gibberish to the baby.

On the second afternoon Ruth caught the Indian staring at her.

"What?" she asked, attempting a genial smile. Though she treated Ruth as nothing more than a servant, Ulele, with her strange herbs and tonics, had most likely saved Dylan's life. Ruth tried to summon gratitude, but mostly she rued the day she and Dylan had accepted the old couple's help. Ruth was accustomed to hard work, but the labor the old woman forced on her was nothing short of a crime. And Nehemiah worked Dylan like a plow horse.

The squaw shook her head, which Ruth had come to recognize meant that the woman was in no mood to communicate. Ruth understood little of what the Cherokee woman said, though Ulele made her work instructions very clear.

"Clean!"

"Wash!"

"Cook!"

"Sit."

Nehemiah seemed proud that his wife's vocabulary was broadening. Ruth preferred the "sit" and "go" commands.

It was no wonder the woman was a domineering bully. The way Nehemiah treated his wife was shameful. He ordered her around in quick, curt sentences, much as he would one of the old hounds lying on the front stoop. The woman did as he ordered and never offered a single rebuke. Ruth would flash a cold stare at the evil man as she dished piping hot stew into bowls. There was no need to speak to a woman in that tone—no need at all.

Tonight Dylan was sitting by the fire, his head drooped from exhaustion. Ruth laid Ulele's mending aside and got up to pour a fresh cup of coffee.

Dylan briefly smiled his gratitude when she closed his hand around the steaming cup. The fire burned low; outside, a cold wind whistled across snow-packed ground.

"Must you leave so early each morning?" she asked softly. She cast a glance at Ulele, who was preoccupied with the baby. Snores rolled from the old man's mouth as he slept by the fire, his pungent stocking feet propped on a wooden chair.

Dylan shook his head. At night it seemed to Ruth that his pain was unbearable. He nodded toward the sleeping tormentor. "He insists we start before sunup."

Dylan rose at three thirty and left the house with Nehemiah a short time later. Ruth made sure he had a warm breakfast of oatmeal and thick slices of toasted bread spread with honey, but the marshal ate very little these days. Night covered the land when the two men returned. Dylan said little about his work, but Ruth knew by their scant conversations over supper that he was doing hard physical labor: cutting wood, setting fence posts, working long hours behind the heavy anvil Nehemiah kept in the barn. Her heart ached for the marshal, but there was nothing she could say or do to lighten his load. When she tried to broach the subject, he'd cut her off and remind her they had to have food and protection for the baby.

Bending close to his ear, she rested her hands on his corded arms and pleaded in a throaty whisper, "We don't have to do this. We can leave."

He closed his eyes. "We need the money, Ruth."

Anger rose up and nearly strangled her. Why did he *have* to be so pigheaded! Nehemiah Ford was killing him. Couldn't he see that?

"Not that badly," she argued. Her eyes darted to Ulele. She had quit playing with the baby and was staring at Ruth. How much did Ulele understand? Sometimes Ruth thought she understood nothing, but at other times she wondered if the cunning female knew more than she let on.

Dropping her voice even lower, Ruth pressed her mouth next to Dylan's ear. "We walked for days without food or shelter. We can do it again. We'll take the goat—the baby will have milk. We can make it." She pressed closer. "Please, Dylan."

Being this near to him set off a strange lightness in the bottom of her stomach. The smell of soap, water, and herbs rose from the poultices. She couldn't bear to watch the way Nehemiah worked a man in Dylan's condition. The punishment was cruel and uncalled for. Yes, they were at the mercy of strangers, but no mercy had been shown them. She feared if they didn't leave here soon, the old man would work Dylan to death.

"No," Dylan snapped. "It's only for a few days. I can make it—I have to make it." He set his jaw. As if that settled the matter, he got up and went to his bedroll on his side of the room.

Chewing her bottom lip, Ruth sat down and resumed the mending. Her back ached and her eyes blurred from the blue mist that continually hung in the cabin. Her clothes and hair smelled of pungent wood, and she longed for a hot bath. Was that possible? She'd spotted an old washtub hanging on the back of the house. Obviously by the way the Fords smelled, the tub wasn't used often. Putting the mending aside, Ruth ran her hand through her hair and scratched. If she only had a brush . . .

She glanced at the Indian woman. "Ulele?"

The woman pretended not to have heard.

"Ulele?"

Ulele grunted.

"Is it all right if I heat water in the morning and take a bath?"

Ulele picked up the baby and shuffled into the bedroom, yanking the thin curtain closed behind her. Ruth resented the fact that the old woman insisted that the baby sleep in the Fords' room. It wasn't fair. Ruth wanted the child with her; she was the infant's caretaker, not Ulele.

Sighing, she scratched her head furiously. She didn't care what Ulele thought; in the morning, after the men left, she was taking a bath.

*   *   *

The next day Ruth washed under Ulele's watchful eye. The old woman eyed the tub suspiciously when Ruth dragged the wooden bathing apparatus in and set it by the stove, while heavy pots of water bubbled on top. Ruth imagined the device was foreign to Ulele.

Ruth felt like a new person once she'd scrubbed away weeks of grime. Afterward, she bathed the baby, laughing when the infant cooed and splashed water in her face. She glanced up to see the Indian's face turn as dark as a July storm cloud. She knew the woman wondered what Ruth and Dylan were doing with an Indian child, but Ruth made no effort to explain their situation. It would only sound worse if the Fords knew that she and Dylan were traveling alone, unmarried. Dylan had been the perfect gentleman, but the Fords couldn't know that.

After the baths, Ruth stood by the fire and dried her and the infant's hair. The baby cuddled affectionately against her bosom, and Ruth felt a rush of maternal pride that rattled her to the very core. She couldn't do this—she couldn't lay claim to the child—or to Dylan. Both were only temporary passersby in her life—ones she hadn't asked for and couldn't allow herself to love. Their paths would part in Sulphur Springs. She would have to find a home for the baby and then her life would be . . . what?

Empty. Empty and unfulfilled. Ruth wondered why the thought bothered her now. She'd never had anyone, and she thought she'd accepted the future she felt God gave her.

But deep down, she knew the reason: she was starting to depend on the arrogant marshal—to look to him for security. The baby was . . . well, who could resist a baby?

That afternoon she wrote in her journal:

Dear God,
    I am so confused. Sometimes I get so angry at Dylan and his refusal to listen to me—then at other times . . .

She stared at the terse paragraph and wondered what she had been about to confide. Whatever it was, the desire now escaped her. Closing the book, she went to start supper.

When Dylan came in that night, he threw her a look that had her on edge during supper. Was he finally ready to call it quits, to leave these terrible people? She fervently prayed that what she'd glimpsed in his eyes was an end to his patience, silently hoping that he had decided that all the money in the world wasn't worth what they were going through.

After supper, Dylan sat by the fire and played with the baby. Ruth smiled when she heard him singing her a lullaby in a soft, resonant baritone. He was very good with children; he would make some lucky child a fine papa some day. He could be tender when the situation warranted, compassionate yet firm when needed.

Ruth wondered why she couldn't openly react to the child as easily. She felt guilty if she laughed when the baby laughed, embarrassed if she spent too much time with her. Once Ulele had sternly scolded her—at least Ruth assumed it was scolding—when the old woman caught Ruth carrying the infant under her arm like a sack of potatoes. She had quickly confiscated the child and demonstrated the proper way to hold a baby: gently, cradled against Ulele's huge chest.

For the rest of that day, Ruth had carefully toted the baby around like a piece of glass until her back hurt something dreadful. Being a mother was hard work; she supposed that's why the Lord had decided she wasn't up to the job.

The next morning Ruth hauled a basketful of dirty clothes to the stream. A thin sun warmed the frozen ground, so she'd convinced Ulele that the baby needed fresh air.

Before Ruth washed and rinsed heavy shirts and pants, she fastened the baby's papoose board to a low-hanging branch where Ruth could watch her. Kneeling beside the rushing water, she stared at the happy child, resisting the urge to grin back. The infant was incredibly charming with her shiny black hair and smiling eyes. As Ruth busily scrubbed a shirt against a rock, she found herself humming the same lullaby Dylan had sung the night before. She sang the song, repeating verses when she heard the baby's soft, cooing response. So the child had an ear for music—that wasn't uncommon.

Ruth remembered when Mrs. Galeen had sung to her sometimes at the orphanage, fanciful songs of butterflies, stardust, and angels. Tears filled her eyes and she swiped them away, blaming the moisture on the cold wind. Where were the baby's mother and father? Somewhere not so far away? Or were they dead? Ruth had no way to identify or return the baby to her people. Dylan hadn't known that a child even existed until she had told him. So many questions would never be answered now, with the death of the old man in the wagon. Was he a kind grandfather—a distant relative, perhaps—or just a plain thief?

* * *

Ruth dried the last dish later that night and then carried the supper scraps to the dogs huddled beside the back step. Dylan got up from the fire and followed her outside on the pretext of gathering wood.

Ruth bent against the sharp wind as she edged closer to meet him. "What was that look about last night?"

He leaned down, picking up a couple of sticks of dry oak. "You're right. We have to leave. The sooner the better."

She shut her eyes with relief, silently thanking God that Dylan had come to his senses. "When?"

He glanced toward the back door. "I'll talk to Nehemiah in the morning. We'll be short some of the pay I'd hoped for, but I can find work when we get to Sulphur Springs."

Ruth nodded, eager to be on their way. She could stretch a penny into a gold coin if she had to. Anything to escape the Fords' house and Ulele's suffocating authority. "Ulele isn't going to be happy about us leaving. She's gotten very attached to the baby."

A muscle worked tightly in Dylan's jaw. "I suppose if we were taking the baby's needs into account, we'd leave her here. Ulele would raise the little girl, and the baby would be reared in her own heritage."

"Never!" Ruth said hotly. "I would *never* leave a child in this stifling household." She wrapped her arms tightly around her middle. Nehemiah was a cold and heartless brute. He'd rarely if ever given the child a second glance. Ulele would raise the child, but not with the tenderness and consideration the little girl deserved. True, Ulele seemed fond of the child. But Ruth shuddered to think about Nehemiah's influence. If he treated the little girl anything like he treated his wife . . . No, Ruth would die before she'd leave without the infant. Once they were in Sulphur Springs, she would search for a respectable couple who would raise her with love and reverence for the Lord. If she wasn't mistaken, that was relief she saw on Dylan's face. He didn't want to abandon the child any more than she did.

"You know I'm right," she whispered. "The Fords are miserable people. You've built fences, trimmed and notched the logs for a chicken house. You've done more work for Nehemiah than he's done himself this year, and you know it. He's taking advantage of you; they're taking advantage of us. We can't leave the baby with people like them."

"But we need money and supplies to get to Wyoming, Ruth."

"I understand and I admire you for thinking of the baby's and my welfare, but we have to leave now, before you collapse."

The rationale seemed to reach him. He nodded briefly again. "All right, tomorrow we leave as soon as I've collected my pay from Ford."

They stood in silence, contemplating the next move.

She glanced at him. "Do we know how to get to Sulphur Springs from here?"

"We follow the road. One, two days, depending on how fast we travel. We'll take it easy. Your feet are beginning to heal. Maybe Ulele will let you have another pair of socks—"

"And maybe Nehemiah will let you have another shirt."

"Maybe."

Their eyes met in the cold moonlight. *Then again, maybe not,* their gazes acknowledged.

Ruth impulsively stood on her tiptoes and gave him a brief kiss on the mouth before she turned and hurried back into the house. She didn't want to arouse the Fords' suspicions, but she was excited about the plan, even though a few days ago they had been in grave danger of freezing to death. In her heart, she knew leaving was the right choice. They would make it; they had made it farther on less and managed. The three were hearty survivors.

Later, she cleaned and dressed Dylan's wounds by the firelight. Ulele's poultices were doing the job; the angry swelling looked less aggressive tonight.

"I'll take the herbs with me," she whispered. "You'll still need to see a doctor once we reach Sulphur Springs."

Dylan caught her hand. Gazing at her with amusement, he teased, "What was that all about?"

"What?" she asked. She could feel heat creep up her neck when she realized what she'd done earlier. Had she lost her mind? Kissing Marshal McCall, of all things!

Why, she had barely noticed the simple gesture of appreciation, and that's all the kiss had meant. Had he taken that *peck* for a real kiss? Apparently he had.

"That wasn't a kiss," she denied. "I was merely

expressing a moment of simple gratitude." She summoned the courage to meet his smiling eyes. "*Stop* that, Marshal McCall. You know it was a harmless peck—nothing more."

His grin widened.

"*Stop* that," she demanded again. She got up and carried the pan of water outside. Her whole body felt aflame from his personal scrutiny!

Early the next morning, Ruth quietly ate breakfast as Dylan and Nehemiah discussed the day's work. Dylan was expected to dig a trench alongside the house where the hogs could wallow this spring—as if anyone would want hogs next to their house—even if the marshal could stick a shovel in frozen ground. Yet Ulele didn't dispute her husband. She fed the baby breakfast, seeming to ignore the conversation. The men left the house soon after, and Ulele went to milk the cow, taking the baby with her.

The moment the back door closed, Ruth started to gather their meager belongings. She packed herbs and clean bandages, a fresh loaf of bread and cold meat left from breakfast. She took two warm blankets from the closet, figuring Nehemiah could deduct the cost from Dylan's wages.

Then she sat down in the silent kitchen, listening to the ticking mantel clock. By now Dylan would have told Nehemiah that they were leaving and the old man was settling up.

While Ulele's poultices had drawn the infection out of the arrow wounds, the physical labor he was doing from dawn to dusk prevented the wounds from healing. Nearly every day they had reopened and were bleeding when he returned to the cabin. Yet every evening when they sat down to dinner, Dylan had asked Ruth how her day had gone, how her feet were healing. Ruth tried not to complain, especially when the marshal was working so hard, but his sympathetic glances told her he knew how worn out she was every night. If Nehemiah was a slave driver, Ulele was not far behind.

Ruth got up to peer out of the kitchen window. Dylan had been gone a long time—long enough to tell Nehemiah and be back.

She returned to the table and sat down. Ulele would be upset when she heard that they were taking the baby, and Ruth wasn't sure how Nehemiah or Ulele would react. Well, she decided, she and Dylan would have to take a firm stance. They'd brought the child here; they would take her when they left.

Ruth wasn't exactly sure how to handle the situation, but she felt that kindness would go further than being brutal about the situation. She would have to find the right words. Though she could hardly stand to be around Ulele, she couldn't be mean about taking the baby. Ulele had no children of her own, and Ruth could understand how she'd fallen in love with the little girl. After all, she'd had to fight the same feeling herself. She might loathe Ulele, but she couldn't deliberately be cruel. The old Indian had a terrible life with Nehemiah. Not only was she isolated from human community, but from the way Nehemiah spoke to his wife, Ruth suspected he wasn't strong in sentimentality. Ulele kept a close eye on her husband when he was in the cabin; Ruth had a hunch that he might have been physically abusive as well. Those suspicions only strengthened Ruth's resolve to be kind.

She got up and looked out of the window again. Was Dylan negotiating for a second horse? She could hardly bear to think about walking a mile—much less five or six—if that was the remaining distance to Sulphur Springs. They couldn't depend on Nehemiah to have told them the truth. She'd learned that much from her experience in the past few days.

She bit her bottom lip, her worry increasing. Dylan had been gone too long. Something was wrong.

Ulele returned to the cabin with the baby. At Ulele's direction, Ruth started to scrub down the walls while the old woman entertained the baby.

The lye soap ate into her hands and water ran down her arms, wetting the front of the shirt Ulele had loaned her. Ruth could hear the baby cooing in response to the woman's native tongue. She wished she could understand what Ulele was saying. Ruth scrubbed harder. Where was Dylan? They needed to be on their way before the day was over.

Just before sundown Ruth saw the marshal coming toward the cabin. By now Ruth was sick with worry. Nehemiah must have stopped off to take care of something in the barn because she didn't see him immediately, which was unusual. Dylan's strides were measured, his shoulders stiff. His posture told Ruth that her suspicions were right: all was not well. The fact that he hadn't come back this morning was troubling enough. Had the marshal changed his mind and consented to stay the day and leave tomorrow morning?

Ulele was busy with the baby, so Ruth picked up the water bucket and slipped out the door to meet the marshal at the edge of the water barrel. His face was pale and his eyes sunken with shadows as he began to wash up. Was it pain or fury that burned like hot coals in his blue eyes?

Ruth shivered as the icy wind whipped around the edge of the cabin. The sky was pewter gray with the lowering clouds. Snow clouds? She prayed that another storm wasn't brewing. "Did you talk to Nehemiah?"

"Yes." The marshal's voice was clipped and concise.

"What did he say?"

Dylan took a deep breath, and a flash of pain marred his features.

Ruth felt so bad for him she almost reached out to touch him. Standing back, she allowed him a moment to recover. "What happened?" she asked.

"He laughed."

Ruth blinked in surprise. "Laughed? He *laughed*? Why?"

"He said we shouldn't be so easily fooled next time."

Ruth didn't understand. "Fooled? What did he mean?"

"He meant he tricked us. We're getting nothing. We've worked for *nothing*, Ruth."

"For nothing?" she echoed. The words refused to register. They had toiled for five days of relentless labor. For nothing?

"You mean you've worked so hard that you've nearly killed yourself, for nothing? He's giving us *nothing*?"

"That's what I said." Fury tinted Dylan's cheeks, and his hands, now calloused and red from labor, made fists at his sides.

Ruth whirled and pretended to dip water as he splashed his face and dried it with a towel. Ruth could hardly believe that anyone—even Nehemiah—could be so deceitful. Dylan had worked from sunup to sundown, working through the fever of infection, hardly able to stand, and Nehemiah was refusing to pay him? He had apparently delighted in his little game, duping them into doing his work when he never *intended* to pay up. She'd never known anyone so dishonest—except the Wyatts. What was wrong with people out here? Were they all out for personal gain at the expense of anyone and everyone?

"I wanted to kill him, Ruth. For the first time in my life I wanted to shoot a man down in cold blood and leave him lying in the snow," Dylan admitted through gritted teeth.

"You should have." Ruth knew the words were uncharitable, callous and cold, but at the moment she couldn't feel anything but hatred for Nehemiah Ford.

"I didn't have a gun." Dylan stared at the horizon,

which was fast disappearing as night approached. "The horse and goat are ours, and I'd say he owes us supplies. I've already taken what we're owed."

Ruth wanted to wring her hands, but instead she kept calm. Bursts of temper had gotten her here in the first place. "I think you're right. We made a bargain and Nehemiah reneged. He agreed to the terms. That's a bargain, whether Nehemiah Ford chooses to honor his words or not."

Dylan met her gaze. "Let's get out of here."

Ruth nodded in agreement. She picked up the bucket of water; Dylan started off for the barn.

The baby was on the floor playing while Ulele stirred a pot of beans on the stove. Ruth set the bucket of water in its usual place behind the stove, pretending all was normal. When the old woman turned her head, Ruth quickly scooped up the two bedrolls, but when she turned for the child, she found herself staring down a double-barreled shotgun.

Ruth's blood froze.

The Cherokee woman held the wide-eyed infant in the crook of one arm. In the other arm she steadied the shotgun. The baby looked at Ruth curiously, clearly happy and healthy after a few days of care and nourishing food. Ulele had taken good care of the child, but the baby wasn't hers to keep.

Swallowing her fear, Ruth remained where she was. Would the old woman really shoot her? The shotgun would rip her in two. She had to be brave. Dylan was just outside the door. She had to measure up.

God, help me, she prayed.

"We're leaving," she said, though she knew the woman didn't understand a word. "Give me the baby." She held out her hands, demanding the infant.

Ulele shook her head no.

Ruth nodded yes, keeping her eyes glued to the gun. "Yes," she ordered, still holding out her hands.

Ulele shook her head. No. The woman refused to relinquish the child, and the shotgun never wavered.

Ruth felt her bottom lip quiver. Suddenly she was angry. Fighting mad. How dare this woman think she had a right to keep this child! Nehemiah and Ulele Ford were mean, deceitful heathens. Nehemiah had noted her Christianity when she'd thanked God for Nehemiah's appearance on the trail, but not once had he offered a prayer before meals or at bedtime. Not once had either Ford said thank you for anything. And now Nehemiah thought he could keep them here by force? By not giving them the horse and supplies they earned? And Ulele thought she could steal this child by holding Ruth at gunpoint?

I don't think so, Ruth decided. Ulele motioned Ruth toward the door with the barrel of the shotgun. Bracing herself for a fight, Ruth lunged for the gun, catching the Indian woman off guard. Ruth grabbed hold of the gun barrel, shoving it toward the ceiling, but Ulele wasn't letting go. While she held on to the gun barrel, Ruth tried to take the baby from Ulele, but the woman was older, taller, and stronger.

All Ruth could do was hold on and fight to

gain control while protecting the child. "No," Ruth grunted with effort, "you're not keeping *her*."

Ulele responded with a guttural word. The baby was howling now.

Suddenly a masculine hand swooped down and grabbed the gun, yanking it out of both Ruth's and Ulele's grip. Before Ruth knew what had happened, Dylan shouldered Ulele aside and snatched the baby out of her arms. Shoving the child at Ruth, he snatched up the two bedrolls, grabbed her hand, and dragged her out of the cabin.

Hand in hand, they sprinted for the waiting horse, on which Dylan had managed to load meager supplies. He hoisted Ruth and the baby atop of the animal and then sprang onto the mare behind them.

"Keep low," Dylan shouted, shoving Ruth down. He covered her and the baby with his body while he held the reins.

A bullet whizzed over their heads, and Ruth buried her face in the smell of leather. She clung tightly to the baby, who was wailing. Glancing beneath Dylan's arm, she saw Ulele standing in the doorway, her hands over her face, the old farmer running a few steps before stopping to fire again. Ruth closed her eyes and concentrated on holding on. They rode at full gallop as far as the horse could safely go carrying double weight.

Finally Dylan drew the animal to a standstill beneath a bare aspen and slid off. He helped Ruth down. "Are you okay?"

"Scared half to death, but I'm fine." Ruth gazed

down at the baby, straightening her blankets so they covered her shoulders.

Dylan grinned. "Was that a fight I just witnessed between two women over one baby?"

Ruth's chin rose a notch. "She wasn't keeping this child." She wouldn't admit that she would have fought a whole tribe of Indians before she'd see this baby fall into the wrong hands. A hundred years would pass before she'd openly acknowledge that she cared for this tiny life—cared so much it hurt.

Part of Ruth wanted the small girl so badly she couldn't stand it, but another, stronger, part of her knew she would never be her mother. The baby needed a home with two parents; that was only fair for the child.

As Ruth gazed at the child in her arms, love nearly suffocated her. "Maybe I should have let Ulele keep her," she backtracked. "After all, she is an Indian baby."

Then why had she fought to keep the child? She should have grabbed the bedrolls and run, and not put the baby in danger again.

Well, she'd done it for Dylan, she told herself.

Dylan had taken to the child; she could see it in his smile, though it did seem odd. He was a marshal, a man accustomed to being alone. He liked his solitary life. He'd said so not once but many times. But she'd watched him holding the child, talking to her every night. While the baby slept, she'd caught him smoothing down the thatch of black hair that persisted in standing straight up. She'd seen him cup that tiny head with his large hand . . . and she had ached with the knowledge that his hard heart was softening toward the child but not so much toward her.

"Ulele wasn't going to let me have her. I knew you'd be upset if I didn't get her."

"Me? Upset?" He looked incredulous. Then he laughed. Hooted, in fact.

The baby started to howl, and Ruth shoved her toward Dylan. He automatically took her, staring at Ruth with puzzlement.

Ruth wouldn't look at either of them. "She likes you better," she said. Her heart ached because she knew it was true. And the knowledge hurt.

9

"The man should be horsewhipped," Dylan observed as they ate bread and cold meat over a small fire that night.

Ruth agreed, wondering how anyone got to be that mean; it would surely take work and the devil's help. How many other unsuspecting travelers had the Fords ensnared?

Ruth steadied the marshal's cup as she poured coffee. Dylan's hands were trembling—a sure sign of his rage. When a person's hand trembled from anger, there would be a price to pay.

Ruth knew the consequences of anger. Lately hadn't she let flashes of emotion overrule good sense more often than not? She hated the feeling of not being in control; she'd prided herself on using good judgment, relying on the Lord, but lately she'd failed miserably. The rigid set of Dylan's jaw reminded her of her own short fuse. But who wouldn't be angry? Nehemiah Ford was an evil man, so evil Ruth doubted the devil would lay claim to his own.

Once when Ruth was small, there'd been a man

who tried to take advantage of Mrs. Galeen's goodness. Ruth had been young, barely able to remember the incident. Mrs. Galeen had paid the worker to help pick apples in the small orchard behind the orphanage. They had agreed on a full day's work— sunup to sundown. Shortly after noon break, Mrs. Galeen had caught the young man snoozing beneath a low, spreading branch ripe with fruit. Ruth could still recall the woman's reaction. She'd whacked the boy smartly on the bottoms of his thin boots. When he'd jumped up in surprise, she'd paid him for the work he'd done and escorted him off the property in a dead run.

The woman had been demanding but fair and compassionate. Character traits Nehemiah Ford wouldn't have recognized.

"Men like Ford should be strung up by their heels," Dylan said. "Shot like a rabid animal."

Ruth released a breath of relief. It was good to know that he was angrier with the Fords than with her. "Well—" she turned to pick up a clean bandage—"maybe not shot. The Good Book says an eye for an eye, but I've never quite understood how far a person could actually go without receiving God's disapproval."

She'd never shot anything but necessary food—and she wouldn't—except she would be mighty tempted right now if Nehemiah Ford caught up with them.

Dylan took a drink from the cup, eyeing her. When he continued to stare, Ruth looked up. "What?"

"You actually believe in the Lord and this Good Book, don't you?"

Ruth gaped at him. "You don't?"

Though in her mind she'd accused the marshal of being a heathen more than once, she supposed she didn't really believe he was. He'd had the tenacity to keep going, to protect her and the baby as best he could under the circumstances. A lesser man might have rid himself of the problem long ago. She didn't know if she could have done all that without the Lord's help, so she had begun to wonder if maybe Dylan was starting to trust more than he knew. He didn't speak coarsely—at least not as much lately— and never the way Nehemiah had gone on, taking the Lord's name in vain with every breath. Though Dylan sometimes made her so angry she couldn't see straight and his stubbornness drove her to distraction, she had to admire his tenacity.

Dylan looked away from the fire. "Never had an occasion to believe in anyone other than myself."

Sorrow twisted in Ruth, deep and hurtful. She hated the way she was softening toward this man. Ruth might not be alive at all if it weren't for this wonderful man. He was a good man. Yet something in Dylan's childhood must have stifled his ability to believe. Some bitterness from his past seemed to haunt him.

Dylan had functioned under incredible odds. Only through God's grace had he managed to travel with his injuries, yet he couldn't seem to see that. The five days at the Fords' place had been torturous.

Dylan was still in no condition to travel. Neither was she; it wouldn't take much to start her feet bleeding again. Could they possibly make it the five or six miles to Sulphur Springs?

Ruth didn't see how the marshal could hold up or how they could feed the baby. They'd left in such a hurry, they'd forgotten the goat. They needed help and needed it badly.

She walked to the brook and wet a cloth, then returned to clean and apply poultices to Dylan's shoulder. Anything placed on the raw flesh made him wince, but this was necessary. The marshal endured the treatment twice daily only by gritting his jaw and turning his head away. It hurt her to hurt him.

"I don't know why you won't let me give you something for the pain." On the second night at the Fords', she'd given him some of the sleeping weed from the store that Ulele kept. When Dylan first drank it, his mood had improved, but in a strange way. His eyes would go wide and soon he would think that he saw spiders running up the wall. The first time it happened, Ruth jumped up and grabbed a shoe, her gaze searching for the offensive bug. But there had been no spiders. Dylan was out of his mind. His hallucinations had lasted for hours until she had given up. She threw the shoe in a corner and let him rave.

After two doses, he had refused any more of the medicine. "I don't want any more of that locoweed!"

He winced now as she applied the herbs. Their eyes met over the firelight. Tonight she found it impossible to break the look, and her touch lingered far too long to be polite. The baby slept nearby, warm beside the fire. "I'm sorry you're hurt," she said. "I feel very responsible."

"Responsible?" His gaze softened. "You had nothing to do with me riding to the old man's defense. When I topped a rise and saw Indians attacking the wagon, I acted out of instinct—I should have realized I was outnumbered. If anyone's to blame, it's me."

She wound a clean bandage around his shoulder. Such a nice shoulder—broad and heavily corded. The past few days he'd lost more weight, but he was still a large, well-muscled man.

"I should thank you, Ruth. I doubt that I would be alive tonight if you hadn't stopped to help."

She smiled. "It was nothing—I would have done it for anyone."

Truth be known, she didn't want to examine too closely what she'd done. If she had known it was Dylan lying near death, would she have passed on without a single backward glance? She didn't want to think so, but at the time she well might have. She was ever so grateful that she hadn't let her fear override kindness. She was glad she'd been able to pull Dylan back from the jaws of death. He was, after all, a decent man.

Perhaps if they had met under different circumstances . . .

But they *had* met under different circumstances—on the wagon train—and Ruth well recalled the marshal's arrogance, the endless teasing when she came into his sights. Yet tonight Dylan McCall was nothing like that man. He was soft-spoken, respectful and, yes, humble. She didn't know how to react to this new man. She was more comfortable with the ornery side of Marshal McCall.

At any rate, she no longer felt animosity toward him, just empathy—for his wounds, for the fact that he had been saddled with a woman and baby so he couldn't carry out his duties. But his trials would be over in a few days, God willing, and hers would have just begun.

"Penny for your thoughts?"

She glanced up. Could her feelings possibly show on her face? "Oh, they wouldn't be worth a penny."

"They might. Are you worried?"

She shook her head. "I'm not worried about me, only about you and the baby."

"I told you I'd help you find a home for the baby when we reach Sulphur Springs."

"I know. It's just that I feel so overwhelmed by the task. I want the child to have a good home, to be raised by Christian parents. What if we make a mistake and give her to the wrong family?" She glanced at the baby, who dozed beside Dylan. The child needed care and love—most of all love.

Tonight's feeding had been an ordeal. Without the goat's milk, Ruth had been forced to chew the baby's food for her. The primitive food chain was unpleasant and sickened Ruth, but the child accepted the fare without protest.

"Tomorrow we'll find another cow or goat," Dylan promised. Was he a mind reader? No, he wouldn't still be with her if he could read her mind.

"It isn't that." She set the roll of bandages and herbs aside and helped him struggle back into his shirt. "I know the baby and I are keeping you from your work."

He shook his head. "I'll wire my boss when we reach Sulphur Springs and explain what happened. There won't be a problem."

"You need to see a doctor before you do anything else."

He grinned, buttoning the shirt. "Yes, Mama. And I'd suggest that you send a wire to your cousin Milford so he will be expecting you."

She dropped her gaze and grinned. He could be as charming as an old-maid aunt when he wanted. "I might very well do that, smarty."

And she would, *if* she had any inkling of how to contact Milford. Regardless, she had made up her mind that she was no longer going to be a burden to the marshal. When Dylan left Sulphur Springs without her, it would be with her blessing and prayers.

They turned in for the night. Her bedroll was on the opposite side of the fire, but when she lay down, she met Dylan's gaze. They looked at each other for a long time. Love stirred inside Ruth; she pushed it down. It was only natural under these circumstances to feel gratitude and yes, even a smidgen of affection for her protector. Dylan had not wanted the job, certainly never asked for it, but he was fulfilling the role admirably. If she was foolishly falling in love with him, it wasn't his fault.

The fire burned low. Overhead a cloudy sky stripped the night of any light. Dylan's eyes closed with fatigue, and he cradled the baby to his chest protectively. Ruth smiled. How she envied that child . . .

Rolling to her back, she closed her eyes. *Don't think that way, Ruth. You're getting soft.* She opened her eyes when she heard Dylan singing now—a soft lullaby—Irish, wasn't it? Ruth had heard the song before but didn't know where. Perhaps from her father's lips.

> *"Oh, Danny boy, the pipes, the pipes are calling*
> *From glen to glen, and down the*
> *   mountainside . . ."*

Melancholy stole over her as she listened to the rich baritone softening the darkness. Her thoughts turned to the only family she knew now: Patience, Mary, Lily, Harper. What were they doing tonight? Was Mary's asthma worse? Would Mary ever find a man to love her—to adore her the way Jackson cherished Glory? Would any of the women be that blessed?

The other girls must be worried sick about Ruth, fearing the worst. She'd been gone almost a month and hadn't written.

She flipped back to her side, stuffing her fist into her mouth to mute her crying. If she hadn't been so willful, so stubborn, she would be with them tonight, in a warm bed or sitting at Pastor Siddons's table, or at Oscar Fleming's. Should she have married the old prospector? The thought still rendered her numb, but maybe God had intended her to marry Oscar. Oscar would be well past the years of wanting children. . . . Perhaps Oscar had been God's way of providing for Ruth, given her barrenness. She didn't want to cheat any man by marrying him and not being able to give him children. God had set her path, but in her self-centeredness she had failed to be obedient to his will, instead running off to Wyoming to build her life. Now she was paying the consequences of her folly.

She would never love another man like she loved the marshal. Hard as she tried to put dreams of a family away, sometimes the hope sprang up to strangle her.

Closing her eyes, she prayed silently. *I will do whatever you want, Lord; only you must show me the way. I am truly blind and cannot see which direction to take at this point. I don't know why I'm here with Marshal McCall and a motherless baby, but I will do my best to find a home for this child and make Marshal McCall's life a little easier—with your grace.*

For some reason God had appointed her— what?—surrogate mother and marshal caretaker? Seemed an unusual responsibility to be given to her, but she didn't question the Father's will. She would function wherever he put her.

She drifted off to the sound of Dylan's singing.

• • •

The first ray of light drew Ruth awake and she lay, listening and waiting, reluctant to face what a new day would bring. She could hear the baby cooing as Dylan talked to her. How was it he could relate so well to an infant but triggered her temper so easily? She couldn't understand that. They could walk together for hours, each seeming to know when the other was tired and needed to rest, always anticipating what the other was thinking. Then Dylan would tease her about marrying Oscar, about her ridiculous decision to follow him, or about her temper, and she would boil over. There was just something about him—

"Do you intend to lie there all day?"

Like now.

"No. But I didn't fancy rising before sunup."

"It's dawn and we're burning daylight."

She sat up and looked at him, holding the baby. "She needs milk."

"And I'm fresh out," Dylan returned, his blue eyes mocking her.

"Grump."

"Let's get moving."

Sometimes he acted like he was running from her as hard as she was running from Oscar.

They rode slowly this morning, sparing the mare since it was carrying double. Ruth sat behind Dylan, who held the baby against his good shoulder. She was careful to avoid touching the marshal's back, to allow the herbs to do their work. Besides, she didn't want to touch him any more than necessary because . . . well, just because.

The baby's serious dark eyes peered at her over his shoulder, and Ruth wished Dylan would change the baby's position. Guilt still nagged her over the decision to bring the child. But as soon as she thought of Ulele and Nehemiah, she praised God that she'd had the nerve to fight. Surely when they reached Sulphur Springs, there would be a family eager to take her.

"Well, well," Dylan said, startling Ruth out of her reverie. "God does provide."

Ruth peered around his shoulder. In the middle of the trail was a cow standing there as if waiting for them to happen along. Ruth could hardly believe her eyes. "Do you think it's . . . tame?"

Dylan's shoulders shook with laughter. "Tame?"

"Yes," she said, stung. "I don't fancy getting kicked from here to kingdom come." She'd been lucky; the other cow had been gentle.

"Guess one of us will have to find out. Should we flip a coin?"

He was teasing her again, laughing at her when she was entirely serious. Well, it was up to him to figure out how to catch this one.

Ruth slid off the horse. Dylan dismounted, too, and handed her the baby. Then he took the rope from the saddle and uncoiled it, keeping the horse between him and the cow. The object in question continued to stare at them, chewing contentedly. Ruth was astounded. Was it just going to stand there while Dylan roped and milked it? Somehow she didn't think so. Finally Dylan stepped back into the saddle.

"What are you doing?" Ruth asked, wondering if he'd changed his mind and decided to ride on. He probably wasn't eager to reopen the wounds a fourth time—or was it the fifth time by now?

"I'm going to rope a cow," he said.

He urged the horse forward, moving parallel to the cow. He began to gently twirl the rope above his head. Ruth watched curiously. He did seem to know what he was doing. When he was within three or so yards of the cow, Dylan sent the rope flying with a flick of his wrist. The cow stood quietly as the noose settled around its withers and the horse planted its hooves in the sod. For about three seconds the cow and the horse looked at one another, and then the cow decided she'd had enough of the game.

With a toss of her head, she attempted to rid herself of the rope. She failed. The mare had, at some point, been a good cow pony, because she stood her ground, keeping the rope taut between her and the cow.

"Good job," Dylan said, patting the animal's neck.

"Now what?" Ruth asked.

"Now we're going to see if that cow has some milk for our baby."

Our baby. His words hit her like a sandstorm. No. She wouldn't even entertain the thought. Dylan's words signified a slip of the tongue—nothing more.

Dylan got off the horse and cautiously followed the rope toward the cow. He spoke gently. Ruth couldn't hear the words, but the cow watched him warily. In a few minutes he was able to rub the beast's nose and apparently convince her that he was harmless. He ran a hand down her side, then knelt gingerly beside her. He tested the udder, then gently squeezed a teat.

"We have milk," he announced softly. "Bring me a canteen."

Taking a cue from him, Ruth moved slowly and quietly, hoping the baby wouldn't choose the next few minutes for a screaming fit. Grace was with them. She handed Dylan two canteens and backed away.

Before long the marshal had filled both containers with milk. When he removed the rope from the cow's neck, he patted her and thanked her for cooperating.

"Well, that wasn't too difficult," he announced, returning to Ruth. "Let's have breakfast."

The baby drank from the canteen greedily. Dylan offered Ruth the first drink from the second canteen. She'd never drunk milk fresh from the cow before, and the warm taste was different. Not distasteful, but different.

"You've milked a few cows in your life."

"Raised on a farm," he said.

She wondered where he'd been raised, and how, but it didn't seem a subject he wanted to open so she left it. There was a lot about Dylan McCall she didn't know, and it seemed, a lot more he wasn't willing to share. At least not with her.

Dylan stood up and stretched. "We'd best move on. I don't want to take a chance on Nehemiah catching up. He's crazy enough to try and snatch the baby and shoot us in the process."

"You think he'd come after us?" Ruth's eyes searched the road they traveled.

"I don't know what that old man might do," Dylan replied, a remnant of his former anger still evident in his tone. "And I don't want to know."

At noon they fed the baby from the canteen again. She cooperated and soon dropped off to sleep in Dylan's arms.

At midafternoon, when Ruth was about to close her eyes from need of sleep, Dylan's soft voice woke her. "Well, well, look at this."

Ruth peered around his shoulder. A wagon drawn by a team of bays was coming toward them. She could see a heavyset woman at the reins. Dylan halted the mare just off the trail, and the woman stopped the wagon beside them. Four children, ranging in age, Ruth guessed, from around ten to four years, peered up at her. Their faces were smudged, as if they'd eaten candy before their ride, their eyes wide with question as they looked up at Dylan.

"Afternoon," Dylan greeted.

"Mama," the youngest whined.

"You hush," the mother admonished.

"But, Mama—"

The woman reached around the three others and thumped the boy on the head. His eyes immediately smarted with tears. Ruth's heart went out to the child as she wondered what the little boy had wanted.

"Mama, Davy needs to—"

"Didn't I tell you all to *shut* yore piehole?"

The youngest child sniffed and swiped his sleeve across his runny nose. The woman turned back to focus on Ruth and Dylan. "What are you two doing out here in the middle of nowhere?"

The woman wore a much-washed blue dress with a round collar. A wool cape hung on her shoulders, and she wore a broad-brimmed bonnet. Her face was rosy from the cold air. The children's clothes looked worn and wrinkled, as if they'd traveled some distance since the morning, and none of them wore a coat that fit properly. Thin arms stuck out of threadbare sleeves, and not one had a coat buttoned up.

Dylan addressed the woman. "We're going to Sulphur Springs. I understand it's not too many more miles."

"Just three or four. Just came from there. Heading to my folks' place," the woman said. "Marge Donaldson's my name."

"Dylan McCall. This is Ruth."

Mrs. Donaldson nodded. "Pleased to meet you."

"Mama, Davy—"

The woman elbowed the oldest child back into his seat.

"Where'd you come from?" another child queried.

"Joshua, you just sit back there and shut up—"

Ruth studied the woman's strong face. She saw a woman worn down from hard work and too many mouths to feed, but she took a chance. "We have a baby who needs a home." The words slipped out before Ruth could stop them. Surprise crossed the woman's face.

"Let's see him."

Dylan glanced at Ruth over his shoulder and then held the sleeping baby up for the woman's perusal. "It's a her."

Marge frowned. "That's an Indian baby. Where'd you come by it?"

"Her—she's a her, and I rescued her from a burning wagon after an Indian attack," Ruth explained.

The woman's frown turned into a scowl. "The red heathens didn't take the kid with them?"

"I don't believe they knew the child was there," Ruth said shortly.

"Well, well. Ain't that somethin'." Mrs. Donaldson's eyes ran over God's perfect creation like she was inspecting rancid meat. And with just about the same emotion.

"Mama—"

"Sharon, I told you to sit down and be quiet!" She smacked the little girl hard and shoved her back into her seat in the corner of the wagon, where one of her brothers quickly moved to shield her.

Ruth wondered if the children ever wished they

could disappear. She'd been raised without parents, along with the other children at the orphanage, except for the time she'd lived with the Norrises. She'd been spared this kind of treatment.

"So yore lookin' for a home for the baby?"

Ruth glanced at Dylan.

"Well, I'd surely be willin' to take her. My husband took off a while back and I'm alone, 'cept for th' kids. Got a homestead not too far from here, cattle to take care of, garden in the summer. Need all th' help I can get. Not too many people out here, ya know, so I got to raise my own help. 'Course, it'll be some time before that one can be anything but a burden, but—"

"Mama, there ain't—"

"You *sit* down, Jacob, and keep yore mouth shut!"

Taking the baby from Dylan, Ruth drew her protectively to her chest. "Ride on," she whispered to Dylan under her breath.

"Don't you have any hands on your place?" Dylan asked.

"Got one. Once in a while some man hidin' from th' law will come through, work for food and a place to sleep. I give him a bunk, and he does a few chores until he up and leaves." She shrugged. "Generally they don't stay long."

"Go," Ruth murmured, giving Dylan a stern look. "Now. She isn't the one."

Clearing his throat, Dylan said kindly, "Well, I think we'll ride on into Sulphur Springs."

The woman seemed unfazed by his dismissal.

"Suit yourself—"

"Mama—"

"Jacob, if I have to tell you young'uns to hush one more time," the woman threatened, turning to catch the ear of the offending youngster and twisting it until the child yowled.

Ruth winced.

Marge looked back. "Say, bet you two could use some grub."

"No," Ruth said, glancing up at Dylan. He wagged an eyebrow.

Marge Donaldson turned on the wagon seat and yelled at one of the middle kids. "Boy! You hand me up four ta five of those turnips back there. Where's yore manners?"

Jacob, his ear fiery red, his eyes brimming with tears an eight-year-old would hate, Ruth guessed, turned and handed the vegetables to his mother.

"Here. Ain't much, but it's somethin' to fill yore belly."

"Thank you," Dylan said, leaning down to take the vegetables, which he handed to Ruth.

"You take care now," Marge advised, then slapped the reins over the rumps of the team.

"Mama!"

"You *hush*!"

As the wagon rattled down the road, Ruth could still hear the children complaining and Marge Donaldson still advising each to "shut up."

"Oh, my," Ruth breathed, hugging the baby tightly.

"Wonder why her husband left?" Dylan said, turning to grin at Ruth.

Ruth stifled a giggle. She felt sorry for the children and wished she could do something to make their lot in life better, but she knew that was impossible. At least she and Dylan hadn't given her the baby to raise and abuse.

"Well, looks like we have our supper," Dylan said, eyeing the turnips.

"Praise the Lord," Ruth agreed, feeling good that God had left the baby in her care a while longer.

It wouldn't be forever, she knew. She accepted that . . . didn't she?

10

The long day had sapped Dylan's strength. As Ruth walked, he clung to the baby and to the saddle, careful not to show Ruth his growing feebleness as shadows began to lengthen.

Ruth had carried more than her share lately, and most of their problems were due to him. If he could live that fateful day over when he'd decided to ride to the old man's rescue. . . . In all likelihood, however, he would make the same decision again, to go in with guns blazing, and that would be all right, but only if Ruth weren't drawn into the fiasco.

He closed his eyes, grimacing when he thought about dying out there beside that wagon, alone, without ever knowing Ruth, really knowing her. He'd have missed discovering that her stubbornness was part of her strength, her ability to focus on an end result without being distracted by her own pain. She cared for the baby, cared for her without complaint. She'd determined to go somewhere new, to begin a new life—whether in Wyoming or elsewhere—and that's what she would do in spite of this major setback. The baby and Dylan were only minor detours in her mind.

While he could appreciate that focus, it bothered him as well. He found himself wanting to distract her, wanting her to think about him in ways other than a responsibility—an unwanted one to boot.

But who took care of Ruth? She was the one who had taken on the job of teaching Glory to read and write, to bathe like a cultured young woman, and to acquire manners. Ruth had worried over Mary's poor health and sat up with her for company and comfort when Mary's coughs racked her slight frame.

But who took care of Ruth?

And why did Dylan find himself wanting things to be different right now? Why was he angry because he was injured and couldn't properly protect Ruth? He wanted to carry the burden of worry and the weight of protection for her and the child. Worry grated on him; she'd had to be the stronger one, even when she had her own problems.

The mental exercise kept his mind off the fact that it was taking four times as long to make the trek to Sulphur Springs as it should have, and that his back felt like a hot poker had caught him between the shoulder blades.

Ruth.

What awaited her once they reached town, found someone to take the baby, and he went on his way? He knew he'd been more hindrance than help, but what would she do without him? What would *he* do without Ruth? The fact that they were together had made the circumstances more tolerable—at least to him.

Then was in the future. Right now Ruth was barely able to put one foot in front of the other. Though it was early, they both needed rest. The baby started to fret.

"Looks like a good place to camp."

Ruth swayed on her feet. "So soon?" She blinked, holding her hand to her head.

"Are you all right?" The question was stupid; she was obviously far from being all right.

"I'm fine," Ruth insisted as she took the baby from him. "But I'm grateful we've stopped early today." She gave him a thankful smile.

"Well, you need to thank the Lord special tonight. We have something to eat." Dylan patted his pockets, which bulged with the turnips Mrs. Donaldson had given them.

"Good idea. Maybe we can both thank him."

The suggestion made Dylan uncomfortable, but he saw her point. The Lord—or whoever—had had plenty of chances to do them in, but for some reason decided not to. It had to be because of Ruth's influence, because he still couldn't bring himself to trust in anyone but Dylan McCall. If he let himself down, he had no one to blame but himself. If Ruth's Lord let him down—well, he'd been let down in that way before, and he might not take kindly to the situation now.

Ruth helped him drag the saddle off the horse and wipe the animal down with dry grass before staking her out to graze for the night. The winter spring trickling into a small pool provided sufficient water. After starting a fire, Dylan dipped water into their single pot and peeled the turnips with his pocketknife, while Ruth changed the baby's diaper. He set the pot on the edge of the campfire to boil.

"We should be in Sulphur Springs no later than late tomorrow afternoon, I'd guess."

"Good," Ruth murmured. She lay back against a tree and closed her eyes. The dark circles under her eyes troubled Dylan. She needed a comfortable place to sleep, decent boots, and a hot meal. How had he allowed the situation to get so far out of hand? He should have turned around the moment he'd realized that she was following him and taken her back to Denver City. If he had, none of this would have happened. He'd have missed the old man and the Indian attack by a good two days, and he wouldn't be here, huddled around a tiny campfire, helpless as a turtle on its back.

But as Sara Dunnigan used to say: If wishes were pickles and *but*s were bread, you'd have a fine sandwich but nothing else.

Ruth got up and unrolled her bed, then collapsed on it in a heap, staring glassy-eyed up at the threatening sky. "I pray we can make it before the weather breaks."

Dylan turned a skeptical eye on the lowering clouds blocking a weak sun. They held snow, and plenty of it. They would be walking knee-deep in the white stuff by the time they reached Sulphur

Springs, but he didn't bother to tell Ruth. She had her hands full with the baby tonight. The child seemed fussier than usual although she'd drunk her fill of milk.

As the turnips bubbled over the fire, Ruth roused herself enough to dress his wounds. He saw the hollow look in her eyes and wondered if she was getting sick. That's all they'd need—for both to be incapacitated and leave the baby vulnerable. He set his teeth, sheer will forcing him to remain alert. Wounds that had shown promise of healing yesterday had broken open today and seeped green pus tonight. Ruth shook her head, her eyes solemn as she cleaned the infection and applied the last of the herbs. Her eyes met his, and he wished that he could erase the fear he saw in their depths.

"It's not good, is it?" He asked the obvious.

"No," she whispered.

"One more day," he promised, answering her mute question. "I'll see a doctor when we get to Sulphur Springs."

She nodded, tying off the clean strip of bleached muslin. Ulele had been smart enough to know that the wound must be kept clean, yet all the herbs in the world weren't going to heal these wounds. They'd had such poor care at the first, then had reopened too many times to heal properly. A doctor would have to lance and cauterize the wounds before healing could set in.

Dylan mutely shook his head. Despite his best efforts, disaster had struck. And it would strike again if he didn't do something to prevent it. Sulphur Springs was only a day away. Yet could they make it?

He had never felt so helpless in his life. How he wished that he believed in Ruth's God—had her peaceful assurances that someone besides herself controlled the situation.

●　●　●

They ate the turnips, each huddled separately in a blanket. The baby fell asleep shortly after dark. Ruth tucked her in, using one of Dylan's blankets to protect her in spite of the dropping temperature. She would stay warm in her wool cocoon.

The wind howled, bending towering aspens, rattling their branches like dry bones. The clouds continually lowered and the constant wind spit random flakes into the air. Dylan watched Ruth refuse to acknowledge the worsening conditions. She moved as if she were sleepwalking, until he told her to roll up in the bedroll to get warm.

Every bone in the marshal's body ached tonight. He closed his eyes, willing the pain to ease. It was an old trick he'd learned from a friend. The Kiowa Indian was a scout for an army fort where Dylan had stayed from time to time early in his career. The brave had taught Dylan survival skills, including how to endure pain. Tonight those skills failed him. He'd never been more exhausted or felt more useless. Though he was bone weary, sleep failed to come.

In its place he thought about Ruth and the baby,

responsibilities he couldn't shirk despite the growing weakness of his body. For the first time he tasted defeat, and he didn't like the flavor.

He opened his eyes to stare at the sleeping infant cradled in his arms. Long, dark eyelashes feathered across her nut brown skin. Tendrils of black shiny hair framed the little girl's face. This was what fatherhood must be like—staring at the miracle you created with the woman you loved. Dylan had never thought much about being a father; that would come years down the road, if ever. He'd never seriously considered being a parent, taking on a responsibility he couldn't walk away from. But here was responsibility nestled in his arms like a purring kitten. The surprise was, he didn't mind, nor did he mind having Ruth around. Most women got on his nerves with their silly giggles and flighty nature, but Ruth was neither silly nor flighty. Independent as a hog on ice, granted. Set in her ways but not fickle.

The admission amused him.

When had he come to that realization? When had he begun to forget she was a nuisance and start looking forward to her nippy responses, that sudden glow in her cheeks when she knew she'd pushed him too far or had embarrassed herself?

He'd never met a woman he wanted to marry, and he'd met his share of females. Attractions had come along, but it had been surprisingly easy to ride away when the time came to leave.

He glanced across the fire and studied Ruth's form huddled against the cold wind. He'd always walked away easily . . . until she'd happened along. This woman wasn't going to be easy to ride away from—but he would. When it came right down to it, women were all alike—actors, deceivers. He'd learned that from a master. Sara Dunnigan had fooled the world—at least her world. She'd burned with religious fervor, thumping her Bible and predicting the imminent end of the world and telling him he'd better repent of his sins. Every Sunday morning Sara and Dylan were in their place on the hard wooden church pew. Second pew from the front, where the preacher would be sure to see them and know righteous Sara was doing her Christian duty by the child God had put upon her.

The preacher—Dylan couldn't remember the name but he saw the face every night in his boyish nightmares—was a pulpit pounder. Sweat rolled from his temples and his booming voice lifted the rafters when he proclaimed that sinners were going to burn in a pit of fire.

One morning, the man had taken off his coat and beat the pulpit with the homespun fabric, his voice bellowing off the walls. Dylan couldn't have been more than six or seven at the time. Overcome with terror, he suddenly sprang to his feet and hopped up on the pew. He looked at Sara and declared in a voice loud enough to be heard over the brimstone, "Let's go, Sara! That man is angry!"

Sara yanked him by the ear and set him down in the pew. "You sit!" she hissed. "God will punish you for this."

He'd sat for the next hour and a half, cowering and crying, confused and angry. How could God love him and want to hurt him at the same time? Suppose he could punish him. Suppose there was a hell. Dylan didn't know how it all worked, but it sounded terrifying.

When they got home that afternoon, Sara had switched his legs and back with a willow branch until red welts formed. With every strike Sara had reminded him that God was angry, that he didn't like smart-mouthed boys, that God had given him to Sara to teach him righteousness, and she would do her Christian duty by him even if it meant humiliation in front of her neighbors.

That was the day Dylan decided he didn't put much faith in God, couldn't love a God that meted out such harsh judgment on a boy who couldn't understand him or his ways. Dylan's feelings hadn't changed over the years. He'd endured the horsewhippings and verbal abuse, but Sara Dunnigan couldn't beat religion into him. He swore that someday he would be on his own, and he'd never answer to another person. Sara's God would have no say over him.

If there was a God who had made women like Sara Dunnigan, Dylan didn't want anything to do with him, no matter what Ruth said about the deity she believed in.

Ruth's sleepy voice drifted to him across the fire. "Penny for your thoughts."

He stirred, uncomfortable. Had he voiced resentment aloud? "I thought you were asleep."

"I am . . . sort of." She sighed, snuggling deeper into the bag. "You were looking so serious. What were you thinking?"

He closed his eyes. "Nothing." He didn't usually think much about his past, but all this stuff with Ruth and the baby had set him off.

Ruth persisted. "You were thinking something. I could see it. Are you worried?"

"Only a fool wouldn't be."

"That's true," she whispered. "But God will see us through."

"God." He shifted, pulling the blanket tighter. He stared at minuscule flakes whipping the air. Conditions could be worse and he figured "God" was about to prove it. "Don't you ever get angry about Norris taking you back to the orphanage?"

A log snapped in the campfire, sending sparks shooting up like a shower of red stars. He thought Ruth wasn't going to answer the question.

"Anger doesn't do anyone any good. It's taken me a while to get that through my stubborn head, but I finally realized anger only hurts the person experiencing it."

Dylan smiled, thinking of the day he'd first met her. A real spitfire, all explosion and bluster. Had that been only weeks ago? Impossible. It seemed she had been in his life always, and yet the past few days he had started to experience something inside him he thought had died. Hope. The first stirrings of real feeling.

He didn't trust the emotion. He didn't want it;

he liked his life. He liked answering only to himself, worrying only about himself and today.

"Tell me about your childhood," she said quietly.

He rolled to his stomach, careful not to disturb the baby. His childhood. Now there was a black page in history.

"Didn't have one."

She laughed softly. "Everyone had one whether they liked it or not. I gather you didn't like yours?"

He thought about the answer, fully aware she wasn't going to give up. She'd find another way to ask the same question.

"I liked part of it. The part when Grandma was alive."

She flipped over and met his gaze across the fire. "You had a good grandma?"

"The best." A smile formed at the corners of his mouth. "Ma and Pa died in a wagon accident coming west. Grandma took me in and raised me until I was six." He hesitated, memories starting to compete with the pain in his shoulder. "The Indian wars were going on then, and a band of renegades rode onto the farm one day. They were hungry and Grandma took them in and fed them. That was her way. She'd take the food off her own plate and give it to a stranger. She sent me to the barn to gather eggs. When I came back, the savages had cut her throat and were sacking up food. I dropped the egg basket and ran as hard as I could. They came after me, but I hid in an old root cellar on a neighbor's property. Sara Dunnigan's root cellar." He laughed humorlessly. "Sara had gone to church that morning or the renegades would have killed her too."

Cynicism seeped into his tone. "Pity that her life was spared. Sara found me the next day still huddled in the cellar. She took me to raise because there wasn't anyone else to do it. She was alone, set in her ways."

Dylan paused, aware he had just told Ruth more than he'd ever told another human being. There was something about her that drew the truth from him, truth that he never intended anyone to know.

"Did she mistreat you?"

He stared up into the black sky, scenes flashing through his mind like a succession of painted pictures: A red-faced Sara with a belt in her hand. Sara making him roll out of bed long before daybreak to hoe and plant, milk the cow, then work in the cornfield under a blazing sun. Sara yelling, threatening, berating him morning, noon, and night until her voice rang in his head like a drumbeat.

"I hated her." He heard Ruth's small gasp and realized that this was the first time he'd ever spoken about it out loud. He hated Sara, simple as that. Nothing about the feeling fazed him; he'd lived with hate for so many years, he'd hardened himself against the sentiment and what it could do to a man. He was content to let the emotion fester and taint his life without ridding himself of the pain. He would never rid himself of the memory of Sara Dunnigan.

"I spent my childhood figuring how to get away from her. When I was fifteen, I escaped and never looked back."

"Oh, my goodness."

Ruth's tone held pity. He didn't want pity. Yet he couldn't keep from telling Ruth more about the evil woman draped in "Christian love and duty." He'd heard her brag to others about her own generosity and goodness of heart—about how she'd taken in the McCall boy, fed and clothed him, "though goodness knows I'm just living hand to mouth myself," she'd say. Given him a pallet and a place at her table was all she'd done, and she'd done that grudgingly. She'd never shown one ounce of love or compassion toward him. He grew up with a willow switch at his backside and the guilt that he was a burden Sara felt forced to bear. With Sara and her friends as examples, God-fearing women had come to mean one thing to Dylan: hypocrisy.

After spilling his bitterness over Sara Dunnigan, Dylan fell silent. He thought of how different Ruth was. In getting to know Ruth, he witnessed a strong faith of a seemingly different stripe. . . .

He mentally shook the thought away. Ruth had tricked him. She wasn't Sara, but she had lied to him. She'd tried to bend him to her will, just like Sara did. Ruth was a contradiction within herself. One part of her was giving and kind, another part as manipulative as Sara had ever been. Well, he'd been fooled by women before, but not lately. Ruth would need more accomplished wiles than he'd seen so far if she intended to coerce him into doing anything he didn't want to do.

Beware, Dylan. Women are still all alike even

though the one on the other side of the fire stirs a long-
ing in you that you never knew you had.

"It's late." He shifted to his opposite side. They
lay in the darkness with only the popping fire breaking the strained silence. He wondered what she was
thinking. He wished he'd never mentioned Sara or
his past. Now Ruth would be trying to pry information from him, and there was nothing more to
tell. She seemed to think that sharing information
was important, like the girls on the wagon train had
done with each other. Ruth had prodded Glory until
she learned all about Uncle Amos and the gold and
how Poppy had died. Glory had embraced Ruth's
friendship and caring like a hungry pup, and she'd
become a part of the "family" of women.

But Dylan wasn't part of the family; he wasn't
part of any family. He was a loner, and that's how he
wanted to keep it. He wasn't going to be swayed by
Ruth's plight, even though he suspected her childhood couldn't have been any better than his.

"I'm sorry, but I want you to know that I care
about you. In a friendly way, of course." She had
spoken so softly he wasn't sure she'd spoken at all or
if his imagination was working overtime.

"Dylan, did you hear me?"

He closed his eyes. "Go to sleep, Ruth. This
snow is going to come down hard by morning, and
the walk will take more energy."

"But I am sorry, Dylan. I'm sorry that a woman
like Sara gives religion a black eye. Most likely she
believed that she was doing the right thing, but

obviously she didn't know the God I worship. He is a God of love and certainly a God to be feared and respected. But he chastens as a loving father, not a vindictive tyrant. Some read the Good Book and try to accept the Word, but deep down they're not willing to let God's Spirit abide in them.

"I make no excuses for Sara. What she did to a vulnerable young boy is inexcusable, but that rests on her soul. My concern is why you let evil continue to ruin your life. Sara will be held accountable and have to face her mistakes. You are responsible for your own errors."

Preachy women drove Dylan crazy. "No sermons." He'd had enough of those to last a lifetime. Empty words meant nothing. "I'm going to sleep now, Ruth. You can stay up and talk all night if you want."

"The Lord loves you, Dylan. You can fight the knowledge all you want. Whether you accept it or not, it won't change how he feels about you."

"Good night, Ruth."

"Good night, hardhead."

* * *

Ruth stared into the fire, thinking how differently life had treated both of them and how differently they looked at life as a result. Dylan absorbed the hurt and let it isolate him from everything and everyone around him. He had built steel barriers around his heart, afraid to let himself care about anyone or anything other than his job. For a moment—just a moment—Ruth let herself resent the woman who'd done this to Dylan. He was a fine man, but a man who couldn't give of himself for fear of being hurt; and that woman, in her zealousness, had taught him hate without realizing it.

Ruth tried to imagine fifteen-year-old Dylan going out into the world to make his own way. She wondered what he'd done between that age and when he'd become a marshal. Had anyone cared about him? Had he ever allowed anyone to get close? Her heart ached for the marshal, for the blessings he'd missed by daily living with bitterness toward Sara Dunnigan— and mistrust toward women in general. He had to put aside that bitterness and accept that not all who professed to follow God knew the truth of his love. Truth is precious, enlightening, and enriching. Truth in the heart crowds out hate and bitterness. *"And ye shall know the truth, and the truth shall make you free."*

She'd experienced that freedom. When Edgar Norris had taken her back to the orphanage, she'd hated him for abandoning her. She'd railed against the unfairness of losing parents not once but twice. She'd blamed God for forgetting about her. But Mrs. Galeen had refused to let her wallow in self-pity or blame God. For a long time Ruth had refused to accept the guardian's insistence that God had a plan for her life and all she needed to do was let him unfold it before her. Over time, by giving of herself to others, Ruth had learned to let go of her bitterness and count her blessings. Dylan had not had anyone in his life to encourage him, to teach him God's ways. As a result, he saw only what he'd lost.

"I always wanted parents," she whispered. She knew Dylan heard, but would he answer? "Someone to take care of me." In the firelight, she saw his face was still set with bitterness even though his eyes were shut.

"When my parents died, that was bad. But I was found by two kind Indians who knew of the orphanage. They didn't take me to their people, where my future wouldn't have been certain. They took me to the orphanage, which was a good thing.

"Then Edgar and Beatrice Norris came to the orphanage, seeking a child. They were both teachers. I went to live with them, and I remember them fondly. Beatrice was so pretty." Ruth turned on her side, her thoughts going back many years. "The Norrises taught me to read and write and to appreciate books. That was a blessing. But Beatrice died and Edgar was so grief stricken that . . . well, he couldn't stay at the school that held so many memories of her."

"But you hated him for taking you back to the orphanage." Dylan's voice intruded on her musings.

"I did," she admitted. "For a while, but then I saw that I was needed at the orphanage. I helped take care of the little ones, read to them, taught them their letters and numbers, helped them with their lessons when they started school."

"So you made yourself believe that his abandoning you was a good thing."

Ruth observed him in the firelight. "Yes, I

suppose I did. But it was better than hating him. Hate hurts only the one hating, not the one it's directed toward. It's a waste of effort."

She could see he was skeptical.

"I don't suppose you could put a good spin on old Oscar's proposal?"

Ruth had to grin. "No, I can't quite get around that one. But I do have to wonder what God wanted me to do about Oscar. Maybe he wanted me to marry the old prospector, and I refused to obey. If so, I will be the loser, not God."

Pessimism was apparent in the marshal's tone. "Why would God want you to marry a man old enough to be your grandpa, an old coot that chews and might take a bath twice a year?"

Ruth suppressed a shiver. "I don't know. I didn't bother to ask God, and that was wrong."

"I don't know about a God who would want to give a pretty young woman to an old codger," Dylan said. "That seems a little unfair—not only to the woman but to the man."

"There could be a reason," Ruth contended. "After all, I'm not someone who will probably ever have a family."

"Why not?"

"I . . . I can't have children." She whispered the words, saying them aloud for the first time. "A man wants a family—children—and I can't give a husband children."

Dylan didn't answer for a long time. Ruth was certain his reaction was what any man's would be—

aversion. An unexpected sadness, a sense of having lost something special, flooded her, and she blinked back tears. Why had she told the marshal something so personal? She felt like a complete fool.

"If a man's in the market for kids, then you may have a point. But if a man's looking for someone to spend his life with, then the problem shouldn't get in the way."

Ruth blinked with surprise. How like Dylan to put something so painful so simply. She swallowed back a cry of gratitude. "You . . . you really think so?"

"I know so. Most men want to find the right woman, not a broodmare."

A light popped on inside her that she didn't recognize—a kind of blossoming of hope. "Well, guess you would know, you being a man."

"Go to sleep, Ruth. Tomorrow is a long day of walking."

"You're right." But she would sleep better tonight knowing that not all men would find her condition appalling. Why, maybe someday, through God's grace, the Lord would reveal such a man to her.

She snuggled into her blankets and closed her eyes. Then they popped open wide. Maybe God already had, and it was Dylan!

She couldn't let nagging doubt override her earlier joy. If Dylan was right and not all men looked at a woman with the idea of producing children, then perhaps she had a chance of marrying one day, having a home of her own. . . . She wouldn't allow herself to think about Dylan, to wish—

No. Better go to sleep and keep such nonsense where it belonged: in the wishful-thinking drawer.

"Ruth?"

She turned, sitting up halfway. "Yes?"

"How do you know your last name is Priggish if you were orphaned at a young age?"

"My father's Bible. The Indian braves brought it with them. My father's name was written in the front: *Harold Priggish.* I don't know my mother's name."

11

Dylan opened his eyes to the sight of snow coming down in blowing sheets. The baby reached out to capture a flake and giggled. Her dark brown eyes shone like a child's on Christmas morning as Dylan handed her to Ruth. A large snowflake lit on the end of the baby's nose, and she looked cross-eyed at the marvel.

Dylan grinned. "She's real cute, isn't she?" Carefully feeding the coals dry leaves, then twigs that he'd dug out from beneath the snow, he soon had a fair fire going.

"The cutest." Ruth touched her nose to the child's. "The very cutest."

"We need something hot in our bellies. I'll warm the milk for the baby."

"All right."

Dylan turned to glance over his shoulder when she didn't move. "Ruth, we've got to get moving."

She drew the baby close, hugging her tightly. "What if I can't? I can barely feel my feet this morning."

Dylan felt his stomach twist with fear. What would he do if she couldn't walk? He squatted in front of her. "We can't give up now. We're going to make it to Sulphur Springs by nightfall."

As he searched her face, he could see that she struggled to believe him. He suddenly wished he had the time or energy to shave. He scratched the prickly growth of beard and realized why he'd never grown a beard before. It itched.

"I'll boil some coffee. That'll make you feel better," he said.

"Do we have any left?"

"Enough for breakfast." He broke ice at the water's edge and filled a coffeepot with water, and then tossed in the last of the grounds and set it on the fire.

Ruth drew her blankets closer to the warmth and changed the baby's wet clothes, hurrying since she was putting up a fuss about the cold air on her skin. Afterward, she fed the baby half the milk that was left in the canteen. Dylan and Ruth drank their coffee in silence while Ruth jiggled the fussy baby.

As gray dawn broke over the mountains, they mounted up, knowing the horse was about played out and needed a good meal and dry shelter as much as they did.

The early morning passed without a single word between them. Ruth tried to pacify the baby. When the little girl finally fell asleep, Dylan could feel Ruth relax against his back.

Midmorning, a speck materialized in the distance. The rocky terrain had leveled to better footing. A small wagon with two figures on the driver's seat appeared. As they neared, Dylan saw a man and a woman dressed in dark clothing. The woman sat close to the man, eyeing the approaching horse with wide, apprehensive eyes.

"Hallo there," the young man called, drawing the wagon to a halt. "Didn't expect to see anyone out here in the storm."

"Neither did we," Dylan confessed. Ruth's free arm tightened around his waist with silent warning. They'd met Nehemiah Ford this same way and look where it had gotten them. Dylan discreetly loosened her grip before inquiring, "How far to Sulphur Springs?"

"Oh, just a couple miles. Should get there this afternoon, but the snow will slow you down if it gets any heavier."

"We plan to make it," Dylan assured him.

"We're gettin' ourselves to home before it sets in for the night," the young man said. He stood up to peer at the bundle Ruth carried. "What's that you got there? A baby?"

Dylan glanced over his shoulder at Ruth. This couple was young—sturdy. The woman looked thin, but kind enough. The child was cold and hungry; she needed solid food, a warm bed, care—care he and Ruth were not able to give. If they didn't reach Sulphur Springs soon, the child would sicken, perhaps die. His uncertainties reflected in Ruth's eyes. Could this couple be the answer to the baby's needs?

Would they be willing to love and care for her, give her the things a child needed to grow strong and healthy?

"Is that an Indian baby?"

"Yes," Dylan confirmed.

The man sat back down, suspicion blooming in his eyes. "Where'd you come up with an Indian baby?"

"Found her in a burning wagon."

Dylan didn't think the couple needed to know the particulars of how they'd come in possession of the little girl. He looked at Ruth again and wondered what she thought. Prospective parents? But they didn't know anything about this couple—they could be fugitives from the law for all Dylan knew. The man had shifty eyes. . . .

And on closer inspection, the woman looked frail—in no condition to care for a small baby. Where were the couple's children? Home, unattended, while their ma and pa rode about the countryside on a snowy day? That was highly unusual—folks out in a snowstorm when they should be home looking after the family—

Ruth broke into Dylan's thoughts when she gently nudged him to ride on.

"We'd better be on our way if we're going to make town before dusk," Dylan said.

"Good luck to you then." The man slapped the reins against the horse's rump and with a wave moved on past.

"I didn't like them," Ruth said quietly. "I think they would have traded the baby or passed her on to someone else as soon as we were out of sight because she's Indian."

"I didn't trust them either."

Dylan urged the horse through deepening snowdrifts as they continued their journey. At noon Ruth fed the baby the last of the milk. Dylan recognized her feeling of helplessness because her face mirrored his own. As each hour passed without a sign of the settlement, he grew more troubled. Snow swirled around them, thicker than before, and Dylan began to seriously doubt that they'd make town before they froze to death. Death was a real possibility, he knew. This was a foolish journey and he was the chief fool.

"Are we going to make it?" Ruth's question was quietly spoken, which gave her fear more weight.

"I don't even know if we're going the right direction anymore," he admitted.

"Oh, God, help us. You're our only hope," Ruth breathed.

Dylan set his jaw. Only Ruth's God knew where they were or if they would make it. For the first time in his life, he couldn't depend on his own conviction and abilities to carry them through a dangerous situation. For the first time since he was fifteen years old, he was thinking—hoping—that God was there, that he had his eye on them. Dylan wondered if he was losing his mind, thinking about God and asking for his help. Still, with his head bent into the blowing snow, he silently asked that for Ruth's sake, God might spare her and the innocent child. What happened to him didn't matter; what happened to Ruth and the baby mattered a lot.

If you're there, help her, Lord, because I can't.

Toward dusk, Dylan was certain that Ruth's Lord was as fickle as Sara Dunnigan's. Both he and Ruth had lost feeling in their hands and feet. Ruth's face would be frostbitten if they remained outside a half hour longer.

Look, God, if you're going to show your hand, do it now. I don't ask anything for myself. I deserve my own fate, but it's not fair to let the woman and child die—

Dylan's thoughts broke off abruptly when he spotted a light in the distance. The glow was dim, but it was a light. Sulphur Springs. They had made it! "There it is," he shouted to Ruth above the howling wind. "There's the town!"

Her feeble grip tightened on his shoulder. "Thank you, Father."

Yeah, Dylan thought as he urged the horse through a drift. *Much obliged. I owe you one.* For the first time in his life, something warm stirred inside him, and he didn't have a name for it.

● ● ●

Ruth stretched out on a feather mattress, exhaustion invading every limb. Transfixed, she stared at the ceiling, reliving the sheer bliss of soaking in warm water up to her neck. She'd sat in the porcelain tub in the bathroom at the end of the hall for over an hour—until feeling returned to her hands and feet.

"Dear God, thank you for your grace," she murmured, for she knew full well that it was only his grace that had brought them this far.

Outside the boardinghouse window, snow continued to fall heavily, mounting on branches and porch railings. Wind howled through alleyways, battering storefronts on Main Street.

At first Ruth had thought she was hallucinating when she'd spotted the outcropping that appeared to be in the middle of the road. The horse was laboring heavily under their weight as they plowed through deepening snow. Once she had suggested that they get off and give the horse a rest, but Dylan had said that was a sure way to die. So they kept moving. The mare had earned a dry stall and the dinner of sweet prairie hay she was now enjoying.

Ruth had resolutely prepared to die in the blizzard. Dylan had taken the baby from her and cuddled the infant inside his coat, grief visible on his frozen features. Ruth had heard his halting prayer for help become a litany. When she'd recognized that he was praying, pure elation filled her. Then fear, the likes of which she'd never known, took over. If Dylan was scared, that meant her mounting anxiety wasn't groundless.

Yet she had refused to give in to panic. Dylan had made the long trip from Colorado to Wyoming more than once, he'd reminded her. But never in winter, and never with an infant and a woman to look after. Or a grave wound in his shoulder. As wind shrieked and snow blew in random bursts, they had pushed on.

Ruth sighed, closing her eyes. She was safe in a warm bed now, wearing one of Annabelle's long, flannel nightgowns that smelled of soap and had been warmed on the woodstove. Images of snow still whirled through her head as she recalled entering Sulphur Springs.

The first building they'd seen happened to be the livery stable. They'd pounded on the wide doors until they roused someone. The door eventually opened, and a small round man with a long white beard and twinkling blue eyes appeared. "Why, he looks like Santa Claus," Ruth had marveled. Eyes widened below the white bushy brows, the friendly man ushered in the nearly frozen strangers. Later Tom Ferry, the town blacksmith, bundled up tightly against the blowing storm, had walked the shivering travelers to the boardinghouse.

Sulphur Springs didn't have such an establishment until last year, proprietor Niles Seaton had explained. Two years ago the town was chosen by Welborne & Sutton Stage Lines as an overnight way station—provided the Seatons turned their residence into a boardinghouse. The town council liked the idea of the stage coming through town, so Niles and his wife, Annabelle, had done a little remodeling and created this right nice place for weary travelers. Folks would spend the night in a spacious bedroom, and the next morning Annabelle Seaton would send them on their way with a hot meal and a friendly smile.

Mrs. Seaton was a solemn woman who had stoically gone about heating water for the weary guests.

She mixed oatmeal in a pan of warm milk and fed the baby. The thin, spry woman had offered little in the way of chatty conversation, but Ruth was ever so grateful for the woman's hospitality. Both Niles and Annabelle saw to the guests' immediate needs and never asked about their circumstances other than to offer them comfortable rooms. Neither Ruth nor Dylan had explained why two rooms were necessary; Ruth guessed she should do that in the morning when she was thinking more clearly.

Ruth settled into the bed, drinking in the smell of clean linens. Pot roast and rich brown gravy filled her stomach. She felt so drowsy she could hardly stay awake long enough to properly thank God for sparing them. She remembered how Annabelle had insisted that she and Dylan have a hot meal, a warm bath, and go right to bed.

"I'm too weary to argue," Ruth said. "Thank you . . . thank you so much."

Annabelle nodded. "I'll lay out towels and soap."

Over Dylan's protest, Ruth had insisted that he bathe, be cared for, and put to bed first. That he allowed her to win the argument attested to his grave condition.

The town didn't have a doctor, but at Niles's request, Tom Ferry went to fetch a Mrs. Fallaby to look after Dylan's injuries. Gert Fallaby had breezed into the room on a gust of cold air, her hearty laugh filling the boardinghouse. After she examined Dylan's wounds, she clicked her tongue and shook her head, then cleaned the aggravated wounds and applied a vile-smelling salve. Ignoring Dylan's skeptical looks, Gert made him open his mouth, and she administered a large teaspoon of laudanum for his pain.

Twisting the cap back on the bottle, she grinned. "That ought to hold you a spell."

"I hope it's nothing like Ulele's locoweed," Dylan muttered.

Gert only smiled. "Let's just say you won't be feelin' much of anything until morning."

Ruth was so thankful Dylan would spend a night free of pain. So thankful. . . . Now he was resting comfortably down the hall from her room. She gratefully pressed both feet against the hot-water bottle Annabelle had thoughtfully placed beneath the covers and thought she'd never be cold again.

Her thoughts started to blur . . . screeching wind, blowing snow . . . anxiety deeply etched on Dylan's wind-chapped features. She knew most of his concern had been for the baby, yet the thought that he might, deep down, harbor a tiny speck of concern for her wasn't entirely impossible. Since leaving the Fords', he'd been kind and tolerant, barking at her far less than before. She opened her eyes and looked at the little girl sleeping next to her. She seemed none the worse for wear, now that she was warm, dry, and fed. *Thank you, God.*

Sighing, Ruth slid deeper into the goose-down mattress and smiled. For the briefest of moments, she pretended that God had made a rare mistake.

She *should* have babies and a loving husband. She *should* love someone here on earth she could truly trust—trust to protect and care for her. Someone like Dylan. Someone like this precious child.

Her lids grew heavier. Annabelle had brought clean clothes for the baby, explaining they were outfits her grandchild had outgrown. Ruth had once more been moved to tears as she'd dressed the child in the flannel gown and crocheted booties. Compared to Ulele, Annabelle was an angel—albeit not a very talkative one.

Ruth was unable to keep her eyes open. Sleet pinged against the windowpane, peppering the glass. They could have been out there in the storm. They could have frozen to death on the outskirts of Sulphur Springs.

Yet she was very much alive, lying here beside the baby. Dylan was sleeping two doors down. Her heart overflowed with gratitude; she hardly knew how to thank God. Dylan wasn't in pain, the baby was safe, her belly was full, she was clean, and she was sleeping in a wonderfully warm bed tonight.

For the moment, life was good. *No, Lord,* she amended. *Good* was such an inadequate word that it seemed close to a complaint, and she didn't have a thing in the world to complain about.

Life was perfect. The words of a psalm floated into her head as Ruth drifted off to sleep: *"Bless the Lord, O my soul: and all that is within me, bless his holy name. Bless the Lord, O my soul, and forget not all his benefits."*

• • •

Ruth didn't stir until well after sunup. She woke to the sound of the baby cooing at her own fingers. Ruth pushed back the mound of covers and bent over the baby snuggled against her. The infant stared up at her with affectionate, dark eyes. Giggling and kicking, she happily thrashed her arms when Ruth stroked her brown cheek with the back of her finger.

"Yes, you just think you're a big girl, don't you?" Ruth cooed. She tickled the baby's tummy. "Yes, you are; yes, you *are*. You're a cutie."

She caught herself up short. A hot flush crept up her neck when she realized she was acting like a silly goose. For heaven's sake! Shaking her head, Ruth rolled out of bed and yelped when her bare feet hit the icy floor. The baby giggled, waving her fists.

"You think that's funny, huh?" Ruth tickled the little girl's tummy. "Well, maybe I'll just put your feet on the icy floor!" In a moment she had the baby laughing out loud. Her uninhibited giggles made Ruth laugh. A knock sounded at the door. She jerked upright at the sound of Dylan's voice.

"Ruth?"

Ruth hesitated. "Yes?"

"Is the baby all right? What's going on in there?"

"We're both fine. Why?" He'd heard! He'd heard her making a fool of herself! The flush grew hotter.

"Breakfast is on the table."

Clearing her throat, Ruth kept her tone neutral. "I'll be right down."

She dressed and entered the kitchen fifteen minutes later. She avoided Dylan's amused gaze and walked to the stove to spoon up a bowl of oatmeal for the baby. Dylan was dressed in clean clothing, freshly shaven, and looking incredibly handsome for a man who had spent the last weeks fighting off death. Annabelle and Niles were nowhere in sight this morning.

Dylan poured two cups of strong black coffee. "Sleep well?"

Ruth nodded, afraid to look at him. He'd be likely to ask what all the laughing had been about, and she didn't want to explain.

"Very well. And you?" She perched the baby on her lap and began feeding her small spoonfuls of oatmeal, resisting the urge to giggle out loud at the sweet smacking sounds she made after each bite.

"I didn't know a thing until this morning." He moved his right arm, then his left, working the stiffness in his shoulder loose. He focused on the little girl. "Did she sleep all night?"

"She never woke once, and she slept late this morning."

Dylan grinned. "That's good. Cream?"

Ruth nodded. Cream. Such luxury! "And two sugars, please."

Dylan ladled sugar, then poured cream into her coffee and set the cup in front of her. "I was talking to Mr. Seaton earlier. The storm has shut everything down, but he says Ed French can use me a week or so at the mercantile to build new shelves. They need to be able to stock more for the winter, though folks say it looks to be a mild one. Since we're not going anywhere until the passes clear, I thought I'd take the opportunity to make up for the money we lost with the Fords, before we move on."

Ruth looked up. "Are you able?" She thought he might be the only one leaving.

He shrugged. "The wound is healing." He grinned as he spread thick molasses on a biscuit. When a drop slipped onto his finger, he leaned forward to let the baby lick it off. His grin widened when she giggled and wiggled two chubby fingers to signal she wanted more.

Ruth grinned too. "I think that's a very sound idea." She took a sip of coffee, still refusing to meet his eyes, though she did glance at him quickly. "Very noble of you." Could that be relief she saw in his eyes?

"We'll stay until the weather breaks—those passes are snow blocked now. Meanwhile we'll ask around and maybe come up with a home for the child."

She broke into another smile. "That sounds good to me." She kept the smile in place even though her mind rebelled at the thought of ever walking away from the child. Could she do it? She *had* to do it. She had no way to care for this child. She needed a mother and a father, a couple with the wherewithal to rear a child.

"Dylan," she said softly, gazing at the little girl in her lap.

"Yes?"

"Could we name her?" She looked up, and her next words tumbled out. "I mean, most folks would expect a baby this old to have a name, and we can't keep calling her 'her' and 'child' and 'baby.'"

Dylan concentrated on his coffee. "I'm sure she has a name, Ruth."

"Probably, but we don't know what it is, and she's too young to tell us." Warming to the idea, Ruth covered his hand with hers. The simple touch sent ripples of warmth up her arm. "Please, Dylan. Let's name her."

The idea seemed to set with him. He smiled and looked at their hands. "What do you have in mind?"

"Rose," she announced. "Look—her mouth is like a tiny little rosebud."

Dylan peered at the child. "Rose? That's sort of frilly, isn't it? What about Maude? There's a good, solid woman's name."

Ruth shook her head pensively. "She doesn't look like a Maude."

"Really?" Dylan studied the baby. "Well, maybe not . . ."

"Rose. Rose Priggish McCall."

Doubt crossed the marshal's features. "McCall?"

"Why not? Rose—for her. Priggish—my last name. And McCall—your last name. Whoever takes her will change her name anyway." Ruth lifted the little girl above her head, the playful action resulting in a cackling drool. "Hello, Miss Rose Priggish McCall. Now you have a name just like the rest of us. In dat *sweet*?" She glanced up, embarrassed. "Isn't that nice?" she amended in an adult tone.

"Yeah," Dylan agreed, "dat's *weal* sweet. Yesitis, yesitis," he teased. Tickling the baby's tummy, he stepped back and admired his namesake. "What do you know? I'm a daddy."

Ruth grinned smugly. *Yeah,* she thought. *And for a short time, I am a mommy.*

. . .

The snow tapered off by late afternoon. Ruth pulled the lacy parlor curtain back and looked out the front window. She counted twenty-five long, thin icicles hanging from the roof. It was still cold as a banker's heart and that made the hospitality of Niles and Annabelle even more welcome. She didn't know when she'd been more comfortable, and the warm bath yesterday made her want a second one soon.

How strange that the long trek into Colorado had awakened in her the realization that simple, everyday things like feeling clean and warm constituted a luxury when one had been without them for a period.

Annabelle bustled into the kitchen carrying a load of linens. She smiled when she saw Ruth. "You got a fine family, Ruth—a real nice husband. Most men wouldn't function with the marshal's injuries. But he's over at the mercantile doing what he can."

Ruth nodded absently. "He's a strong man."

Annabelle stored the sheets in a side drawer of a bureau and closed the door. "Been married long?"

Ruth went silent. She couldn't lie to the woman; the Seatons had been too good to them, and besides, she wasn't going to ever lie again. Lying didn't pay; goodness knows she'd learned that, if nothing else.

"We're not married, Mrs. Seaton."

The woman turned, censure mirroring in her eyes.

Ruth hastened to explain the situation and ended by saying, "The marshal is escorting me to Wyoming, where I hope to locate a distant cousin. Mr. McCall has been the embodiment of a gentleman, although at times I've been quite a trial to put up with, I'm sure."

Annabelle nodded. "Don't surprise me. I can read a man like a book, and I was telling Niles this morning that Dylan McCall is a fine soul." She paused behind Ruth's chair to rest her hands on the young woman's shoulders. "Don't let him get away, honey. If you're lucky enough to find a man like McCall in your lifetime, don't play coy."

Ruth smiled sadly. "He doesn't love me, Mrs. Seaton. He's deeply fond of the baby and he protects me with his life, but he isn't a man looking to settle down. Not now and most certainly not with a willful, foolish girl who tricked him into taking her to Wyoming, who nearly cost him his life."

Annabelle's clasp tightened. "Don't know about the willful part—you'll have to answer that—but I'd say there's nothing foolish about you, my dear.

Otherwise, you wouldn't be here. It takes a hearty soul to survive in these mountains, and it looks like you and the marshal have pulled it off." Annabelle left the room, bustling toward the stairway.

Ruth was sitting at the kitchen table drinking a cup of hot tea when the back door opened and Dylan came in. He stamped his feet and wiped his boots on the woven rug inside the door. "Hi."

"Hi."

"Sent my boss a telegram." He winced as he shrugged out of his coat. "Told him where we are." He poured himself a cup of coffee from the pot on the stove.

"Is he angry with you?"

Dylan shrugged and sat down opposite her. "No. Kurt wired me back immediately. He says he knows travel is dangerous right now, but Dreck Parson's leaving a trail a mile wide. If I don't get to Utah soon, though, I'm going to be too far behind him to catch him." His features sobered. "I don't know if I can let that happen, Ruth."

She leaned closer, her eyes shadowed with concern. "Of course not—we'll leave immediately."

He reached out to cover her hand with his large one. The contact sent an electrical current through her—like lightning on a hot summer day. "I'm torn. I've worked hard on the Parson case, and I don't want to lose Dreck. But I don't want to endanger you or Rose any further. Can you understand?"

She nodded. "We made it this far, Dylan. I'm not afraid."

Her concern was much larger than physical danger: Dylan's inability to accept and trust the Lord. She could never marry a man and be unequally yoked. Of course marriage was the last thing on Dylan's mind, but the idea had started to crouch in the back of hers—like a hungry lion. How could she walk away from this man? Yet how could she fall in love with a nonbeliever?

"I think you should stay here. You'd be safe—and so would Rose."

Ruth shook her head. "I've already asked. Mrs. Seaton says there isn't any work for me in town—that even the residents are having a hard time keeping food on the table. If I stayed, the baby and I would surely be a burden—and I'm not willing to impose like that."

"But the weather, Ruth. It's not safe. We almost died yesterday. I can't put you and Rose in danger again."

She closed her eyes. *Lord, what on earth do I do? There's nothing for me in Sulphur Springs. How can I just let Dylan walk away?*

After a few moments, Dylan said quietly, "I asked around and found out there's another town not too far from here that's bigger and more prosperous because there's gold there. Perhaps you can find work in Deer Lick. And a home for Rose. We can set off as soon as the weather clears and we're strong enough to travel. I don't see any other way, Ruth."

Ruth nodded mutely. As usual, God wasn't giving her more than the next step of the way. "The

weather will break—you'll see. And if I can't find
work in the next town . . . I might just follow you
all the way to Wyoming, Marshal McCall."

Dylan grinned. "I just can't seem to get rid of
you, can I?" They gazed at each other for a moment.
What was that she saw in his eyes?

Dylan broke contact and glanced over her shoulder. "Where's Rose?"

"Asleep." Ruth stretched like a lazy cat. "I wanted
to just sit and enjoy a cup of tea. Is that silly?"

He smiled, and it hit her anew how wonderful
he really was. Dylan McCall was an attractive man,
even with his flaws. He was stubborn and single-
minded, but he could be caring too. He had made
sure nothing happened to her on the trail even
though she thought she was alone. The whole time,
Dylan had her in his scope much like God kept
her in his sights. That suggested a man who cared,
whether he wanted to admit it or not.

"No, that's not silly," he said. "But I'm concerned
about you, if you travel on with me any farther. We
have a chance to end this right now with your reputation still intact."

She bit her lower lip. "We both know that nothing indecent is going on. I'll dress like a boy again.
We can go into town separately." Her gaze met his.
"I can't stay here, Dylan. I don't know whether God
has something for me in Deer Lick or in Wyoming,
but I do know I want to move on with you. Please,
Dylan."

Dylan sighed. "I know you, Ruth. If you have a

mind to follow me, I wouldn't be able to stop you. I don't think I can take the strain." He grinned. "All right. We'll set off in a day or two, as soon as we're rested up."

She nodded and changed the subject. "Did you have Mrs. Fallaby look at your injuries again?"

"Not yet. I was over at the mercantile. I'll start on the shelves soon."

"Be careful—"

"—you still have infection," he finished for her. He took a drink of scalding coffee. "If you're set on worrying, worry about yourself. How are those feet?"

She glanced down at her toes encased in the soft slippers Annabelle Seaton had supplied. The blisters were better—much better now that she could stay off her feet. "They'll be as good as new in a few days. And you're the sickest." She reached to lay the backs of her fingers against his face. "I would wager that you've got a fever right now."

He seemed comfortable with her touch. Embarrassed, she felt her cheeks warm. What was she thinking? He could take care of himself, except that she wanted to take care of him so badly it hurt. But the marshal wouldn't want that. He was a solitary man; he'd made that clear.

Ruth got up from the table and busied herself at the counter. "Perhaps before we go, we can ask around and see who can take . . . who would want Rose." Giving an Indian baby away wouldn't be easy. There was a lot of prejudice in the world.

"I mentioned that to Annabelle. She said she

would ask around. There's a specific couple who might be interested in taking her," Dylan informed her.

"Oh," Ruth said faintly. *It's the right thing,* she told herself. *The only fair solution for what's best for Rose.*

When the door opened again, ushering in another burst of cold air, they both looked up.

"Well, well, you two look better," Niles boomed.

After he unwound his bright red muffler, he pulled off his gloves and jammed them into his coat pocket. He shrugged out of his coat and hung it on a peg.

"It's amazing what a good night's sleep and a bath will do for a man," Dylan said.

"Saw Gert a minute ago. Said for you to come on down and let her look at those arrow wounds again."

Dylan got up and set his cup in the sink, then began putting on his coat. Noting the difficulty he was having, Ruth went over and helped him, though the marshal looked a little self-conscious about needing help.

"Want me to go with you?" Ruth offered.

"No," he said, "you stay with Rose."

"Oh, th' missus said she'd already talked to the Carsons about taking Rose. They thought they might like to consider it," Niles said.

"Oh," Ruth managed, "that's good. Your wife hadn't mentioned the Carsons earlier—I'll talk to Mrs. Seaton about it later. She said she was going to the church."

"Yes, decorating for a wedding, you know. Nice young couple. Known them all their lives."

Apparently Annabelle Seaton was a pillar of the community in spite of her quietness. Of course, it wasn't every day three frozen strangers materialized out of a snowstorm. This morning Annabelle was as friendly as Ruth could have asked.

"Yes, she told me," Ruth said to Niles.

She felt distracted, as if she couldn't concentrate properly, and she didn't know why. Rose needed a home. A real home. And if Annabelle had found a good family, well, that was good.

Dylan opened the door. "I'll be back later."

"Yes," Ruth said absently. "Have Gert make sure you have no infection."

He gave her a tolerant grin. "I'll do that."

As the door closed, Ruth heard Rose start to awaken. She hurried out of the kitchen to see about her. Annabelle had pulled out a spare drawer to make a bed for the baby and promised to look for a more appropriate crib today. Ruth was afraid Rose would crawl out of the cramped space.

Rose had a wet diaper, so Ruth quickly changed her, grateful that Annabelle had provided the luxury of diapers. She hugged Rose close, enjoying the baby's clean scent. Her heart ached. Rose needed parents—real parents—but Ruth was going to miss holding her little body close.

"I bet you'd like some milk," she murmured.

Since they'd reached Sulphur Springs, Rose wanted to eat all the time.

"Making up for all those weeks when you had so little, are you?" Ruth said softly. She laughed when

Rose gurgled happily, but guilt assailed her. When they moved on, would the baby go hungry again—and cold? Ruth sat at the kitchen table, holding the cup, avoiding Rose's efforts to grab it. Soon the little girl settled down and drank the milk.

"Oh, Ruth," Annabelle said as she came in later, her cheeks rosy. "I forgot to tell you. I found a couple who might like to have Rose."

Ruth knew she should be elated, but she just felt empty.

"The Carsons. Henry and Clara have no children. They're about . . . well . . . forty, perhaps. It's so hard to tell," Annabelle finished, reaching to brush a work-worn hand across Rose's hair. "I don't think I've ever seen a child who enjoyed milk so much," she said. "It's good to see her contented."

Nodding, Ruth ignored the moisture suddenly filling her eyes. "Tell me about the Carsons."

"Oh, they're fine, churchgoing people. Wanted children for years but none seem to come along. Henry breaks horses for a living. There's a real need out here, you know. In fact, they've got a bunch of horses in the corrals right now. Got some for sale," Annabelle said.

Once Annabelle warmed up, she was actually rather chatty.

"What is Mrs. Carson like?" Ruth asked.

"Well . . . Clara's a hard woman to get to know." Annabelle poked up the kitchen fire in preparation for the evening meal.

"Why is that?"

"She's very quiet—and very neat and orderly. Hardly says a word. But she's a fine woman. Henry's quiet as well. They have a peaceful home, I think. They live just outside of town. A small house, but there's room for a baby. Would you like to go talk to them tomorrow afternoon?"

Ruth didn't, but there was no way around it. Rose needed a home and the Carsons sounded ideal. "That would be fine. If the snow has cleared enough."

The concession tasted sour. Her heart twisted at the thought of going. But she'd made a commitment to find a good home for Rose, and she would do it.

"They're not far out. We'll be all right in the buggy. If not, we can wait a day or so."

Ruth played with Rose while Annabelle prepared supper. When Rose discovered the joy of playing with a ring off a pickle jar, Ruth sat her on a blanket on the kitchen floor where she would be warm, so Ruth could help Annabelle cook.

By the time the meal was ready, Dylan had returned, looking a little pale.

Ruth helped him off with his coat. "Are you all right? What did Gert say?"

"I'm fine—"

"I'll go ask her myself," Ruth warned.

Dylan appeared uneasy, as if he wasn't used to someone worrying about him. "There's some infection, but she poked around and said she didn't think it needed to be lanced. Gave me something for pain."

"Let me see what she gave you." Ruth stood in front of him and extended her hand.

Dylan reluctantly surrendered the brown bottle. Ruth sniffed at the contents and wrinkled her nose. "How much of this are you supposed to take?"

"A teaspoon three times a day, if I can get the stuff down. Smells like rotting garbage."

Ruth sniffed the vial. "Have you taken any yet?"

"Gert made me choke down a teaspoon of the medicine—it's strong enough to drop a buffalo." He sat down in the nearest chair. "Would you get me a cup of coffee, Ruth? If you're not too busy."

Concern filled Ruth. His request for her to get his coffee must mean he felt worse than he'd ever admit. "Are you sure that's all Gert said?"

"That's all she said." Dylan looked at Annabelle. "Chicken sure smells good, Mrs. Seaton."

"Going to make some gravy to go with it," Annabelle promised.

"I may have died and gone to heaven."

Dylan's grin set the woman atwitter. Ruth hid a smile by turning away. Dylan had not lost his charm. It still oozed from every pore. Even Annabelle had fallen under his spell.

Ruth met his eyes solemnly. "Mrs. Seaton said she's found a family who might be willing to give Rose a home."

"Oh?" Something flickered in his gaze—Ruth wasn't sure if she saw relief or disappointment. "Are you going to talk to them?"

"Tomorrow afternoon."

Dylan studied her for a long moment. "What if they're a good family for her?"

"Then—then Rose will have a family."

Ruth picked up the baby and put her into the wooden high chair that Annabelle had brought down from her attic.

As if he'd received a silent call, Niles strolled into the kitchen as his wife set the food on the table. Ruth spooned potatoes and gravy for Rose, letting the mixture cool while Niles and Annabelle came to the table.

"Offer a blessing, Father," said Annabelle.

Niles had a voice that could carry halfway across town, and when he prayed, he made sure every word was heard. Ruth caught Dylan's eye as she bowed her head and hid a smile. Niles liked to hear his own voice, but he was truly a man of God and she liked to hear him pray.

They enjoyed a fine meal of fried chicken, mashed potatoes with gravy, and the last of the green beans from Annabelle's garden. The conversation flowed as if it were any other day. But for Ruth it was anything but normal. By tomorrow night Rose could belong to a couple of strangers.

•   •   •

After lunch the next day Ruth and Annabelle climbed into the buggy and tucked thick robes around themselves. Dylan had insisted on going with them despite Ruth's urging him to stay and rest.

"Not on your life," he'd proclaimed as he put on his coat. And so the threesome set off to talk to Henry and Clara Carson.

The Carson place was, as Annabelle said, not far outside of town. The house was surrounded by corrals, many of which held five to eight horses each. No doubt Mr. Carson was a prosperous horse wrangler. The dwelling itself was small, with a porch across the front. Rosebushes, now winter-dead, had been trimmed back, but their branches still poked out of the snow.

Annabelle, Ruth, and Dylan had barely stepped out of the buggy when the front door opened and a tall, pretty woman stepped onto the porch. She was wearing a blue-flowered dress with a rounded collar and a white apron covering the front. She looked like a perfect mother for Rose, but Ruth couldn't conjure up one smidgen of happiness about it.

She swallowed hard and summoned up a pleasant smile as she walked toward the porch. Her only hope now was that Clara kept house like a gutter rat.

12

"Clara, this is Ruth and Dylan, and the little one is Rose," Annabelle said. Ruth hugged the baby protectively as Dylan took Ruth's arm and steadied her.

Clara Carson looked nervous. She clasped her hands in front of her and smiled. "Come in."

Ruth followed the others into the house, taking in every detail. The front room was neat and smelled clean. *Rats*, Ruth thought.

A Christmas tree adorned with white candles stood by the fireplace. Brown, braided rugs, faded by many washings, covered the floor. Heavy curtains hung at the windows, blocking out winter's feeble light. Crocheted doilies graced the backs of three chairs, books were neatly and evenly stacked on a small table, and a framed picture hung on the wall. Ruth thought it was a landscape but the colors were so dark she couldn't tell.

Ruth let the baby's blanket fall away and removed the small pink crocheted hat Annabelle had found among some baby things she'd packed away.

The woman took a step backward, her eyes noting the child's heritage. Her features twisted.

Dylan squeezed Ruth's arm reassuringly. If it had not been for his presence, she couldn't have done this. She looked at him, and a silent, compassionate message passed between man and woman . . . father and mother.

"As I mentioned, Clara, this is a tragic circumstance," Annabelle began as the four were comfortably seated in the immaculate room. "This baby was found in a burning wagon, with the only man who might know whom she belongs to dead from Indian arrows. Ruth rescued the child and has been caring for her ever since. But the baby needs a good home, and Ruth and Dylan are not in the position to keep the child." Ruth noted how skillfully Annabelle skirted the truth.

"The mister and me are God-fearing folks," Mrs. Carson said in a strangely flat voice.

"I've assured Ruth of that."

Rose reached toward a glass dish that sat on a lamp table.

"That's not for play," Clara warned.

Ruth distracted the baby by jiggling the jar ring she'd brought with her. "Sorry."

Clara leaned forward, cautiously touching the child. "She's a pretty little thing—even if she is one of those savages."

Ruth caught back a sharp retort.

Clara looked up and met Ruth's eyes. "The mister and I have need for children what with all the work to be done around here, but the good Lord has not seen fit to send any until now."

Rose reached out and latched on to Clara's hand. The woman smiled, tears shimmering in her eyes. Rose brought the hand to her mouth, and Clara paled as drool pooled in her hand. Gently prying the tiny fist loose, she reached for a crisp handkerchief and lightly blotted her hand. "My, they are messy, aren't they?" She smiled.

Ruth glanced at Dylan. Messy. Yes, Rose could be very messy.

"May I get anyone coffee? Tea?" Clara asked.

The three guests declined.

"Would you like to hold her?" Ruth hesitantly lifted the baby and held her toward Clara. For a moment the woman looked as if she didn't know what was expected of her. "Oh . . . I don't think that's necessary." She patted her stiffly starched apron. "I have my Sunday best on this afternoon . . . the mister thought it appropriate. Perhaps later . . ."

Nodding, Ruth lowered Rose back into her lap.

Dylan spoke up. "Will your husband be along shortly?"

Clara shook her head. "No, he leaves family things to me. He's a very busy man, you know. He has little time for outside interests." She smiled again.

Ruth lifted her eyes sourly. Rose was *not* an "outside interest." This was a child they were talking about, not a hobby. As far as Ruth was concerned the interview was over.

Dylan stood up, twisting the brim of his hat.

"We'll not keep you, Mrs. Carson. Ruth and I will give this some thought."

Surprise crossed the woman's face, and she slowly stood up, carefully straightening her blouse collar. "You're leaving so soon?"

"We need to get back to town," Annabelle explained. "Looks like it could snow again anytime."

Clara nodded. "You will let me know when you might want to bring the child here? I'll need a few days' preparation. . . ."

"We'll let you know what we decide," Ruth managed. "I want to pray about this."

"Certainly prayer is called for," Annabelle agreed.

Ruth held Rose close as they made the silent trip back to town. As Dylan and Ruth got out of the wagon, Annabelle laid her hand on Ruth's arm.

"You weren't satisfied with Mrs. Carson?"

Ruth felt a thrill when Dylan pulled her and Rose protectively against his side. A muscle worked in his jaw. "No, but Ruth will pray about it."

Annabelle gave him a curious look. "Of course. Only God knows what he has planned for this little one."

Niles Seaton was leaving as they approached the boardinghouse. "Old Mrs. Brown is feeling poorly. Thought I'd stop by to see if there's anything she needs from the mercantile. How did the visit with the Carsons go?"

"Why don't I walk with you to Mrs. Brown's?" Annabelle looped her arm through her husband's. "We can talk later, Ruth."

"Yes, thank you for taking us to meet Mrs. Carson."

Dylan took Ruth's elbow and steered her toward the door. "What did you really think of Mrs. Carson?"

"She's not getting my child."

"*Your* child?"

Ruth whirled to face him. "Dylan, she wouldn't even hold Rose or talk to her. Her only concern was that silly glass dish. She was . . . cold, Dylan. And she called Rose a savage." Ruth stiffened her chin. "Clara Carson is the savage."

"Annabelle seemed to think the Carsons are good people."

"I'm sure they'd do all the right things. The house was nice. Clean. Mrs. Carson appeared to be affluent and well mannered. But that doesn't make a parent." Ruth rested her hand on the crop of black hair. "A baby needs someone to get down on the floor and play with, Dylan. Even I know that. I can't let Rose go there." She pleaded silently for him to understand.

Dylan met her gaze for a long moment. "Then she won't go there."

As simple as that? She wouldn't go? Relief flooded Ruth. She drew a shaky breath. "Then she won't go." When she met Dylan's smile, she thought her heart would burst right out of her chest. *Then she won't go.*

The next afternoon Niles delivered a note to the Carsons informing them that the child would remain with Ruth and Dylan for now.

• • •

Sunshine glinted on the crusted snow so brightly it made Ruth squint. She took a cleansing breath of air, turning her face to the warm rays. They were on the trail again. They'd started out not long after sunup.

Niles and Annabelle had stood on the front porch of the boardinghouse and waved them off. Ruth had to laugh when she thought of how Rose had melted Annabelle's heart. The night they'd arrived, Annabelle had been woken from a sound sleep and seemed distant, but oh, how she had warmed to Rose and Ruth and Dylan while they were there. Why, by the time they left, the woman was practically conversational.

A part of Ruth regretted leaving Sulphur Springs. But another part, the bigger part, felt a rightness about being with Dylan and Rose. There was hope for her future, wherever she ended up. Hadn't she just read Jeremiah 29:11? "For I know the thoughts that I think toward you, saith the Lord, thoughts of peace, and not of evil, to give you an expected end." She clung to the hope that God would do good things for them, and that God would lead her to her expected end—a new life, either in Deer Lick or in Wyoming. Perhaps she could find a job in Deer Lick that would allow her to support Rose. . . .

Dylan had agreed that when they reached Deer Lick, he would see a doctor about his wounds. If the doctor said he needed more time for them to heal, he would stay, even though she knew he was eager to move on and not lose Dreck Parson. What if there was nothing for her in Deer Lick? Well, she'd just have to go on to Wyoming with Dylan after all. How long had he said it would take to reach Wyoming? Two or three weeks, depending on weather. It could take two months.

Ruth smiled. Thanks to Ed French and the new shelves Dylan had built in his mercantile, Dylan had a few dollars in his pocket, and the saddlebags bulged with enough food to last them well into the next territory. They had two fresh horses, a cow for fresh milk for Rose, and a pocketful of dreams. At least she had dreams. Dreams that someday a man like Marshal McCall would fall in love with her and she—

She stopped the thought. Whether they reached Deer Lick or Wyoming, she would just be plain Ruth again. Ruth the orphan. Ruth, the woman who was destined to spend the rest of her life alone.

Oh, God, why did you allow me to experience the joy of motherhood—of loving one man so much that I don't think I will be able to exist when he leaves me? It would have been so much better for me to have never met Dylan, never known the joy of little Rose.

Was it possible she had misunderstood God's direction? Her pulse hammered at the idea. Yes, it was possible . . . but not likely. Once they reached Deer Lick, once they found a suitable home for Rose . . .

Then she must concentrate on building a new life, the one she'd hoped to find in Denver City. Those days seemed so long ago, though it had only been a few weeks. She glanced at the baby nestled in Dylan's coat, wisps of dark hair peeping out from under her wool cap. Already her arms ached to hold her . . . to hold the man who carried her.

She angrily shook the notion away. She had never held Dylan, not in the truest sense. Never close to her heart, whispering all the hidden longings bursting inside her.

"Cold?"

Ruth jerked at the sound of the marshal's voice. Shaking her head, she took a firmer grip on the reins of her horse and rode ahead a short distance. She needed to put distance between herself and this man she had come to cherish. *You're daydreaming, Ruth. Of all people, you should know better than to daydream.*

By midafternoon they were approaching the small community of Shadow Brook when Ruth spotted a small gathering ahead. Men on horseback. She peered in the distance, wondering if bandits had waylaid some innocent traveler. She set her jaw. They were not stopping this time. She reined up abruptly and allowed Dylan to catch up.

He rode up beside her and asked, "What's going on?"

"I don't know. Look—ahead." Eight figures gathered in a tight circle. Ruth noticed a corral to the left—with a horse standing by the railing.

Dylan leaned over and handed Rose to her. "You and the baby stay here. I'll find out what's going on."

Fear shot through Ruth. "Dylan! Remember

what happened the last time you rode to a stranger's aid!"

"Yeah." He glanced at Rose. "The best thing that's ever happened to either one of us." Her protest fell on deaf ears as Dylan kicked his mare into a gallop.

The snow had thinned to almost nothing as they had ridden west, and Ruth was grateful. It certainly made the trip easier. She grew almost ill every time she thought about how close to death they'd come before reaching Sulphur Springs. Dylan couldn't take another setback. She watched cautiously as he rode off, her heart offering a wordless prayer for protection.

The circle of men opened as the marshal approached. He reined in and the men talked. The wind was slight and voices didn't carry. Ruth wished she knew what was happening, prayed that it wasn't more trouble.

Finally Dylan motioned for her to join them. Clucking her tongue, she nudged the horse forward. As she rode toward the group, she saw Dylan shaking hands with one man, glancing toward the horse in the pen. Well, at least the strangers were friendly.

Reining in, she smiled as Dylan made the introductions. Pointing to Ruth, he said, "This is . . . Jim, and the baby's name is Rose."

Ruth still wore trousers and boots as well as two layers of flannel shirts because they were warmer and it was easier to ride astride in pants. By now she was accustomed to receiving odd looks, but it still made

her slightly uncomfortable. The cowboys acknowledged the greeting by ducking their heads, their gaze
sweeping over her and the child. Rose and a bulky
coat hid Ruth's telltale curves from the men's views.

Dylan grinned at her. "They're having a contest."

Lowering her voice the best she could, Ruth
repeated, "A contest?" She turned and looked at the
horse prancing nervously in the corral, his low whin-
nies edgy. When she looked back, Dylan met her
gaze. "They've invited me to join in."

An alarm went off inside her. "What kind of
contest?"

He motioned toward the waiting stallion. "A riding contest."

Her eyes darted to the corral, then back to
Dylan. "Riding what?"

"That horse there. Bert." He nodded toward the
spirited animal. "Fifty dollars to the man who can
ride him the longest."

Ruth's jaw dropped. "Dylan—"

The marshal quickly took her mare by the reins
and pulled her aside. Out of earshot, he pleaded
with her. "I can double our money, Ruth. I can ride
that horse longer than any man here."

Ruth was aghast. Gamble? She didn't hold with
gambling—the Good Book clearly advised against it!

"How could you think of such a thing?" she
demanded. "We have enough money to last us to
Wyoming if we're frugal. Besides, you're a sick man!
Your wounds have barely begun to heal!" she hissed,
staring over his shoulder at the horse in question.

Why, riding a bucking stallion would be suicide for him. "What is wrong with you? I thought you had better sense—I will not allow you to kill yourself or squander money on a horse!"

She looked at the prancing stallion. He was lively for an animal bearing the innocuous name of Bert. Bert. He wanted to ride a horse named Bert. True, it would be easy money, but clearly against God's instructions.

Dylan's eyes narrowed. "Since when do you make my decisions?"

She met his gaze stringently. "Since you clearly lost your mind."

"I can ride that stallion, Ruth." His stance softened. "Okay, look. I won't wager the money—I'll put the cow up for entry fee." He stepped closer, his eyes shifting to the waiting men. "Shadow Brook is only a half mile or so away. Even if I lose the cow—which I won't—we'll make it there this afternoon and I'll buy you another cow."

"No." She looked away. "You're not wagering the cow or the money. Rose needs her milk, and I won't risk you losing the cow on some silly man thing. I forbid it."

Dylan's jaw firmed. "You're not going to make me look like a henpecked husband—I'm riding that horse."

"You are not! And I couldn't make you look like a henpecked husband because I look like a boy, Dylan, and even if I didn't, we're not even—" She caught herself and lowered her voice when the men turned to gawk in their direction. "You're not riding that horse. Now let's go."

"You're right. We're not married." Throwing her a defiant look, he turned and rode back to the men. "Gentlemen," he announced—loud enough for the dead to hear, Ruth noticed—"I'd be honored to take your money if you'll accept the cow as entry fee."

Ruth fumed; she was mad enough to spit nails. How could he! How could he do this to her and the baby? Just when he showed signs of thawing, the conceited worm threw her a curve hard enough to flatten her.

"Okay," she yelled, "have your own selfish way! Go ahead, kill yourself and starve poor Rose to death! See if I care!"

The marshal shot her a withering look. The men shuffled their boots, looking to Dylan for explanation. He met their puzzled gazes. "When do we ride?"

"Be a couple of hours yet," one of the men said, glancing at Ruth. "We're waitin' for Hank Grisham to show up."

The marshal nodded. "I'll be ready." He turned his mount and rejoined Ruth.

Ruth gritted her teeth. If the man wanted to kill himself, there was obviously nothing she could do. *I told you not to get your hopes up, Ruth. Dylan McCall cares nothing for you or the baby. Hasn't he just proved it?*

Dylan was checking the cinch on his saddle, purposely ignoring her, which stirred her temper even more. Was he being stubborn or was it a man's pride? She didn't have the right to order him around, and this was his stubborn way of showing her that he answered to no one—most certainly not a woman.

Oh, Sara Dunnigan, if you were alive, I could cheerfully wring your coldhearted neck, Ruth stewed. *You've made the man distrust all women, when in truth only one woman has betrayed him. You.*

Ruth knew she shouldn't have pushed him. But somehow, someway, she had to stop Dylan from killing himself to prove to her he was his own man. Straightening in her saddle, she turned to face the marshal, who was stoically going about his business. "Dylan," she called sweetly.

He glared at her.

"If you're going to do this, could we go into town first? The baby will be hungry soon, and I'd like to feed her some warm mush. Might as well get a room for the night, if there's a hotel or boardinghouse." She left the "because you lost the cow" go unsaid.

He shrugged his agreement. Leaving the cow behind, they rode to Shadow Brook, which could hardly be called a town. The main street was a rutted track. Half a dozen cow ponies were tied to hitching rails in front of a mercantile, and another building stood farther down. The travelers stopped at the general store, and Dylan went inside to ask about a place to stay the night. He learned that there was a boardinghouse located just behind the saloon.

The establishment was smaller than the Seatons', but it looked nice enough. When Ruth and Dylan

approached, the owner, Jess Clark, was just leaving
to go care for his sick brother.

"If you don't mind fending for yourselves," he
said, "you're welcome to stay the night. You being a
U.S. marshal," he told Dylan, "I trust you not to run
off with the family silver."

Dylan laughed as they went inside. "We'll need
two rooms—the baby's crying keeps me up at night."

The clerk barely raised a brow, but Ruth kicked
Dylan in the shin for the ridiculous explanation.

They paid for a night's lodging and chose rooms
on the first floor, handy to the bathing room and
kitchen. Jess Clark had let the fire in the woodstove
burn down to coals. Ruth poked the flames alive
and fed the fire kindling as she plotted how to keep
Dylan from killing himself on that horse.

When a rosy flame burned, she bit her lower lip
and prepared to do battle. Dylan was going to be
awfully mad at her, but he was going to be awfully
alive when this was over.

Dylan sat at the table playing with Rose, who
was settled contentedly on a soft blanket on the
floor. Ruth laid her hand lightly on his broad shoulder as she paused beside his chair. She meant the
touch to be warm and comforting, though still he
tensed. "Dylan."

He eyed her suspiciously. "What?"

"If you insist on doing this, please let me clean
your wounds and apply fresh bandages. I'll bind the
injuries tightly so they won't break open again."

She looked at him pleadingly, using all of her

feminine wiles. She didn't feel good about tricking him, but she loved him enough to do anything to keep him alive. If those wounds broke open again, he might not be so fortunate this time. Didn't the marshal realize his mortality? Or was he so intent on besting her that he was blind to danger?

"Please?"

"Gert said I was healing okay. I don't need new bandages."

"For me?" she insisted. "I would feel better if I knew the wounds weren't likely to break open."

He didn't want to appease her; that was evident when resentment flared in his eyes. But maybe the part she'd hoped existed—the tiny part of him that was finding it increasingly hard to ignore her—finally made him consent.

"All right."

She released a pent-up breath. "Thank you. And why don't we have a cup of coffee before you ride? Something hot would make us both feel better."

He shrugged.

The smell of fresh-perked coffee saturated the air as Ruth cleaned and rebandaged his wounds. She worked quickly, her nimble fingers now familiar with the task. Dylan sat stoically, refusing to confront her. When she finished, she got two mugs from the cabinet and poured coffee. As she handed him a cup, she suddenly turned toward the baby, who was happily chewing on her fist.

"Oh . . . I think she's choking, Dylan!"

When Dylan turned his full attention to Rose,

Ruth reached in her pocket and withdrew the bottle of laudanum and dumped a healthy dose into Dylan's cup. She hurried to screw the cap on and shoved the bottle back in her pocket before the marshal turned around.

"She wasn't choking."

"Honest? Sorry."

She picked up her cup and took a sip, eyeing him over the rim. He watched the baby a few moments before he took his first sip. He grimaced. "This is the worst coffee I ever tasted."

Ruth shrugged. "I've had better, but at least it's hot. Dylan, why don't you go lie down a minute? I'll wash these cups and feed Rose."

"I'll take the saddlebags to my room."

"Thank you."

Ruth prayed that the laudanum would take effect quickly. She'd given him enough to fell an elephant, and even though he hadn't finished his coffee, she hoped it would do the trick. She heard him leave the house, then return. When she didn't hear him come back down the hall, she waited several more minutes, then tiptoed to the door of his room.

Listening outside, she heard his soft snores and grinned. Success. In a flash she darted into her room, tucked her long dark hair beneath her hat, and ran back to the kitchen to check on Rose. She might be as foolish as Dylan, but she was healthy—at least for now. She was saving the marshal's life, she told herself.

Bert would throw her in two seconds. She was

light, and if the fall didn't break her neck, she could withstand the impact. She'd been thrown by a horse before and had learned how to fall. But Dylan, she knew, would try to win—and that meant he could die. This way, they'd lose the cow for sure. But they had enough money to buy another one, and no amount of money could replace Dylan McCall.

She pulled on Dylan's gloves, eyeing the sleepy baby. She'd have to take Rose with her and ask one of the men to watch her while she rode. They would find the situation curious, but she was good at bluffing. At least she'd had lots of practice along those lines over the last few weeks.

"Come on, Rose. Let's go save Daddy." She picked her up, then went to make sure Dylan was all right. He was out cold, breathing evenly, stretched out across the bed as if he'd fallen over asleep. She hoped she hadn't given him too much laudanum, but enough to keep him down for at least a couple of hours.

This was her first opportunity to study him. He was always on the move, except for the days he'd been unconscious after the attack. But then she'd been afraid to look for fear he was dying, and she'd had the baby to care for as well. But now, oh, my. Dark lashes against tan skin, the faint shadow of beard, defined cheekbones and square jaw . . . she sighed. She was risking her neck to keep him alive for another woman. She frowned.

Soon he'd be an angry man. *Furious* wouldn't describe what he'd be when he woke up and found that she'd tricked him. But he'd be alive and thanking her when he cooled off.

At the last minute, she decided to take his boots. She set Rose down on the floor. Straddling Dylan's unconscious form, she tugged, finally dislodging the left boot, then the right. She tucked the boots under one arm and hurried out of the room with Rose, closing the door behind her.

When she reached the corral, the cowboys were gathered to watch the stallion try to rid himself of his first rider. Ruth was careful to carry Rose the way a man would, letting her head bob like an apple in a barrel. She carried Dylan's boots tucked beneath her right arm.

Hank must have shown up, because nine men turned to watch Ruth approach. She dropped the boots and shifted the baby to her right hip, then turned and spit in the snow. The spittle wasn't enough to make a blotch, but it made a convincing show. Swiping her hand across her mouth, she said gruffly, "Me and the marshal decided I'd best do the competin'."

The men cast a glance at the boots and then back toward town as if they expected to see the marshal approaching.

Ruth eyed them harshly. "Any problem with that? The cow's still up for grabs."

The men shrugged. "No problem," they chorused.

"Guess not."

"Suits me."

"Care to keep an eye on the young'un whilst I

ride?" She hawked up another wad and spat on the ground, gagging. Whew. That tasted awful! Why on earth did men find it necessary to do that all the time?

The men grumbled under their breath. Finally one agreed. "I'll keep an eye on the kid."

The cowboys turned back to the corral, where the rider was picking himself up from the ground. Over to one side Bert snorted and pawed the frozen ground. Ruth kept both eyes on the horse, swallowing against a dry throat.

Lord, have mercy on my soul. How did that horse come by his name?

She stood by, jiggling the baby as the second man prepared to ride. Grasping the stallion by the mane, he swung up as two men tried to control the angry beast until the rider was set. At his signal, they let go and bolted for the fence.

The stallion gave a couple of spirited bucks with a twist and sent the rider flying over its head. The cowpoke sprawled in the snow, looking dazed.

Contestant number three mounted a few minutes later.

One by one Ruth watched Bert pitch each rider in record time. She cringed, turning away as the fourth rider flew past her over the fence, taking out a row of oak pickets. He rose out of the snow, trying to shake off the blow. A front tooth hung by its root.

"Hey, kid," someone yelled at Ruth. "You're next!"

Ruth swallowed and handed the baby to the man standing next to her. She ran her tongue lightly over her front teeth, praying she could keep most of them.

"I can do all things through Christ which strengtheneth me." She prayed silently as she dragged her feet toward the four-legged keg of dynamite. *"The Lord is my shepherd; I shall not want. He maketh me to lie down in green pastures: he . . . he . . ."*

The stallion turned a jaundiced eye in her direction, seeming to smirk, as if he was amused at the idea that she'd even think of getting on him. He looked meaner than Satan himself.

Approaching the animal, Ruth caught her breath and tried to hoist herself onto the broad back. It took three men to hold the horse now. Bert snorted, his eyes wild. After several minutes of her feet flailing the air and failing to get a leg up, someone took pity and hefted her onto the brute's back.

For a moment the stallion stilled. Taking a deep breath, Ruth dug her hands into the mane to get a firm grip. Then she waited.

The men stepped back, freeing the horse.

The stallion stood meek as a lamb.

She flashed a lame grin. What was wrong here? Praise God! The Lord had seen her point and he was assisting—

Suddenly the horse lunged, jarring Ruth's teeth. Horse and rider shot out into the middle of the corral. Bert jumped straight up, as if someone had lit dynamite under him, and landed stiff-legged. Ruth's brain ricocheted against the top of her head. Bert, all twelve hundred pounds of him, jumped again, humping his back and twisting in midair. Ruth slid to one side but by some miracle managed to right herself when the horse went the opposite direction on the next jump. She saw stars, then planets shattering around her. Stark terror of being pounded into the ground beneath Bert's hooves was all that kept her hanging on to his mane.

On the next buck she lost her grip. A wicked spiral of the stallion's back sent Ruth sailing though the air, straight toward a water barrel. She crashed into its side, splitting the timber wide open. Icy water gushed everywhere, and she landed in the snow face-first.

The last coherent sounds Ruth heard were the men hesitantly, but politely, clapping.

• • •

Silence. Dylan heard nothing. Why was there no sound? For weeks now the first sound he'd heard every morning was either the baby or Ruth.

His eyes popped open. He didn't recognize where he was at first and then remembered they were in Shadow Brook. A boardinghouse. He rolled over, wincing when his shoulder reminded him he wasn't healed yet.

He groaned.

His head felt like it was stuffed with cotton, his mouth dry. When he sat up, he couldn't focus.

He blinked, trying to clear his head. He tried to stand, but his legs and arms didn't feel a part of his body. He stumbled and nearly fell face-first into the braided rug. Holding on to the bedpost, he managed to remain upright but felt on a tilt. What was wrong?

Drugged. Someone had slipped him something!

Ruth. What had she done to him this time?

Hearing a commotion outside, he looked out the window to see a number of cowboys hightailing it out of town . . . toward the corral. Now, why did instinct tell him that whatever was going on involved Ruth?

His mind began to clear. Jamming his hat on his head, he took a step toward the door before realizing he was in his socks. His boots were nowhere in sight. He'd had them on when he—

Ruth. She'd taken his boots. If she thought that would stop him, she had another think coming. If she thought she could talk the cowboys out of holding the cow as collateral for his bet or use his injuries as a reason for letting him out of the competition . . .

The more he thought about her embarrassing him, the madder he got. Thankful that he hadn't stabled the horses yet, Dylan mounted and galloped toward the corral, intent on stopping Ruth before she made a fool of him.

As he neared the corral, he heard yells and calls. His horse skidded to a halt and Dylan slid off, dropping the reins. The sound of men's laughter and hooting filled the charged air.

Walking gingerly across the snow-packed ground, Dylan gravitated toward the noise. Something told him that the answers to why he'd been drugged—and where his boots were—were there. The closer he got to the melee, the more certain he was of it.

He reached the corral in time to see Ruth fly through the air and into the water barrel tied to the corner fence. He winced when he heard the dull thud of her body hitting wood and bouncing off like a rag doll, her black hair flying when her hat flew off.

Two men jumped off the fence and ran to divert the still-bucking bronco, while two other hands grabbed Ruth's arms and dragged her outside the fence.

Rage cleared the last of the fog from Dylan's mind. Rage and cold fear—fear like he'd never experienced before. Had the woman lost her mind?

Ignoring his stocking feet, he jumped the fence and sprinted across the corral in the direction they'd dragged Ruth. She lay unconscious, her head cushioned by her crushed hat. A cowpoke bent over her, patting her cheek in an attempt to bring her around.

"You okay, girlie?"

Dylan jerked the man away from Ruth and dropped to his knees to pull her into his arms. Feelings he'd never had before washed over him. Warmth. A need to protect. A need to love.

Too late. Ruth was dead. Crazy, stubborn, misguided Ruth. Ruth, who'd rescued Rose from fire but had tried her best not to love her. Ruth, who had stubbornly followed him across a territory with the idea of finding some distant cousin. Ruth, who had bullied him, saved his life, stood beside him, cared for him. Ruth. His Ruth.

Closing his eyes, he rocked, tenderly cradling her close to his chest, her coal black hair spilling over his arm.

"I'm sure sorry," one of the cowhands said. "We had no idea she was a woman. Then when we realized she was a girl dressed like a boy—"

Dylan looked up at him. "Couldn't you tell she was a woman? How could you miss it?"

"Well, we didn't know at first," another put in, "but then when we did, it was too late to stop her."

"You let her ride that horse anyway?"

"She was determined," another said.

"We didn't think she'd get hurt," the first added.

Dylan bit out, "You should have known she wasn't an experienced rider. The bet was for *me* to ride!"

The men looked at each other. "We just thought . . . well . . . we thought we'd play a little trick on her, 'cause she dressed like a man, tried to fool us—"

"She wanted to keep me from losing the cow," Dylan said softly, "and keep me from killing myself."

He continued to rock Ruth gently, his mind filled with memories. Memories of this woman on the wagon train taking care of the other girls, reading her Bible, teaching Glory to read and write, trying to persuade Glory to take a bath. Ruth laughing in the firelight, sunlight tingeing her hair.

He saw a spirited Ruth determined to follow him

though she hadn't a clue how to survive on the trail. But she *had* survived. Ruth, who wouldn't hold the baby more than she had to, but still found a gutsy way to keep her alive those first few days. A furious Ruth facing an irate Ulele and then jumping on a horse and making a run for it, clinging to him like she'd never let him go.

Never let him go.

But she had let him go. Why? Perhaps she *did* love him. Had she taken his wounds because she loved him?

Tears stung his eyes and he held her closer, the pain of loss nearly suffocating him. He'd never wanted to care. Not about her. Not about anyone. He'd pushed her away because she got to him. Made him hope for things that were impossible. He'd been ornery and rude to her, made her think he'd ridden off and left her to fend for herself in an unforgiving land, but she'd stood her ground all the way. He'd been surprised by her determination, shamed by her willingness to take on the responsibility of a homeless child. She was a good mother, once she got used to the idea. Then she'd taken to it like a bee took to honey.

She'd pulled those arrows out of his shoulder when a weaker woman would have fainted. She had refused to let him die. She had found water, worked day and night to bring down his fever. When he was sharp with her, unreasonable, she'd stood up to him and gave back as much as he dished out. He'd never met a woman like her.

He loved her.

The power of that revelation hit him in the middle of his chest like a sledgehammer. He'd never thought love would find him, never wanted it to. But love had attacked him in the guise of this good-to-the-bone woman. He'd been a fool to tell himself he could leave her, that he could live without her or the baby. They were a family—an unusual one, but a family nonetheless.

Suddenly the cowhand's admission registered. They'd known she was a woman and yet they'd set her on that bronco. A bronco that had never been ridden and, from the looks of at least three limping cowboys, hadn't been yet.

Dylan gently put Ruth aside before his rage clicked in. He stood up and lashed out with his fist, which landed solidly on the nearest cowboy's jaw. The man rocked back on his heels, his knees buckling before he recovered and threw a solid punch into Dylan's belly.

The two men rolled on the snowy ground, going after each other with a flurry of fists and shouts as the other men formed a circle and cheered their chosen opponent. The melee gathered steam as the cowhands joined in. Fists flew as they all waded into the brawl, yelling and shouting.

13

Ruth slowly gained consciousness, aware first of a piercing pain in her left side, followed closely by a whole new host of aches and pains throughout her body. Then she became aware of men yelling. Yelling loudly. The noise was deafening, causing her head to pound even more. She wanted them to stop. Someone had to make them stop!

She tried to move, but she couldn't. She tried taking a deep breath, but a sharp pain near the base of her skull rendered her helpless. She lay back again. Then she remembered.

Bert. The bronco— the ornery horse had thrown her. *Rats.* There went Rose's milk.

She'd warned Dylan against betting the cow; she'd warned him that this would happen. But would he listen? Noooo. He had to enter this silly contest. It didn't matter that he was barely able to remain upright on a tame horse, much less a bronco that nobody could ride.

Ruth opened her eyes. Blur. She was blind!

No. That was sky. Blue sky. She relaxed and her

eyes focused. She realized she was in the middle of a free-for-all. Snow and fists were flying everywhere. Grunts of pain and fury filled the air. Blood. Men's feet flew out from under them like broken stilts. The group was going crazy.

Then she saw him.

Dylan. Smack-dab in the middle of the whole mess! Well, if he hurt himself, it served him right!

Then she saw Rose. The cowhand still held the baby, but Rose's head was bobbing like a cork as the man egged on one of the fighters. Rose was clapping and laughing at every blow Dylan landed, as if she was cheering him on. Ruth sat up gingerly, amazed.

Then it occurred to her. Bert. That bronco had never been ridden, had tossed several experienced cowboys straight into the ground, and yet she'd been put on him. They tricked her! No wonder the cowpokes had snickered when she hadn't been able to muster enough leverage to mount without help. They had known she was a woman—why, they probably made side bets on how far the bronco would throw her!

Did Dylan know? A slow, warm fuzziness crept over Ruth. Somehow she knew that he did know, and that was what had sparked the brawl. He was fighting for her—the woman he swore he'd throw to the wolves without a second thought. Her insides turned to mush and tears filled her eyes. He loved her; the big buffoon was fighting for her and the baby—the family they'd created.

Happiness puddled from the corners of her eyes as she watched the marshal down one cowboy, then another. She loved this crazy man, this man who'd been so afraid to care about her. She loved him heart and soul and loved the baby as much, maybe even more, though she didn't see how that was possible. Love was love, and she had enough to supply both Rose and Dylan for the rest of her life.

Now she had a choice. Would she admit her love, stay and help him fight, or get up and walk away from it all? Walk away from the baby, away from Dylan? She could ride until she found a town that had work for her; she could earn enough money to return to Denver City. She could do that.

Then she remembered a Scripture verse she had read this morning before they set out on the trail. It was from Jeremiah 18. God told Jeremiah to go to the potter's house. As Jeremiah watched him work on a clay vessel, it "marred in the hand of the potter: so he made it again another vessel, as seemed good to the potter to make it."

The words struck her because one day in Sulphur Springs, she'd encountered an old Indian inside the livery. He'd been working there in the warm barn, forming pots from the earth, his hands making a beautiful vessel out of a shapeless lump. The old man's face was weathered and lined with age, his eyes ageless. Ruth had stood watching him, commenting on his skill.

In broken English he'd told Ruth that people were like his pots. Some were already baked—set in their ways, inflexible, hard. "They miss out on a lot of good in life," he'd said.

But then he picked up a lump of unformed clay and began to mold it into a pretty shape. "Some are like this clay, ready to become something useful. They go through the fire and come out of the oven beautiful."

She'd held a pot in her hands, almost sad that it could no longer be molded. One of the pots had a bump along the bottom edge, a bump that would be there until the pot was broken. A flaw. The pot had a flaw, like all people.

She had a flaw too. Many of them, actually. The Jeremiah verse gave her hope that perhaps God could still mold her life into something useful, even though she was marred. Perhaps she could be useful, despite the flaws.

But not if she was already "baked," already set in her ideas of what God was doing in her life. She'd assumed that because she could never have children, a husband and family were out of the picture. She'd hardened her heart against the possibility. But was she being so headstrong in her prior notions that she was blind to God's taking her in a new direction? Was it possible that God was now bringing love into her life—and a child—and that she had been too much of a "baked pot" to recognize the gift?

So, Ruthie, what are you going to do about it? Are you going to set aside those old beliefs and open yourself to a new direction? Or are you going to walk away with your old thoughts and patterns and miss out on the blessings God stands ready to give you?

Of course, there was still one barrier left before

she could give her heart to Dylan. Unless they were spiritually matched, she couldn't think of a life with him. Could she trust God right now, even if she had no idea of the outcome?

One thing she knew: she hadn't come this far to see some cowboy destroy this man she loved. Holding her aching side, Ruth pushed herself up and managed to roll to her knees. She squinted against the sea of brawling fists, searching for a weapon. A shovel leaned against the corral railing.

Shoving herself to her feet, she stumbled through the fighting cowboys and grabbed the shovel. A moment later she was in the middle of the chaos, her screaming pain forgotten, fighting alongside Dylan.

When Dylan spotted her, his mouth fell open as he stared in amazement and relief before he ducked a roundhouse by another cowboy. "I thought you were— " he yelled.

"Dead?" Ruth smacked the shovel against a cowpoke's head, knocking him out cold. "You're not that lucky, McCall!"

Grinning widely, Dylan hooked his arm around Ruth's waist and pulled her to him for a long, thorough kiss while the battle raged around them. When their lips parted, he smiled down at her. "You're some woman, Ruth Priggish."

"You're some man, Marshal McCall." They both ducked swinging fists and reentered the fray.

A man knocked Dylan down. As he crawled out from between the legs of two fighting cowpokes, he called out, "Hey, Ruthie?"

"Yes?" She took a wide swing and clunked a man over the head.

"Been meaning to ask you something."

"Can't it wait?" She dodged an oncoming fist, bringing her weapon squarely down on the man's hand. The cowpoke yelped and backed off.

"Don't think so—at the rate we're going we're not likely to live to a ripe old age." Dylan swung a hard left.

"Yeah." She brought the shovel down, nearly tripping over her feet. At the rate they were going, life was mighty risky. "You're right. What's the question?"

"Want to get married?" he asked, shoving aside a windmilling cowboy with a left hook.

Her eyebrows shot up.

"Later," he added, felling another attacker.

"Later?" She swung the shovel and leveled a cowboy, who went down like a shot.

"Not too much later—say, later this evening?"

She bit down on her lower lip and hauled off and let another man have it. She had some serious thinking and praying to do, but "later" sounded good to her.

•　•　•

"How's that rib, cowboy?" Dylan smiled as they rested on their horses before the last descent into Shadow Brook. Rose lay contentedly in Dylan's arms.

Ruth gingerly touched her aching side. The doctor had bandaged the cracked rib at the horse corral and shook his head over the angry dark blue bruises, which proved to be plentiful. Bert had done a job on Ruth Priggish.

"I'm fine, Mr. McCall." She flashed a merry smile. "Never better in my life."

Dylan sobered. "I still can't believe you'd love me enough to risk your life for me."

"It wasn't entirely unselfish. If something happened to you, what would happen to me and the baby?" She leaned closer to touch his sleeve. "Love isn't that difficult to understand, Dylan. Sacrificial love is mystifying, but maybe that's because it comes from God. God's love for you, Dylan McCall, knows no bounds. Is it so impossible for you to accept such perfect love? A love that's true and born of grace and compassion, not the twisted form Sara practiced."

He sat very quiet, his eyes focused on the town ahead. She didn't know if her words had reached him; she could only pray that the Holy Spirit had finally found an open door.

"God did the same for you, Dylan. He gave his only Son to die for you. And for me."

"The years have hardened me, Ruth. Until you came along I spent my life scoffing at God. It was easier to convince myself that he was the outlaw and not Sara." His eyes sobered. "If the Lord will have me, I'll do my best to honor him—start making him first consideration in my life."

"Oh, Dylan!" She leaned over and threw her arms around his neck and showered his face with kisses. The horses shied, but Ruth held on tightly.

"It's shoutin' time in heaven! When you invite God into your heart, he will remain with you forever. Forever, Dylan."

Leaning back, Dylan blew out his cheeks before he offered a brief, tentative smile. "Forever. That's pretty overwhelming."

"But true." She kissed him soundly on the mouth. When she would have pulled back, he pulled her closer and lengthened the embrace.

Later, he confessed, "I accept the Lord and his salvation, Ruth, but I still have much to learn."

"I know . . . but you will learn, Dylan. You will learn." Filled with the Holy Spirit, Dylan would grow in faith and forevermore walk in the light of the truth. How could anyone want more?

"All right, then." She picked up the reins, grinning.

"All right what?"

"All right. I'll marry you." *Thank you, God, for leading this wonderful man into your fold. Help us both, Lord, to grow and trust in your Word.*

Maneuvering his horse closer again, Dylan bent from the saddle and kissed her. "Then why are we wasting time sitting here? Let's go find a preacher."

• • •

"Not much call for rooms in the winter," Jess Clark repeated as he handed Dylan the keys to their rooms. He grinned when he heard they were hoping to get married yet that evening.

"Don't see a problem with matrimony. The missus and I were hitched forty-three years before I lost her five years ago."

"Thank you so much," Ruth said. "I . . . Could I order a hot bath?"

"Is it possible to get hot water for two baths?" Dylan asked.

"Sure thing. Just give me an hour."

* * *

Ruth took in her spacious bedroom with a huge triple window facing south. Snow fell outside in a heavy blanket, but warmth from the woodstove had begun to seep into her chilled bones. Favoring her left side, she pulled back the lace curtains to look outside. The world was beginning to look like a fairyland.

Mr. Clark was warming kettles of water for their baths, and Rose was sleeping on the bed that was covered with a colorful Double Wedding Ring quilt. The friendly room contained a comfortable, overstuffed gingham chair and massive, dark cherry furniture: a dresser, chest of drawers, a cheval mirror, and a washstand with a pretty porcelain bowl and pitcher.

Ruth stared at her image. It was the first time in weeks that she'd seen her whole self in a mirror, and she winced. Long days on the trail had dulled her hair; it felt like straw. Wind and rain had left her skin tough as cowhide, and she hadn't been careful enough about wearing a hat in the blinding sun. Traces of tan rimmed her eyes and reddened her cheeks. She wanted to be beautiful for Dylan, especially today, their wedding day. But instead, she looked like a tired, bruised scarecrow.

Later Ruth joined Dylan in the parlor to wait for their baths. Dylan wrapped his arms around Ruth's waist. His gaze met hers. "You've never looked prettier," he whispered.

"I look awful—my skin—"

He caught her hand and brought it to his lips, lightly kissing her fingertips. "You're a beautiful woman, Ruth."

She closed her eyes, relishing the warmth of his breath on her hand. How was it possible to know such happiness? Such contentment? Six weeks ago she would have said it wasn't possible, not for Ruth Priggish, but she'd been mistaken.

As he held her hand tightly, Dylan's kisses explored her neckline. She leaned back, allowing him further access to the graceful curve. The baby slept soundly upstairs; snow fell gently outside the large windows.

"Dylan?"

"Hmmm?"

"How long will we stay in Shadow Brook?"

She wasn't sure of his plans; the marriage proposal had come so suddenly. Did he regret the impulsive moment, or had he clearly thought the proposition through? She prayed for the latter.

"We're in no hurry to leave."

She snuggled closer against his warmth. "I'm going to be generous and allow you to retract the proposal. I know everything was so hectic, and you thought I was dead."

His grip tightened. "A jury couldn't make me take it back." Turning her gently to face him, he smiled, his eyes openly adoring her. "I love you, Ruth. I've waited all my life for you to come along. I didn't know that day I joined the wagon train that you were the one, but somewhere along the way I got a pretty good hunch." He kissed her again, and to Ruth, the world was suddenly as perfect as God intended.

His gaze darkened with desire. "You can have the first bath."

"All right." She touched his features lovingly, wanting to memorize the character lines she saw. He had a strong face, gentle yet resolute; eyes as blue as an October sky. The dark growth of beard would soon vanish, and the clean-shaven marshal would be handsome enough to break any woman's heart. Ruth surmised that Dylan McCall had broken more than his share of hearts. She felt a prick of jealousy when she thought of other women and her man. Funny how possessive of the marshal she'd become practically overnight.

"And—" he kissed her earlobe—"then we get married. I paid Mr. Clark to send for the preacher."

Ruth threw her arms around his neck. Her slight weight impacted his, and they staggered back into an overstuffed chair. Ruth held her left side, wincing in pain as she giggled. She showered his prickly face with kisses.

Chuckling, he caught her face between his hands and stilled her long enough to catch his breath. "I have never proposed to you properly."

"That's all right. You did ask—" He usually ordered her to do things, which would have been all right in this instance.

"But not properly." Sitting her upright, he sank to his knee beside the chair and caught her hand. Gazing into her eyes, he asked softly, "Will you spend the rest of your life with me, Ruth Priggish? Will you be the mother of my children—?"

Her pulse quickened and she stopped him. "Dylan—"

"Let me fin—"

She brought her left hand to cover his mouth. The air had suddenly gone out of the room. In her blissful state she had forgotten to remind him of her condition. Her heart ached. Once he remembered, he would surely take back the proposal, and she couldn't blame him. "I can't . . ."

"You can't?" Disbelief flickered across his features. "You can't marry me?"

She shook her head, tears spurting to her eyes. "I can't be the mother of your children. Remember? I told you—that night we were talking about our childhoods? I thought you understood."

Her heart was breaking. Holding her side, she got up and walked to the window. As she stared out, she sorted her words, wondering why she had let herself get so excited. Why hadn't she even thought that perhaps he had not understood the seriousness of her condition that night under the stars, when they had shared their deepest secrets? They would have Rose, but Dylan would desire a son and eventually other children. And she wouldn't be able to provide him heirs. Oh, God, why hadn't she made sure he understood sooner?

He remained on one knee, viewing her tolerantly. "You're going to have to be a little more specific, Ruth."

Ruth bit her lower lip, trying to stem her rising tears. "I wasn't born like other women, Dylan. I'm physically unable to bear children. . . ." Hot tears rolled from the corners of her eyes. "I'm so sorry—I should have been more specific but . . ." She licked away salty wetness. "It's my fault . . . I'm so sorry."

He came to her, turning her and taking her tenderly into his arms. She closed her eyes and relished the moment, probably the last time he'd hold her like this. If he ever held her again, it would be out of pity, and she couldn't bear that. They clung to each other while her tears dampened his shoulder. It seemed like hours before she found her voice again.

"I know it matters . . ."

His voice was as soft and gentle as she'd come to expect these last few days. "Well, sure it matters, but probably more to you than to me, Ruth." He held her away from him, his eyes searching hers. "Until I met you, I didn't think I'd ever have a wife and children. I know how badly you want to be a mother, Ruth, but we have Rose. I'm sorry that you want more—"

"Me?" She reached out to trace the curve of his chin with her forefinger. "It isn't me I'm concerned about—it's you."

The light of everlasting love shone from the depths of his eyes. "I love you, Ruth. That's all that matters. Mothers aren't born—I know that from living with Sara Dunnigan. You're a mother at heart. That's what counts. You thought you'd never have children, but God put one right in your lap. You just didn't realize it."

She smiled up at him, almost unable to believe how God had blessed her with this man. Oh, there were still wounds, wounds Sara Dunnigan had caused. Emotional scars like Dylan's didn't heal overnight, but there'd been a good start. With love and God's grace, Ruth felt she could help the process along. She'd love him so fully, so completely, that he wouldn't have time to think about the past; he would only look forward to the future—a future with her and Rose.

"So you're not so mad at God anymore?" She kissed his cheek softly.

"I'm not mad. You have shown me that Sara Dunnigan did not worship a God of love, the God you know . . . the God who must have been watching over us all along the way. I'm hoping you can show me how to know more about your God . . . no, my God too, now. I'm willing to learn. Right now, though, the road looks pretty steep."

She caught his hand. "Not with both of us walking."

"Oh, Ruth." He kissed her. "I have a lot to learn if you're willing to teach me and be patient—"

"I would be ever so glad to help you get to know our Savior and heavenly Father." She moved back to nestle in the crook of his arm. "God willing, we're going to have a good life together, Dylan."

"No doubt," he whispered, stroking her hair. "And about those babies you can't have—well, we can adopt more children if that's what you want. Then there will be grandchildren and great-grandchildren . . ."

She didn't let him finish. She turned and kissed him, murmuring her love. "I love you, Dylan McCall. I love you so deeply it hurts."

Lifting her gently off her feet, he swung her around, holding her tightly. The excruciating pain in her left rib was well worth the price. "I thought after we got married this evening, we'd stay around here a few days, then ride back to Denver City."

Ruth's smile faded as he set her back on her feet. "Denver City?"

"Well, seeing as how we've traveled no more than thirty miles since we left and winter's set in, I thought with your cracked rib, Christmas coming on, and my being so late anyway, we'd go back to Denver City for the winter. I'll have to let Dreck Parson go and trust that another marshal will bring him to justice. Anyway, after all the excitement, I could stand a little recovery time." He grinned wryly. "You can spend the next couple of months with Patience, Lily, Harper, and Mary and get adjusted to having a husband and baby before we move on." He kissed her again. "Maybe you should write to your cousin Milford and tell him you won't be coming."

"I never told—oh, you!" she said, swatting him lightly when she realized he was teasing. She shrugged, looping her arms around his neck. "Finding Milford would have been a long shot anyway."

"I'd say—but thank God you chose to bluff it out and follow me."

She drew back and peered up at him hopefully. "You truly do thank God?"

He smiled, holding her tightly. "You're a hard woman to please, you know that?"

He did trust God, though; Ruth could feel it, and it erased the last vestiges of doubt that this new path was the one God wanted for her.

That night in Jess Clark's parlor, while snow fell outside the windows, Marshal Dylan McCall and Ruth Priggish exchanged marriage vows. Jess witnessed the ceremony with a smile and a dutiful shower of rice.

The fee: one bucket of milk from the cow Ruth and Dylan hadn't lost after all.

Epilogue

Dylan, Ruth, and Rose McCall rode into Denver City three days before Christmas in a stagecoach, in relatively luxurious fashion considering the way they'd left.

The treat was a gift from Jess Clark, who claimed that he made investments in the future—young folks' futures. In this particular case, Ruth and Dylan McCall's shining future.

"You kids be happy—that will make my speculation one of the soundest I've ever made," the good man had said as he put the new family in the coach and shut the door.

"I'll send the money as soon as I collect my pay," Dylan had promised.

"No need. Send it, don't send it. I'll simply pass the money along to some other struggling stranger."

The world needed more Jess Clarks, Ruth decided.

"Whoa, there!" the driver yelled, sawing back on the reins, drawing the coach to a snow-fogged stop in front of the stage office.

"Den-ver Ci-ty!" he yelled, wrapping the reins around the brake handle. "Everybody out!"

Dylan glanced at his new bride. "Ready?"

"Sure am," Ruth said, smiling up at the handsome marshal. Her husband. She'd never been more ready or happier in her life. All her dreams had come true. She had a wonderful husband—a man who cherished her, a man who had proven his love and whose smile restored her faith in miracles.

And she had a baby.

A charming, captivating little brown-eyed child whose laughter was the light of her life. Each time Ruth held her sleeping daughter, she experienced God's love afresh; when the baby reached for her, she felt complete. She'd changed. She'd become pliable. She'd become a usable pot, even with her flaws.

Dylan climbed from the coach and reached for the baby. Settling Rose on his hip, he reached for Ruth. He smiled up at her as sun broke through the clouds.

"Ruth!"

"Harper!" Ruth stepped down from the coach and threw herself into the black girl's waiting arms.

"I can't believe it! What are you doing here?" Harper exclaimed. "We thought by now you'd be in Wyoming!"

Ruth laughed, taking the baby from Dylan. "I'm bringing my family to meet my folks."

Harper's puzzled gaze traveled from Ruth to Dylan to the baby. "I'm not even going to ask. Not before I get the others. Then we want to hear the whole story." She shook her head, her black eyes sparkling. "I know it's got to be a good one."

"It is." Ruth laughed. "It *surely* is."

Dylan retrieved the small bag. "How are you, Harper?"

"Fine, just fine, Marshal." Harper glanced at Ruth. "How are you?"

"Never better." Dylan adjusted the brim of his hat and winked at Ruth. "I'll get a room at the hotel," he said. "I need to send Kurt a telegram as soon as we're settled."

Harper tripped behind as the couple walked toward the hotel, Marshal McCall proudly showing off his baby girl and his new wife. Ruth knew Harper was fairly bubbling over with curiosity about how she and the obstinate marshal had gotten together and where the Indian child fit into the picture.

"I'm getting the others," Harper announced. "Then we'll have tea and you can tell us everything. *Everything*," she emphasized. Her eyes traveled to the good-looking marshal and she repeated, "*Everything*, Ruth."

"I'm hungry," Dylan said. "And I'd bet this one would like something to eat." He tapped Rose's nose with the tip of his finger and she giggled.

"We'll be in the café," Ruth told Harper.

Harper dashed off and Ruth grinned up at Dylan. "Hope nobody gets in her way."

"She'll mow them down if they do."

They settled at a table and studied the one-page menu. They'd barely ordered before Mary, Patience,

Harper, and Lily burst through the doorway, their faces animated with excitement.

They all spoke at once, but somehow Ruth managed to tell the story of her trek into Colorado Territory, the baby's rescue, Dylan's injuries, Ulele and Nehemiah Ford's deceit, their escapades trying to find a home for baby Rose, and finally how they had managed, through it all, to fall in love and get married.

"Married! You got *married* without us?" Patience demanded.

"I didn't plan on getting married," Ruth said softly. She reached over and took her husband's hand. "But this handsome man simply swept me off my feet."

"Oh, you two." Mary chuckled. "I am so *happy* to hear the news, but, Ruth, Oscar was rather put out by the way you up and disappeared." She took Ruth's other hand and held it.

"I'm sorry," Ruth said, feeling sorry for the old prospector in spite of her aversion to his smell and manners. She squeezed Mary's hand. "What's been happening here? Tell me everything."

"Well, nothing like what's happened to you, but we've been doing quite well," Lily said.

"Harper and I take in sewing," Mary said softly. "Denver City is growing so fast that Rosalee Edwards can't handle it all. Why, just the other day two wagon trains pulled into town and decided to stay the winter. The families might even remain when spring arrives. Families get settled and sometimes,

Pastor Siddons said, they like it so well here that they don't want to move on." She shrugged. "That's good for the sewing business. Plus, the cowboys can't even sew on a button, and there are a lot of cowboys around here— ranchers and the hands who work for them."

Ruth grinned. "I'm so happy for you." Everything seemed to be working out splendidly.

"I'm working on a wedding dress right now. It is so beautiful," Mary enthused. "The wedding is going to be quite an event."

"Surely is," Harper added. "The bride comes from the Hawthorn family, who has been involved in a feud with the groom's parents, the McLanes, for over a year. The fathers hate each other and the mothers won't speak. It's real shameful the way those two sides carry on—why, they even designated certain days to come to town for supplies. The Hawthorns come on Thursdays, the McLanes on Fridays. Both sides decided that shortly after the feud broke out."

Dylan bit into a piece of cherry pie. "What are the families arguing about?"

Mary shrugged. "Water rights—what else?"

"I bet Ben's folks don't even know what his intended looks like," Lily surmised. "Last time the McLanes saw Lenore Hawthorn was five years ago." Lily shrugged. "The young couple met at a church social. The parents don't go to the church socials, but this time they let their children attend. Ever since then Ben and Lenore have been meeting secretly, refusing to let their parents interfere with true love. They're so happy together, but the shine's taken off the engagement since both sets of parents vehemently object to the love match."

Harper nodded. "They both really love one another—you can just tell. It's very romantic."

The match didn't sound romantic to Ruth. It sounded like trouble waiting to happen, and she'd witnessed enough trouble to last her a lifetime.

Patience joined the discussion. "The dress is so beautiful, Ruth. Lenore will be a gorgeous bride, but I don't know how she and Ben are going to carry this wedding off with their folks so dead set against it."

Mary looked sad. "Lenore's folks won't even let her come to town to try on the dress—Patience has been helping me, modeling the dress so I can mark hems, fit the bodice. She's about the same size as Lenore, or I'd never get the dress done in time. They're getting married on the thirty-first . . . New Year's Eve. Lenore's grandmother is paying to have the dress made, or poor Lenore would have to get married in a regular gown."

"If you'll excuse me, ladies, I need to send a wire." Dylan leaned over and kissed Ruth. "The Good Book mentions something about gossip, doesn't it?" He winked.

The girls reserved further comments until the café door closed behind the marshal's back.

Mary slid to the front of her chair. "How long are you going to stay?"

"Until my rib heals and the worst of the weather is over." Ruth sighed. "Maybe two months or longer, Dylan promised. Then we're off to Utah."

Mary clapped her hands. "Wonderful. We'll get to spoil this precious baby." Mary reached for Rose, and the baby happily made the transfer.

• • •

Several days later the girls had caught up on all the news. The town had surprised Ruth and Dylan with a bridal shower two days after Christmas. The Siddonses hosted the festive event at the church.

"I am overwhelmed by your generosity," Ruth told the women in attendance with a grateful smile. Mounds of unwrapped household gifts piled around her chair. "I have never felt so loved."

The next morning, Ruth visited Mary and Harper's sewing room— a small cubicle at the back of the mercantile. When Ruth entered the establishment, Patience, wearing Lenore's wedding dress, turned from her perch on a stool, while Mary knelt at her feet, fastening Irish lace along the hem and train.

Harper, Lily, and Ruth sat near a cheery fire, admiring Mary's handiwork.

"It's so beautiful," Ruth praised. "Mary, you have such a talent."

The young woman blushed. "I've really enjoyed designing the dress."

The women turned abruptly as the back door

suddenly burst open and a masked man entered the store. He stood for a moment, beady eyes surveying the situation.

Ruth gasped, reaching for baby Rose, who played at her feet.

"Nobody move, ladies."

The women did as they were told. Mary coughed, and the man leveled the gun at her. "I said *quiet*!"

Patience stepped off the stool, wide-eyed. "What do you want?"

The outlaw motioned for her to step forward.

Patience's hand flew to her chest. "Me?"

"You. Get over here."

When Patience obeyed, he hooked his arm around her waist and dragged her out the front door.

Ruth and the other women sat frozen in place, shock paralyzing them as Patience's screams echoed up the street.

Recovering first, Ruth raced outside in time to see the bandit riding away, Patience imprisoned on the saddle in front of him. Ruth started running for the sheriff's office, bumping smack into Dylan when he stepped out of the telegraph office.

"Whoa." He reached out and caught her. "Where's the fire?"

"Patience. *Man*," Ruth panted, pointing down the street. "Took her."

The marshal whirled. "Calm down. Catch your breath. Someone took Patience?"

"We were . . . in the shop. Mary was pinning . . . hem on Lenore Hawthorn's wedding dress—bride's parents forbid her to try it on . . . so Patience was wearing it. A man burst into the mercantile . . . and grabbed her. They went that direction." She pointed west of town.

"You go back with the girls. I'll get the sheriff, get a posse together." Dylan kissed Ruth soundly. "We'll find her. Don't worry."

Tears filled Ruth's eyes. "Oh, Dylan, be careful."

His hand brushed her hair. "I'm always careful."

They had come too far to lose each other now!

Late that night the posse returned to town without Patience. A deputy and Dylan met Ruth and the other women gathered outside the mercantile.

"You didn't find her?" Ruth wrung her hands at the sight of the two men's solemn faces.

Dylan shook his head. "Not a trace of her. We'll have to wait until someone contacts us—see why the man took Patience, and what he wants."

Ruth walked into his arms. "I'm so afraid for her."

Dylan held her tightly. "I know, and I'd do anything to bring her back." He spoke over Ruth's head to the assembled women. "Any idea why someone would want to kidnap Patience?"

"We've discussed that all afternoon." Ruth stepped out of his embrace and wiped her eyes.

"And we can't come up with any reason," Harper reported.

"She's not had a problem with anyone? Didn't turn away from a suitor?" the deputy asked.

"No," Lily protested. "Conner Justice has called on her a few times, but there's been no problem."

Sheriff Jay Longer rode up just then and climbed out of the saddle. "Just been talking to some of my men. You said Patience was wearing Lenore Hawthorn's wedding dress, right?"

Ruth nodded. "Yes."

The young man frowned. "Well, there's our answer. There's been bad blood between the Hawthorns and McLanes all year. Ben and Lenore's wedding has set them off again—I'd bet a dollar to a doughnut the kidnapper is from the groom's side."

Mary feebly lifted a hand to her forehead. "Oh, dear goodness. The outlaw mistook Patience for Lenore?"

The sheriff nodded. "That'd be my guess. What about you, Marshal?"

Dylan nodded. "It would seem that way."

The women murmured their distress.

Ruth's eyes grew wide. "What will he do when he discovers he's got the wrong person?"

Dylan drew her back to him. "I don't know, honey."

"But *why*?" Ruth argued. "Why would any-one snatch a bride? What do they plan to do with Lenore—Patience?"

The sheriff and marshal exchanged grave looks.

"Let's not panic," Dylan said. "Maybe when they find out they got the wrong woman, they'll bring Patience back."

Ruth and Dylan trailed the sheriff and deputy to

the sheriff's office while Lily watched Rose. Dylan told her Jay Longer had been sheriff in Denver City for three years and was considered an effective lawman. "You're not to worry," he ordered.

"Jay, we've got a problem," Dylan said as the three men stepped inside the sheriff's office.

"Well, like you said, let's not panic until we see if he brings her back."

"And if he doesn't?"

Jay took off his Stetson and hung it over a peg. The sheriff was maybe a year or two older than Dylan, powerfully built, ruggedly handsome, Ruth noticed. "That's not good," Jay said.

Perched on the side of a battered desk, Dylan put his arm around Ruth. He said softly, "Don't worry, Ruthie; we'll find her."

Closing her eyes, Ruth tried to take comfort in her husband's assuring words. The past weeks had been so hectic—she'd hoped their lives would settle down, but apparently peace wasn't to be. Someone had taken Patience in place of Lenore Hawthorn, someone with a grudge.

Lord, please watch over Patience, Ruth silently prayed as she succumbed to the warmth of her husband's embrace.

There just seemed to be *no* end to trouble in Denver City.

TURN THE PAGE
FOR A PREVIEW OF

And don't miss the rest
of the books in the series,
Faith, *June*, *Hope*, and *Glory*.

Available now in stores and online

CP1632

1

Patience Smith might have been surprised to know that her life had just changed dramatically. Sheriff Jay Longer didn't realize his had changed at the same instant.

Swinging a long leg over the saddle, the sheriff of Denver City, Colorado, climbed aboard his mare. His eye caught Dylan McCall hugging his wife on Main Street, right in broad daylight. And in front of the sheriff's office, too. He frowned. Was that any way to uphold the dignity of law enforcement?

A moment later Jay rode up to the waiting couple, sliding out of the saddle before the mare came to a stop.

Ruth McCall whirled to face him, her pretty face a mix of warring emotions. "We were in the shop. Mary was pinning the hem on Lenore Hawthorn's wedding dress—the bride's parents forbid her to try it on, so Patience was modeling it. A man burst into Mary's millinery and grabbed Patience. They went off in that direction!" She pointed west. "Go!"

"Honey, slow down," her husband warned. "I don't want you upset."

Tears brimmed Ruth's eyelids. "You have to *do* something, Sheriff!"

Jay frowned. Deliver him from newlyweds and estrogen-produced hysterics. All that sweet talk between the marshal and his bride should take place in the privacy of their home, not in the presence of people who might find it scratchy to watch. Of course, time was, when he still had Nelly, he might have been as lovestruck as Dylan, but he'd have had enough sense of propriety to keep it to himself.

Sure, he would.

If he had Nelly back, he'd get down on his knees right out there in the middle of the street and tell her all the things he wished he'd said when he had the chance.

Jay casually straightened the brim on his Stetson. "She was wearing Lenore Hawthorn's wedding dress when she was abducted?"

Ruth nodded, tears rolling down her cheeks. "She was standing in for Lenore for the final gown fitting."

Jay glanced at Dylan, then back to Ruth. "Well, there's our answer. There's been bad blood between the Hawthorns and the McLanes for years. Ben and Lenore's wedding has set them off again—my guess is that the culprit has a connection with the groom's family."

With the Hawthorn/McLane wedding scheduled to take place tomorrow night, Jay figured that had to be the circumstance. Old man McLane was a crusty old reprobate, and he'd sworn to stop the nuptials between his oldest son and Hawthorn's youngest daughter. Apparently he'd found a way to interfere.

Ruth lifted a shaky hand to her forehead. "Sakes alive. The kidnapper mistook Patience for Lenore?"

Jay nodded. "That'd be my guess. What about you, Marshal?"

Dylan agreed. "That's the way I have it figured."

Denver City hustled in the background. An hour from now it would be dark, and a posse would find it impossible to track the young woman. Jay would have to set out alone and follow the trail until it got cold—or until he found Patience Smith.

"But *why*?" Ruth argued. "Why would anyone snatch a bride? What do they want with Lenore—Patience?"

The sheriff and the marshal exchanged sobering looks before Jay finally admitted, "Well now, that's hard to say." Could be a million explanations, but only one thing mattered. What would the kidnapper do with the girl once he discovered his mistake?

"Let's not panic," Dylan said. "When Patience tells the man that he's got the wrong woman, he'll probably turn her loose."

Whirling, Ruth bolted back into Mary's millinery shop in tears, and Dylan approached the sheriff.

"We've got a problem," the marshal said.

"Could be—then again, he might have realized his mistake instantly and let her go at the edge of town."

"Maybe—but if he didn't?"

Jay took off his Stetson and wiped his forehead. "Then you're right—we have a real problem."

Dylan stood by while Jay slid a Winchester Model 1873 into the hand-tooled rifle scabbard tied to his saddle. A cold wind buffeted the men's sturdy frames. Tomorrow night 1873 would be ushered out with parties and noisy celebrations, but Jay wouldn't be part of the festivities.

Dylan ran a hand across his face. "I still think I should be the one to go after her. Those girls and Ruth—they're like family to each other."

Longer busied himself checking cinches and stirrups. He knew the girls had come all the way from Missouri to be mail-order brides, an arrangement that hadn't worked out. The orphaned young women were as close as sisters, so Dylan's bride's tears were understandable. "You're newly married, and you're the marshal. I'm single, the sheriff, and the crime was committed in my county."

Not that Jay wanted to go after this particular orphan. He'd had more than one disagreeable run-in with Patience Smith, the last occurring a couple days ago. She'd burst into his office carrying a bird with a broken wing and asked if he knew anything about setting bones. He'd calmly pointed out he was town sheriff, not town vet. He'd eyed the critter that scattered droppings on the office floor.

She'd eyed him back sternly, then asked if he was coldhearted.

He had to admit that he was—had been for a long time. And he wasn't in the bird-fixing business.

She'd left with the bird in hand, and the last he'd seen of her, she was crossing the street, head held high, determination evident in her squared shoulders and stiff back.

Dylan's voice broke into Jay's musings. "The kidnapping took place in my town."

Jay sighed, knowing how stubborn McCall could be. "Look, let's not argue. I'm going after her, and I'm going to bring her home. That's my job; it's what I get paid for."

Conceding, Dylan stepped back. "I'll look after the town while you're gone. That much I can do."

Nodding, Jay gathered the reins between his gloves and mounted. "Finding her—finding anyone—in these mountains isn't going to be a cakewalk." The sheriff settled his hat more firmly on his head. He'd be lucky if he survived the search this time of year. January wasn't for the fainthearted. But he had another reason for going, one he wasn't going to mention. The wire he'd received today crackled in his shirt pocket. He knew what it said by heart. His gambling debts had caught up with him. The people he owed were coming to collect, and he didn't have the money to pay. If he wasn't here, there wouldn't be much they could do, and if he could buy enough time, maybe he would recoup his losses. And then again, maybe he wouldn't.

Turning the horse, he rode out of town due west. Somewhere out there a young woman was in danger, and as sheriff, it was his responsibility to rescue her.

He could only hope that Patience Smith was as

tenacious with her kidnapper as she'd proven to be with him.

*   *   *

Patience decided that getting rid of trouble was like sacking fog. You grasped, fumbled, and blocked, but it kept coming. She shivered. The late-afternoon air was cold as granite, and she was wearing little more than lace and tulle.

She wanted off this horse, and even more, she needed to make sense of what had just happened. She glanced sideways at the man who held her on his horse and wondered about his intelligence. How could anyone mistake her for Lenore Hawthorn? Lenore had blonde hair, angular features, and blue eyes. Patience had brunette hair, a round face, and dark brown eyes.

The swarthy man's hold tightened. "Stop squirming, Lenore!"

"I'm not Lenore!"

"Yeah, yeah. That's what they all say." He set his spurs deeper into the mare.

"But I'm not Lenore!" Patience yelled.

"Shaddup!"

She swallowed back her mounting hysteria. The outlaw gripped her tighter around the middle and galloped around a curve. This mistake had something to do with the ongoing feud between the Hawthorns and the McLanes, she was sure. Hatred between the two families ran as deep as still water, and she feared there was no telling what fate awaited her if this man thought she was Amos Hawthorn's daughter. The families' insane feud had been going on for decades.

She frowned when she thought of Mary, Lily, Harper, and Ruth. The girls had all looked thunderstruck when this man had burst into the sewing shop and seized her. If the situation wasn't so grave, she'd laugh; but right now all she could do was cling to the horse and pray she'd survive the frantic ride.

The scoundrel was dirty and his rancid breath repulsed her. Where was he taking her? How soon would he accept the fact that she wasn't the intended bride? And then what? Would he dispose of her before she could convince him that he'd made a terrible mistake?

Relief suddenly flooded her. *Dylan.* Ruth's husband—or maybe the town sheriff, Jay Longer—would come after her. The bigheaded sheriff and she mixed like oil and water, but right now she wasn't particular about her rescuer. Considering their simmering animosity toward one another, she wondered if he'd even bother to come after her—but Dylan would make him. His job would make him. With his piercing blue eyes and hair as red as a Colorado sunset, Sheriff Longer was a hard man to understand. But whether he liked her or not, the toughminded sheriff would not let this brigand get away with kidnapping a woman from his territory.

She clung to that belief as the horse's shod hoofs pounded the frozen ground. Wind stung her face and cold seeped through her bones. She had no protection from the wintry elements—no coat, only the lace sleeves of Lenore's wedding dress to protect her from the icy wind.

Suddenly, as if the hand of God swooped down and smote the enemy, the horse stumbled and pitched forward, throwing Patience and her captor over the animal's head. Patience went airborne. Seconds later she slammed into the frozen ground.

Lying motionless, she struggled to catch her breath, and then, dazed, she sat up in a feeble attempt to regain her bearings. She was alive! The horse lay prostrate on top of the kidnapper. She wished she felt compassion, an urge to offer assistance to the poor, unfortunate villain, but relief flooded her. She was free! The man must surely be dead, or very close to death; she didn't have the strength to even budge the horse to look.

Rolling slowly to her feet, Patience groaned. She tentatively tested her weight on one foot and then the other, and discovered that she could walk. Which she did, as fast as her injury would allow, grasping the hem of the fragile gown, trying to protect the sheer material from the rough trail.

Limping over the frozen ground, she sucked in deep drafts, the cold air stinging her lungs. Where was she? She had no idea; she wasn't familiar with the region. From the time the five mail-order brides had come to Denver City, she hadn't ventured far from the outskirts of town. Her eyes searched the barren, snow-swept land, and she shuffled faster. She'd heard talk of prospectors in the area, how fiercely the men vied with each other for gold. Hysteria now threatened to overtake her as she realized she would freeze to death if she didn't find shelter soon. Her teeth chattered and her breath came in ragged gulps. *Walk, Patience. Walk like your life depends on it.*

Heartsick, Patience realized that in these circumstances, it actually did.

● ● ●

A blast of winter wind buffeted the sheriff, and he huddled deeper into the sheepskin-lined coat. The girl had only a thin, silk wedding gown to protect her from the cold. If he didn't find her soon . . .

Jay rode slowly, leaning from the saddle to search for tracks, but the frozen ground made tracking difficult. He didn't stand the chance of a snowball in a skillet of finding her, but he set his jaw in determination.

And then he spotted the dead horse. Dismounting and hanging on to the reins, he approached the carcass. His mare was skittish, and he had no desire to be stranded out here on foot. This was unfriendly country. If a man didn't freeze to death, he stood a good chance of running into a belligerent miner defending his claim.

Jay examined the animal, noticing a boot half-hidden beneath the horse's body. When he had satisfied himself that Patience wasn't there, he mounted again. He had no shovel; he couldn't bury the miscreant. Animals would take care of what he couldn't. He nudged his horse and rode off slowly. Supposing the woman was still a captive, for it was possible the dead horse and victim had nothing to do with Patience Smith.

Then again, there was nothing to suggest that he *wasn't* the kidnapper, and when the horse stumbled she'd gotten away. If that were the case, where would she have gone? Running the questions through his mind, Jay came up with the same answer to both: most likely to one of the mining camps dotting these mountains or an isolated shaft, which would make finding her even more difficult.

He had been in these parts long enough to know that he couldn't go riding into camp dressed like a lawman. That would tip off the kidnappers that he was on their trail if she was still being held somewhere. He studied the rugged landscape, weighing his options. As far as he could see, there was only one choice open to him. Miners were a rugged lot, suspicious of strangers, so he'd ride into the closest town and get himself a shovel and a gold pan. Going undercover wasn't his style, but he was going to hit those camps disguised as a miner.

A Note from the Author

Dear Reader,

When I first began the Brides of the West series, I thought I would tell only the Kallahan sisters' stories: Faith, June, and Hope. Then Glory came along, and she opened a whole new realm of possibilities. Ruth, Patience, Harper, Lily, and Mary were created—and as you see, the Brides of the West just keep involving themselves in the most unlikely knee-slapping escapades. As the Brides of the West continue, I hope you will see something of yourself and your own life in the stories of Ruth or Patience or any of the other courageous young women. My prayer is that this fun-loving fiction containing simple truths will minister to you, my reader, and put a song in your heart and a smile on your face.

In his name,

Lori Copeland

About the Author

Lori Copeland is known for her fast-paced historical and contemporary romantic comedies. She is a two-time *Romantic Times* Lifetime Achievement recipient, a RITA and Christy Award nominee, and an inductee of the Missouri Writers Hall of Fame. In 2014, Hallmark Movies produced her contemporary title *Stranded in Paradise*.

Lori has published a combined total of 120 books in both the general and Christian market.

She makes her home near Branson, Missouri, with her husband. They have three grown sons and an ever-growing family.